Paul Stuart Kemp was born in Gravesend, England in 1972. As an English writer, he has managed to resist the mainstream American influence that dominates popular fiction, and casts dark tales throughout major British cities such as London and Liverpool.

Paul Stuart Kemp lives i͟

by Paul Stuart Kemp

## Novels

**Eden**
**The Unholy**
**Bloodgod**
**Ascension**

## Short Story Collections

**The Business Of Fear**

# THE UNHOLY

## Paul Stuart Kemp

decapita

Published in Great Britain in 2002 by
Decapita Publishing
PO BOX 3802
Bracknell RG12 7XT

Email: mail@paulstuartkemp.com
Website: www.paulstuartkemp.com

Cover artwork by Andrea Fioravanti
Illustrations by Paul Stuart Kemp

Photograph of author by Jeanette Kemp

The Author asserts the moral right to be
identified as the author of this work

ISBN 0 9538215 4 4

Set in Meridien

Printed and bound in Great Britain by
Cox & Wyman
Reading, Berkshire

# THE UNHOLY

# CONTENTS

## PART ONE
## INVITATION

## PART TWO
## THE VALUE OF FORCED CHOICES

## PART THREE
## MASKS AND MAGICS

## PART FOUR
## BENEATH THE MUCK AND MIRE

# THE UNHOLY

**unholy**, *un-ho'li, a.* Not holy; not
sacred; unhallowed; profane;
impious; wicked.

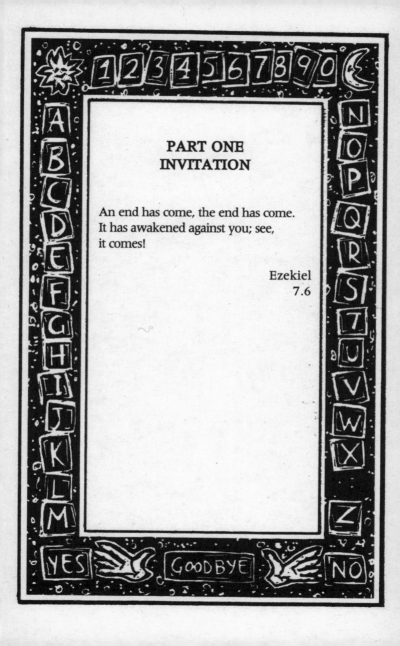

# PART ONE
## INVITATION

An end has come, the end has come.
It has awakened against you; see,
it comes!

Ezekiel
7.6

# ONE

## BENEATH THE GLASS

Cassandra eyed them sternly across the table, the tip of her index finger hovering over the heart-shaped planchette. Michael was looking at his wife, his eyebrows raised slightly with bemusement. Cass could see what was going on, the same as every other time her sister had wanted to 'play the ouija' as she called it; Michael would snigger and demean the board. Cass wouldn't have it.

Irene hissed at her husband, telling him to be quiet, but her sister was already close to her limit.

"If you're not going to take this seriously..." she threatened.

"I am, Cassie, I promise."

"There are other people who value what I do."

"I'm sure there are," Michael tried to say solemnly, but Cass caught his raised eyebrows again.

She pulled her pointer back across the table as if to leave but Irene stopped her swiftly with a hand across her wrist.

"Take no notice of him, Cass," she pleaded. "He'll be good."

"He has to be more than good," Cassandra instructed her firmly. "He has to be focussed. We won't achieve anything with him playing the fool."

"You said you'd try this with an open mind," Irene said, turning to look at him.

"I know, I know," he replied, holding his hands up, "but this just seems ridiculous. I mean, how are we supposed to channel wandering spirits or whatever with little wooden letters set out around a tiny card table?"

"As long as there are letters and numbers it doesn't matter what we use," Cassandra was indignant, the planchette held tightly to her breast now as if it was a wounded creature.

Both their eyes were upon him, and eventually he had to relent.

"Okay, I'll try and keep an open mind."

Irene smiled at her sister, and finally Cassandra replaced the pointer gently upon the green felt surface of the card table. She'd made the letters and numbers herself, small wooden tiles carved with intricate precision, personal to her own contact. She had tiles and cards hidden away at home too, some made by spiritualist craftsmen from America and Western Europe, but whenever she was asked to somebody else's house, as was the case this evening with her sister, she liked to bring her own set.

They each placed the tips of their index fingers on the top of the wooden planchette and watched Cassandra as she concentrated on the board in front of her. Her eyes seemed almost to flicker up inside her head, as though she was slipping into some kind of trance, and yet she always kept the appearance of mostly being with them.

As she began to speak her first words, however, a strange kind of chill immediately seemed to circle the room, prickling the hairs across their forearms.

16

"Is there anybody here with us?" she murmured.

Michael felt the chill more readily now and shuddered perceptibly. Irene shot him a glance but saw his face was like stone, and let him be.

"Is there anybody here?" Cassie asked again.

The room was dimly lit; a couple of candles burning on the side table, the glow from the kitchen coming in through the open door. But now they seemed to visibly dim, as though the table and the three of them sitting around it was slowly descending into a creeping dark void the more Cassandra spoke.

"We need to know who you are."

Michael felt his hair lift off his forehead by an impossible breeze, followed by a compulsion to swallow. In his head, a hundred different words for fear began to conjure themselves. This didn't feel right.

"Tell us your name."

Michael felt a twitch beneath his finger, and he realised that he'd forgotten about the board. His eyes flickered downward to see that the pointer had actually moved to the far side of the table without him even realising. It moved beneath his touch to the letter E, and then the letter N.

"Ben," he heard his sister-in-law murmur, her voice now low and soft.

He had missed the first letter.

He would have to pay more attention.

A sweat had broken, he could feel it cooling rapidly on his forehead, on his top lip. He swallowed hard, the pointer itching beneath his fingertip. This wasn't right at all.

"How old are you, Ben?"

His eyes went wide as he watched the glass move to the number 3 on the table in front of his wife. The cold sweat broke a trickle of ice water across his brow,

17

and as a second shiver coursed across his body, he snatched his finger back and cried out in terror.

"This is bullshit," he screamed, his voice louder and more hysterical that he'd intended.

His wife stared agog at him but he didn't care. That fucking thing had stopped right in front of her, for Christ's sake.

He could feel his hands shaking, and as much as he didn't want to admit to Cassandra that maybe there was something in this ouija stuff after all, the board had given him the shits.

"Sit down," Irene said to him, but there was no conviction in her voice. She'd never tried playing the ouija before, despite how many times she'd harangued her sister about it, and now it seemed that she didn't like it either. She didn't look as though she was as frightened as he had become, but he could see in her eyes that terror had found its way in, and if this continued for just a few more minutes, she'd be right there with him.

"Sit down, Michael," Cassie hissed at him. "You can't just leave in the middle of this. We've called Ben here. We can't leave him here."

"Fuck him –"

"Michael," she persisted firmly, her eyes focussed hard upon him like steel bearings. "If you want to stop, that's fine, but we have to finish this properly."

He stared at her for a few moments but it was clear that she believed in what she was saying. Very slowly he retook his seat.

"Please put your finger back on the planchette."

"No way," he hissed. "Look, I don't know what's going on, or what you're trying to do, but you're moving that thing yourself."

"We're all touching it."

18

"No, you take your finger off as well. You too Irene. If this thing's for real, it should do it itself."

Cass looked at him, looked at the terror that had taken him over, and finally relented and pulled her hand back into her lap. Irene likewise looked at Michael, before she too removed her hand. Then Cass began to speak again, talking to whatever spirit had entered their home.

"Do you have a message for us?"

All three of them studied the heart-shaped pointer in the middle of the table but it refused to move. The frantic rate that Michael's heart had been hammering slowed a little at this. So it *was* bullshit, he thought. That wooden thing wasn't going anywhere.

"Do you have anything to pass on to us?" Cassandra tried again, and once again the glass remained motionless.

Both Irene's and Michael's eyes flickered up towards Cassandra, but she stubbornly refused to return their gazes, and instead persisted with the spirit she'd claimed was with them.

"Is there anyone else with you?" she tried.

They stared at the pointer hard, as though their combined will could move that thing, when suddenly it seemed to jog to the side. Michael's heart turned to ice, and then cracked in two, his stomach slipping like greasy eggs in a frying pan. His forearms were knotted with tension, his fingers shaking and numb. The pointer jogged again, this time a whole sickening inch, across the table towards the end of the alphabet. Cassandra asked her last question again, and Michael hissed at her to stop it, stop it right fucking now. But the question had been asked, and now the spirit wanted to answer.

The pointer suddenly shot across the table, taking

one of the wooden tiles with it as it flew right off the table. Michael stared at it in horror as it hit the floor and skittered into the skirting board with a dull thud.

The three of them sat in stunned and sickened silence for a moment as the wooden pointer slowly spun to a halt. Only then did anyone say anything. It was Cassandra, and all she could utter was a shuddering inhale.

"What's wrong?" Irene asked her, her voice trembling.

"The planchette," Cass stammered. "It left the table before we said goodbye. The spirit wasn't sent away. It's still here. In this room."

Even as she spoke the air seemed to darken even further. An eerie thick chill came swiftly on its back so that their breaths fogged visibly in front of them. The whole house had become deathly silent, and a clammy, almost hand-like weight, seemed to press down upon their shoulders from behind.

Their eyes tracked around the darkness of the room. The candles had gone out, and the only light that illuminated the room now was coming from the kitchen. With his breath still fogging into white clouds in front of him, Michael glanced back down towards the card table and at the wooden tiles still set out around its perimeter in a rectangle. The letter that was missing, the letter that the nervous pointer had ripped right off the board, was the letter Y.

# TWO

## WHAT CRAWLS BEHIND THE WALLS

Irene tugged on the light cord in the bathroom and stepped in front of the small mirrored cabinet over the sink. Her face was pale, her eyes bloodshot, and her heart hammered beneath her blouse. She wanted to swear repeatedly, but not in front of Michael. They been married less than two years, and although she'd sworn some in her youth, it was a side of her she didn't want him to see, despite how shitted up she felt.

Michael, on the other hand, had seemed flustered at the time, Cassandra's pointer hitting the floor just inches from him, but he'd had a couple of beers from the cooler and that had seemed to recompose him. She hoped it wasn't just her who felt scared. Cass was a veteran at this kind of thing, and she'd left quickly afterwards, blaming her sister and her husband for what she called negative psychic turbulence.

She looked hard at her own reflection in the small oval mirror, and for a moment became aware of just how silent the house had become. She held a breath, her focus drifting into middle distance, listening even for the TV downstairs, but there was nothing but the drumming of her own heartbeat.

She looked back at herself. Her pupils were stark inside her eyes, and brutally sharp. She could make out the flecks around her iris, the veins at the edge of the white, all with unusual clarity. The silence of the house was suffocating now - Michael must have turned the TV off for some reason – all except for the thump-thump-thump inside her chest.

Her head conjured the sight of seeing the heart-shaped pointer whistling across the table, tumbling through the air, before hitting the hard floor. She remembered looked across at her sister and seeing her face aghast, and that had scared her more than the accident. Her expression had been one of terror, as though she'd actually clasped eyes upon one of the ghosts she claimed to communicate with. Irene might almost have sworn to have felt something, not like a hand upon her or anything even as physical as that, but more like a breath, a passing touch of a cold exhale.

Something brushed past her cheek suddenly, a chilling whisper in the still air of the bathroom, and she shuddered away from it, stumbling to the door with a sudden fright as she screamed out her husband's name. She felt stupid even as she cried out, but when he did not reply, she hurried to the top of the stairs and called out to him again.

The house was still in silence; no TV, no fridge opening in the kitchen, nothing.

Irene stood for a moment at the top of the stairs looking down, waiting for him to appear, but there weren't even any footsteps; the house was simply dead.

She called out again, a note of panic creeping into her voice, but his name echoed off the walls like a dull clarion, the sound sucked into a void.

The hairs had risen on her neck now, prickling like nettles. He wouldn't have gone out without telling her, she thought quickly to herself. Where would he go? Cass had already left, angrily too, and Michael wouldn't have gone after her anyway.

A door slammed shut, and her heart skipped a beat, her stomach lurching.

"Michael?" she almost wept his name now, but still he did not reply.

She put a foot on the top step, stooping to try and see through the banisters, praying that he would appear out of the living room with a reassuring smile on his lips.

"Michael?" her voice was quieter now, timid even. What if something else had heard her. What if there was something loose in the house after all.

Something creaked above her head, from the roof or the attic, and Irene almost stumbled down the stairs as she cowered away from it, her head swivelling to stare up at the ceiling. But there was nothing there, nothing visible anyway. Then came the soft padding of footsteps, thump-thump-thump, as if somebody was treading slowly across the rafters.

Her breath froze in her throat. A cool breeze suddenly lifted her hair delicately off her face. Her skin raised gooseflesh, the hairs on her arms itching. And then came a footstep in the hallway just below her. She shot a glance down through the banisters and saw Michael standing there looking up at her, another beer in his hand. His expression was bemused, and as she stared back at him, she realised that she could hear the TV droning in the background behind him. There was no mistaking it, it was on, and she could hear the theme tune to his favourite show playing too.

"What are you doing sitting on the stairs, hon?"

23

he asked her, taking a gulp from his beer.

Irene opened her mouth but nothing came out, nothing that made sense anyway.

"Come and watch TV," he went on, half turning, the motion unsettling his balance. It was clear that that was not his third beer in his hand.

"I'll be down in a minute," she murmured, unable to take her eyes off him. "Where did you go?"

"The kitchen."

"No, before that. Did you go outside for something?"

Michael shook his head.

"I've been here all the time."

Irene looked back up at the ceiling. The slow padding had stopped, the upstairs rooms now quiet once more. She suddenly didn't want to go back into the bathroom, and even though she'd left the light on, she hurried downstairs to sit with Michael for a bit. It'd be bedtime soon, she thought crazily to herself, and they could go up together.

## 2

The clock on the bedside cabinet ticked steadily in the darkness, but it wasn't that that had woken her. Something was moving in the attic, in the space above their heads.

The rafters creaked gently, and Irene stared wide-eyed up at the ceiling, tracing in the darkness its route by the sounds across the attic floor. Michael made honking noises beside her, submerged in a deep sleep, and Irene did not want to wake him. He'd have thought her crazy about someone walking in an empty attic if she woke him, and only a couple of years into their marriage, to actually wake him in the middle of the night for so ludicrous a notion would put an unnecessary strain where one didn't need to be. His hours had already become longer and harder than they had been, and he needed his sleep. They'd moved to Hunton for the fresh air of the countryside, thinking that when they raised a family, which Irene hoped was soon, their kids would grow up healthier than if they'd stayed in grimy old London.

The creaking stopped suddenly, and for one horrible moment Irene thought she was being watched, as though whatever had been tramping across the rafters had suddenly stopped and looked down at whatever was watching it.

Her skin ran icy cold, and a shiver scuttled across her flesh; she didn't like it at all.

Her entire body tensed with fear, the feeling of being looked at immense and frightening, and she almost took hold of Michael's arm with the intention of shaking him awake. Almost. But her hands stayed where they were. The creaking started again, continuing in the direction it had been going, fading as it moved away from above their bedroom and out over the landing, sending the house into silence once again.

But the feeling of dread would not leave her. As much as she tried to reason it – noisy pipes, contracting timber – the image of something treading carefully from one rafter to another would not leave her head. She could visualise, in the darkness of the bedroom, a shadowy black figure with thin gaunt legs striding from beam to beam, a large black hat perched on its head, obscuring features she knew would be hideous, ghost-like.

The word ghost screamed out at her. Why had she

used it? It made the whole cottage feel haunted, possessed, and the shiver of fear shot rapidly through her body, chilling her bones utterly. Oh how she wanted Michael to snort himself awake. She would hug him then, under the pretence of passion. She never felt afraid when she was with him. Terror only came to her when she was alone. Perhaps she thought that he would always protect her, no matter what might face them. Perhaps it was just someone else to share the fear with her, halving it, who knows? Perhaps that was why she felt so terrified now. With Michael snoring beside her, it felt as though she was alone, with no one to protect her from whatever was creeping about in the attic.

Something whispered behind her ear and Irene shook violently. It was only a few words, enough to make her think afterwards that perhaps she had heard nothing at all, but tears welled quickly, her pulse thudding a sudden furious beat. She clutched at her husband now, her fingers clenching his pyjamas inside the ball of her fist, but he didn't wake. He snorted loudly as he rolled halfway over, but then slid back into his former rhythm of wheezing breaths.

Irene's eyes were white in the blackness of the room. Her hands were shaking, her icy skin prickled with gooseflesh, and her breathing had become insanely ragged. The whispering did not come again, but she lay in a horrible silence for at least an hour, unable to move in case this thing should see her awake, unable to breath in case it should hear her.

What she saw next was sunlight illuminating the room. Her eyes flickered open to see Michael creeping out of the room. She spoke his name, wanting him to stay with her, at least for a while, and he stopped and looked back at her with a warming smile on his lips.

"I didn't mean to wake you," he said to her, his voice still hushed.

"I'm glad you did."

"Are you okay? You look pale."

"I didn't sleep well."

He came to the edge of the bed and perched on it, pressing the palm of his hand against her brow.

"You don't have a temperature."

"Nothing high anyway."

Michael's brow furrowed.

"Doesn't matter," Irene said, taking his hand and holding it firmly in hers. "What time is it?"

"Six."

"Do you have to go so early?"

"The cattle won't look after themselves."

Irene pursed her lips. She knew this new life would be so much healthier for them, but the hours were crippling. They'd not been here a month, but she could see the tiredness at the edges of Michael's eyes already in the darkness that circled them. He'd not complained, although the work was hard, but she suspected that he wouldn't quit even if he wanted to. They'd made the decision to stay, for the benefit of raising a good family. What kind of living could London offer their kids? Here they would have fields and woods to play in and explore, while the city could only offer dirty streets full of speeding cars and criminals. There was no question really.

Her eyes went past him to the ceiling, but it was just as it should be, the thin shaft of golden sunlight breaking through the gap in the curtains and painting itself through its centre like a long magician's staff. There were no noises now either, no creaking of rafters, and as much as she wanted to tell her husband about what she had heard during the night, she did

27

not want to upset him. It was an old cottage, a forester's cottage. It was supposed to make noises. It was just that last night -

"I'll see you lunchtime," Michael said, bending to kiss her.

He ruffled her hair with his hand, stroking it away from her face with his long delicate fingers, the skin of his fingertips roughened from honest manual labour. It felt nice to have his touch upon her, the abrasiveness of his skin, and she could only help but think that it would have been nicer to have had it during the night.

"I'll make you something nice," she said, taking his hand in hers and kissing it tenderly.

He got up to leave, smiling before making his way to the door.

"I'll look forward to it," he said, and went to close the door after him.

"Leave it open," she said, a little more loudly and abruptly that she'd intended.

His face appeared back round it.

"I need to get up in a minute anyway," she added.

"Sleep some more, honey," he said to her. "There's no need to get up so soon if you had trouble sleeping."

"No, it's okay. I think some fresh air would do me more good."

"Sure?"

Irene nodded.

"Yes. I'm sure."

# THREE

## INFLUENCE OF THE TREES

Michael came home at one o'clock, his work clothes dappled with green. Irene greeted him warmly as he came in the back, his muddied boots left outside by the step, craning her neck to plant a kiss upon his lips so that she didn't dirty her apron.

"I've made you a pie," she told him excitedly, almost skipping back to the log-burning oven, "from those apples you got from the orchard."

"I haven't had a home-made apple pie in years."

"I know," she said with a grin. "I only hope it tastes okay."

"And why wouldn't it," he said, siding over to her and laying a kiss upon the back of her neck.

Irene curled from the contact, the sensation tickling the hairs at her nape, and turned swiftly to take hold of him, forgetting the greenery that covered most of his front.

"You shouldn't have done that," Michael said to her, kissing her anyway. "This stuff is a swine to get off."

Irene backed away a little to examine it.

"What is it?"

"Just greenery off the trees. I've been doing some pruning up at the copse on the hill."

"And it won't brush off?"

She wanted to have a go, but didn't want a kitchen full of dirt with her pie almost ready to come out.

"Mostly," he said, glancing down at his chest. He lifted a hand but Irene stopped him.

"Not in here."

"Sorry," he said with a grin, and turned to go back outside.

"What's that?" she asked, stepping after him.

"What's what?"

"That, on your arm."

Michael raised both his arms and cast an eye over them both, but Irene had already taken hold of the one she had seen and was manoeuvring it towards the light.

"It's just a twig of something stuck to the skin," Michael said dismissively, waiting to take his arm back. But Irene wasn't about to let it go so easily. She put her face nearer to it, lifting the sprouting stem gently with her fingers.

"That's not stuck," she said quietly, as she scrutinised it further. "It's like it's growing out of you."

"That's ridiculous," he said. "It's just something that's got snagged, that's all."

"No, look," she said adamantly. "It's sprouting out of your arm."

Michael looked closer now, to humour his wife if nothing else, but to his amazement, the twig did indeed seem to be growing out of his flesh. He pulled it a little but it was in there alright.

"Just what sort of trees are you pruning up there?" Irene wanted to know now. "Are they dangerous?"

"There's no such thing as a dangerous tree," Michael said to her, pinching the stem between his thumb and index finger, teasing it out.

"I think you ought to ask Mr Oates."

"I'm not wasting his time with something this silly."

The roots were firm inside the flesh of his arm, but Michael continued to ease it out. He winced in pain as the growth refused to let go of whatever it had adhered itself to, but with a thin snapping sound the twig came free and Michael went over to the kitchen bin to drop it inside.

"There," he said, with a kind of uneasy flourish. "It's gone now."

Irene regarded him with an uncertain expression. It was clear that she wasn't convinced.

"You should tell Mr Oates anyway," she said to him.

Michael went over to her and kissed her forehead.

"It's gone now, honey," he said with a smile. "Now, how about a slice of that pie?"

Irene turned and went back to the oven, hooking open the heavy metal door and peering inside. A wave of dry but sweet-smelling heat parched her face, but she could see that the pastry had turned the colour of caramel. Reaching up for her oven glove and a spatula, she guided the metal dish off the shelf and out onto the counter. Steam plumed around her like mist on a rolling moor, and she closed the oven door to find Michael standing over her, inhaling the steam with closed eyes.

"I'm going to have to pay the orchard another visit," he said dreamily.

"I take it you still want a slice?"

"And make it a big one."

"There's something else I've been thinking about, Michael," she said, pulling a knife from the cutlery

31

drawer. "It gets a bit lonely with you all out all day, so what would you think about getting a pet?"

Michael looked at her.

"What sort of pet?"

"A cat or a dog or something."

Michael stared at her as she balanced a large slice of pie out of the dish and set it onto one of her dessert plates. Handing him a fork, she added:

"It'd keep me company."

Michael pondered the notion as he picked up his plate.

"I don't see any reason why not," he said at last, lifting the pie up to his nose and smelling it with half-lidded eyes of bliss.

"And it would get plenty of exercise, living out here."

"You can be sure of that."

"So what do you think?"

Michael separated a chunk of pie with the edge of the fork, the apple steaming madly, but he left it to cool a few moments more.

"A dog might be a bit of a bind, you know?"

"A cat then?"

Michael smiled, and then finally nodded.

"Sure," he said. "Why not."

Irene grinned with happiness and then prompted him to try the pie. She watched him keenly as he picked up the chunk of pie before blowing on it and slipping it into his mouth.

"Well?" she wanted to know eagerly.

"Good," he stammered, the word coming out on a cushion of steam. "And hot."

# FOUR

## FERTILE

Irene was stirring her cup of coffee and thinking of names for cats when a sudden wave of nausea broke. She was still in the kitchen, bending over the counter, and she clamped one hand to her belly instinctively, her other to her head as it went light. Her eyes glazed, her vision finding middle distance, as her stomach convulsed wildly. Michael had already gone back to work some twenty minutes before, leaving her alone in the house, and even though it was probably only a bout of sickness, she suddenly wanted him to be close by.

Dashing through the house to the small downstairs bathroom, Irene held her breath for fear of vomiting across the hall carpet, but when she reached the toilet and bent over the white porcelain, nothing came up into her mouth.

She stood there for a few moments, one hand against the wall for support, but the feeling of sickness and light-headedness had evaporated just as quickly as it had come. Her eyes focussed on the clear water in the bowl, her other hand still clasping her belly, but the nausea had passed.

Slowly she stood upright, waiting for any further

sign - a convulsion, a head rush - but there was nothing, and so hesitantly she wandered back along the hallway to the kitchen.

Taking up the spoon from where she had dropped it, Irene resumed stirring her coffee, her forehead knotted with confusion. It was a little after one thirty. Breakfast had been cereal and some toast, a slice of apple pie for lunch, nothing that would cause an upset stomach. She picked up the milk bottle still sitting on the counter and put her nose to it, but it smelled fine. Taking the mug up, she went out through the back door, slotting the milk back into the inside of the fridge door on her way past.

The air outside was cool and fresh, and she breathed it deeply as she sat down on the wooden bench at the back of the cottage. The view stretched for miles, down to the tree-lined stream just past the end of the garden, and up to the fields of one of the other farms, all the way to the copse-dotted horizon. It was idyllic, a perfect place to raise a family, and she smiled to herself as she took a sip of her coffee.

Michael had taken a job at Manor Farm. The front of the cottage looked out over it, but she could not see any of its fields from where she was, and imagined him lifting bales of hay of walking out to the sheep in the fields. Irene had met Mr Oates, the owner of the farm, only once before Michael had been offered the job, and he'd seemed a nice enough man. He was married to a woman called Lizbeth, and without any children to help on the farm, Mr Oates had advertised. She'd been dubious about leaving the city, leaving everything she had ever known and moving to a cottage in the middle of nowhere. But as they'd driven to Michael's interview, the grey grim streets had changed to rich verdant greens of woods and fields, and she'd sat breathless, wondering about all the possibilities, as Michael had driven her through it.

They'd not been moved in two months yet but Irene couldn't imagine moving back. To sit at the back of her new home and look out over sheep-filled fields, with birdsong in the hedgerows and skylarks in the air, with a sighting of a fox skirting a low stone wall only a few days ago; why, it was almost too much to believe that it was true.

She put her hand back upon her belly as she sat on the wooden bench, and dared imagine what it might be like to have a child inside there. Would it be a strong boy with dark hair and a mischievous grin, or a beautiful girl with blonde curls that she could tie up with bows. She found herself smiling insanely, and chastened herself for being so in love with idea. She and Michael were trying, of course. That had been the main reason for moving out to the countryside, after all. But so far there had been no success. She only hoped that Michael's long hours and strenuous work wouldn't take their toll on him too much.

But their bedroom time had not suffered. In fact the fresh air seemed to have increased his enthusiasm, and as she sat and drew images of him in her head - his wide sweating body, his heaving muscular torso - she found another huge smile spreading across her face that she had trouble controlling. She even held her hand up over her face, concealing the sight of this woman sitting alone and grinning to herself, as if someone might be watching her and thinking her insane.

Let them watch, she wanted to think, but the hand remained in place, giggles coming as she let love for her husband overwhelm her with a blissful warmth.

Later that night, after they'd eaten and Michael had showered, Irene suggested an early night. Michael had looked up at her, his eyes wide with surprise.

"I've only just put the telly on," he said.

"I know, but I've missed you all day," Irene said softly, perching on the arm of his chair and sliding a hand across his shoulders.

It didn't take long for Michael to catch on, and he slipped his arm around Irene's waist and lifted his head up for a kiss. Irene obliged, and their lips came together passionately, Michael's other hand finding bare flesh beneath her skirt, rising up to knead her thigh.

"God I love you," he murmured between kisses. "I love you so much."

Irene had her fingers in the depths of his hair now, teasing his locks, urging him.

"Take me to bed then," she breathed, pressing her lips against his cheeks, his forehead.

Michael climbed out of his chair then, reached to turn off the television, and then turned to scoop her up into his arms, before carrying her out of the living room towards the stairs.

Irene pressed kiss after kiss across his face and neck as he negotiated the stairs, carrying her across the landing, before pushing the bedroom door open with his foot. Irene reached blindly for the light switch as Michael staggered in a kind of uncertain limbo in the darkness of the room, and they both giggled as they then stumbled onward towards the bed.

He dropped her onto the mattress before falling at her side, finding her lips with his own once again as he sought to undo her blouse. Throwing her head back to allow him access to her neck, Irene breathed heavily with delirium as she felt his lips and tongue rove down to her throat, and to her breasts as they became bared. The sensation was hot and deeply erotic, his mouth upon her breasts, his hands teasing between her legs, and she wanted him deep inside her, wanted his seed to fertilise her there and then tonight and make her a child. She opened her eyes now and saw him busy beneath her open blouse, but she hauled him away from her, her fists grasping great tufts of hair, and pulled his lips against her own once again, tasting his tongue like she had never tasted him before.

Her hands moved down to his shirt, unbuttoning him roughly, before forcing her hands across the thick mat of hair across his chest. They went down even further to unbuckle him, and found him already hard and straining, and she struggled to expose him, so restricting were his trousers at his crotch. She felt his fingers at the small of her back, trying to undo her skirt, but she didn't want that, didn't want the neatness or the conformity. She had his cock in her hands, and it was all she wanted.

"Leave it," she snapped, pressing her lips back hard against him.

She felt his body tense, and she realised quickly his confusion.

"My skirt," she said, "leave it where it is. Just pull my knickers down."

But Michael did not respond, either with words or actions, and Irene realised too that she had never spoken this way with Michael before, either in the bedroom or out. She opened her eyes to see him looking uneasily at her. The mood was shifting rapidly, the heat dissipating. She wanted him to fuck her right now. She'd waited all day for him, all day since her morning coffee and her dreams of bearing a child.

"I want you inside me," she said quietly, her words less filthy, her tone less bestial.

"And I will be."

"Oh Michael, I love you so much, I can't bear it. I don't want to wait until we're both naked, I want you *now*."

As she said this last word she yanked on his member still clutched in her hand. She didn't know if she meant it as a catalyst or whether it was purely unintentional, and frankly she didn't care. It had the desired effect, and Michael hoisted her skirt up to her waist before taking hold of her knickers and tugging them down across her thighs, pulling them off her feet and tossing them away behind him. He looked back up at her with a grin of wild desire, and she pulled him back over her eagerly, kissing him hard once again as she felt his cock butt hard at her hips before slipping deeply inside her.

The sex was hard and aggressive, quick too, and he filled her more fully than he had ever done before. It seemed to take its toll on Michael too, for he rolled away from her with heavy groans after he was spent and sank into a deep slumber almost immediately. Her eyes grew leaden too, and she had barely pulled the covers over their sweating bodies, or pressed a kiss against his chest, before she too fell headlong into a deep and heavy sleep.

It was dark and warm. Encased inside a sweet-smelling fluid, her limbs slow to move through its rich viscosity, she felt herself being lulled by the red and orange luminescence around her. She was happy, of that she was more aware than anything.

Then something moved just ahead of her, unseen as yet, but she was already moving through the nurturing fluid towards it. A tiny shape appeared, curled like a pale bean, and she felt herself loose a delicate gasp.

She was inside her own womb.

And there in front of her was the child she and Michael had just conceived.

The larger end of the bean suddenly sprouted into a more recognisable skull-shape as she watched, two deeply-pink and bulbous eyes appearing to stare blindly back at her. Tiny fingers unfurled from barely-developed hands and clutched weakly at the supporting water in which they both swam.

This was so obviously a dream, she thought distantly, watching this tiny baby develop at incredible speed, but it was still so blissful to lay eyes upon him, imagined or otherwise.

She watched breathlessly as his fingers continued to grasp without strength, watched spellbound as his tiny legs unfolded from his body, and kicked out with little regard for his mother's stomach. And then his eyes swivelled and roved behind lids only membrane thin, opening to return her gaze with utter focus and insane dread.

The fluid that encased her suddenly began to thud, echoing the heartbeat of this infant loud in her head. The stare that met hers was red and fierce, horrific like that of a rabid dog, and it chilled her insanely as a spine-toothed grin suddenly cracked his face in two, loosing a sickening blood-curdled cry like that of a butchered baby.

*          *          *

Irene loosed a half-strangled scream as she sat bolt upright in bed, crying and shaking, convinced that she was indeed pregnant, but with what? Her thoughts jerked back once again to Cassandra and her hateful ouija and the sounds that had thumped in the attic and behind the walls after it had all gone so horribly wrong. Why had they even tried it? Why had they summoned the dead? Had that been the face of the expectant father inside her? Not Michael, but the thing that they'd failed to say goodbye to.

She looked down at her hands and saw, by the pale light coming in through the undrawn curtains, that they were physically shaking. The thudding of her child's heartbeat continued to pulse inside her head, louder than it had been, pounding against the inside of her skull and punching at her very thoughts.

She reached down and put a trembling hand against her belly. Could she feel it kicking? Could she feel the ridges of its needle grin piercing through the flesh of her womb even now? No, of course she couldn't. It was a dream, just a dream.

Irene clasped both hands to her head and clenched her hair in two great fists, wringing it until it hurt. Oh God what was happening? What was this thing that haunted their home?

She was sure she was pregnant. She had felt so happy with the thought of bearing a child, and now this nightmare had stolen that joy, replaced it with a horror that she didn't think could exist.

Slowly she lay back down, the sweat-soaked sheet icy upon her back, and stared up at the darkened ceiling above her in terror. Was there something up there looking down at her? Was it watching her even now, watching the mother of its child? Tears came again, of agony and frustration, coursing down her cheeks and staining the fabric of her pillow. Why was this happening to her? Why had she been robbed of a joyful pregnancy?

She had to go to the doctor in the village first thing in the morning, she realised desperately, clenching her eyes shut against the oppressive darkness of the room, forcing the tears out more readily. She had to find out for certain, and only then could she hope to find a smile for the thing that she was sure she was already carrying inside her.

# FIVE

## THE DOCTOR

There's no possible way I can tell whether you're pregnant or not," the doctor tried explaining to her for the second time.

"No way?"

"Not for at least four weeks. I'm afraid the human body just doesn't work that quickly."

Irene slumped back in her chair and stared at him. She knew he was right, of course, and in hindsight it seemed ridiculous her coming into the village to see him. They'd been trying for a baby for a while, but the previous night's dream had seemed to prove her conception, despite the horrible face it had worn. Here and now in the doctor's surgery she could explain that face rationally; it was psychological, of course it was, the fear of motherhood, it was terrifying really. Had it not been for the house, or rather her sister's visit with the ouija board, she would almost certainly not be this scared.

"Do you want to make an appointment to come back in four weeks time" the doctor asked her.

Irene realised that she'd been staring into space.

She smiled apologetically.

"I'm sorry, Dr Walton," she said. "It's just that... I had this dream."

42

"Of being pregnant?"

Irene nodded again, embarrassed.

"You'd be surprised how common that is."

"Really?"

"Many women dream of their unborn babies before there's any sign. It's like the first test there can be, if you will, the connection between mother and child."

"I'm glad to hear I'm not the only one."

It was Dr Walton's turn to smile now, and he got up to escort Irene to the door. She rose and went with him, her fears only marginally assuaged. She knew the reality of the situation, the jitters, the nerves, and here her new doctor had confirmed her fears as commonplace. She halted at the threshold as he pulled open the door for her.

"Four weeks, you say?"

"Make an appointment with my receptionist," he said with another smile. "Better to be safe than sorry."

"Of course, doctor. Thank you."

And with that she left, her head busy with dizzying thoughts.

Once outside, Irene made her way along the high street towards the post office. She had only walked perhaps thirty or forty yards when she saw an elderly woman on the other side of the otherwise empty street staring at her. It wasn't a wide street and they could see each other plainly, but the old woman's eyes seemed black and unnatural, staring right into her. Irene tried to keep moving, tried to ignore her, but she glanced at her a few paces on and found that she was still staring at her, motionless but for turning her head, her cavernous eyes hypnotic. Irene stopped, her skin crawling with unease. She wanted to call out to her, to ask her if they knew each other, but before she could, something else snatched her attention.

Off to her left, perched on the limb of a tree, was a crow. It too did not move, but regarded her in much the same way as the old woman. It's eyes were hollow and penetrating, and the hairs on the back of her neck prickled at its attention. She gazed back quickly at the old woman but saw that she was now looking from her to the crow and back again, as if Irene and the crow were somehow inextricably linked. But that was crazy.

Irene shuddered visibly, and her head went as light as it had the previous day, only this time it threatened to take her consciousness. She could feel herself growing weaker, a flurry of sickness sweeping through her belly. Suddenly she didn't want to be in the village any more, and blamed it readily on her nausea.

She turned quicker than she'd intended, ignoring her trip to the post office, and swayed unsteadily, blackness waiting behind her eyelids. Her sight came in blurred snatches, of the road and the shops along its length, but she hurried away regardless, back along the pavement away from both the old woman and the crow, her hands outstretched in front of her like a blind man.

Tears were welling now too, but for what reason she didn't know, and they contorted her vision further as she staggered back the way she'd come, where there were more creatures waiting for her behind that parked car, up in the eaves of the chemist and hanging from the tree out front of the church. How dare that old woman stare at her, as though she was some kind of monster herself, as though all the secrets and the horrors of the world could be pinned upon her.

By the time she'd turned the corner and found her

way back onto the road that led home, the tears of anger and desperation had burst, and skipped freely down her cheeks. Sobs came too, and she was glad that they had stifled themselves so that they wouldn't be seen by the old woman or anyone else on the street.

She'd made her appointment with the doctor for four weeks time, only now she wasn't sure whether she wanted to go back there ever again. Something wasn't right in the village. She'd not noticed it before, but then she hadn't noticed a lot of things before. She suddenly wanted the familiarity of the city, the busy roads, the crowded thoroughfares. This place was too quiet, too unpopulated. The lanes were empty and the creatures had begun to watch her. It wasn't right, wasn't right at all. But how could she explain any of it to Michael? How could she explain that she didn't want to have her family grow up in this place after all?

# SIX

## THE SECRET HEARTS

All Dorothy Grace could do was stand and stare at the woman on the other side of the street. The spectacle was almost too much to bear, and yet it was right there in front of her, waiting to be witnessed, on the other side of the high street.

A pillar of eager flame licked across the young woman's body as she watched, rising to a flickering cone of brilliant yellow heat a full yard above her head. She seemed not to feel the ferociousness of the inferno, but merely returned her gaze with something close to indignance.

Dorothy had felt her stomach turning, witnessing something so terrible as this human fire, and yet so little of her body seemed to be consumed by its fury.

Her skin remained white and unblemished, her hair silken despite how it danced on end, but most of all her expression renounced all knowledge of the very fire that engulfed her.

Even as she watched the woman turn tail and flee, her consciousness threatened to slip as the flames flailed behind her, contorting and guttering as the bonfire fought to keep its fuel of human flesh.

She watched the inferno rage until the woman turned the corner and disappeared from sight, and then like a finger snap inside her skull, the spell seemed broken, and Dorothy staggered sideways, clasping the wall of the nearest shop for support as the world became a little darker, a little bit more slippery to hold onto.

Harvey Keits had already returned home from his job at the slaughterhouse, had taken a hot bath and was now sitting at the kitchen table idly flicking through the newspaper. Kitty, lost inside great plumes of steam from the largest of their casserole dishes, was busy serving up two platefuls of sausages in onion gravy. It was one of her husband's favourite dishes, despite the stories that he'd reveal about what went on in the abattoir, and what actually constituted a sausage.

Kitty turned with a plate in each hand, but as she laid eyes upon her husband, or rather what had become of him, both dinners slipped from her numb fingers, smashing across the tiled floor, and spattering thick gravy up the magnolia walls like the brains of the dead.

A fleshless skull grinned back at her, sunken eyes rising from the sports page to look blankly up at her. Why have you ruined my supper, those eyes seemed to say? Do the dead not deserve sausages?

The scream that lodged in her throat grasped the air in her lungs too, throttling her as she staggered away from this monstrosity. The zombie clambered out of his chair, his once black hair now grey and decayed and sagging like rotten string, his skeletal hands reaching up and out to take hold of her. Kitty ran screaming now, her voice found, straight out of the front door and straight under the wheels of the local meat van as it thundered out of control past the house.

*       *       *

The lamp still burned on the floor beside Len Barrett's mattress, and showed to him again the handiwork of his first day's decorating. It had been a full day too. He had worked deliberately and methodically, getting everything just right in the bedroom. His sight followed the perfectly hung wallpaper from the doorway right across to the curtainless window, the glass like a void of solid blackness, reflecting everything inside the room so deeply that he could not even see the bright stars out in the cloudless night sky.

He lay there gazing contentedly up at the reflection of his perfect room. Everything was right. Everything was his and his alone.

Then he heard the rumble of a van approaching somewhere outside in the night, and as its headlights found the window through which he looked, it illuminated an ugly and cruel face sitting right outside, its gaze returning his as it watched him.

The van passed and went, snatching away its light, and he could see it no more, yet he was certain that it saw him still, its eyes still hollow, its gaze still creeping.

It had been but the briefest of glimpses, too brief to discern anything other than a glimpse of its hideous face, but its features had been burned upon his imagination like deathly black phosphorus.

Len lay stricken, certain in his mind that it was still perched upon his windowsill, returning that glance that they had shared. The chill of fright had caught him. He was suddenly no longer blissful in his new home, but troubled now, and distraught in an old cold house, a shell of a building that suddenly offered no hope for the future.

\*          \*          \*

Lizbeth Oates trod the steps down to the cellar, pulling on the light cord that illuminated the jars of pickled vegetables. Something seemed to move in the uncertain shadows cast by the single yellow bulb, and for a moment she halted near the bottom of the wooden stairs.

The door suddenly banged shut behind her, even though there was no wind, sealing her in the cellar. Something was down there with her, and just before the bulb blinked out, she saw its face, vast and grotesque, coming at her.

She screamed as she started back for the door, but her heel caught on the unlit stairway, and she tumbled, striking her head on one of the wooden steps, and knocking the horror from her consciousness.


On the roof of the church, a flock of crows descended beneath the wash of moon and stared out across the panicking village. In unison they had landed, and like one they all stared across the rooftops and fields towards the copse of trees that stood on the hill, the same copse of trees that Michael Rider had pruned the day before.

Their feathers were blacker than the night, and glinted coldly beneath the moonlight, shining like burnished coal, as their unblinking eyes regarded this secluded society.

There was death on the wind, bringing with it the smell of carrion. There would be pickings, of flesh and of souls. Something was coming, they knew, and it had no name.

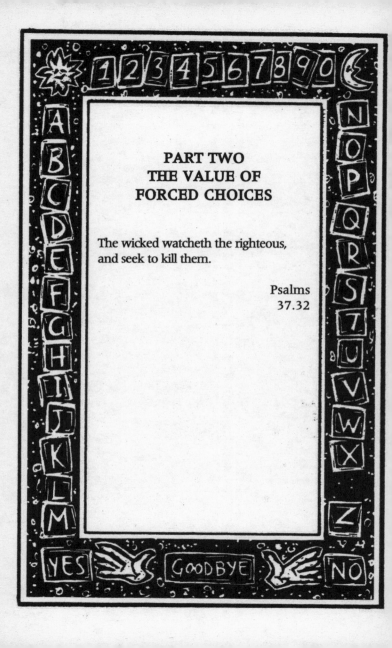

# PART TWO
# THE VALUE OF
# FORCED CHOICES

The wicked watcheth the righteous,
and seek to kill them.

Psalms
37.32

# ONE

## DOOR TO A DARK WORLD

Aunt Cassie was already there when the two of them got in. She was sitting by the window gazing out at the sheep-dotted fields, her head resting limply on one hand, her hair barely combed and hanging down across her shoulders like a muddy-brown fleece snagged on a barbed wire fence. She turned to look at them as they entered, her face not one that spoke of having had a good day. Her expression was grim, almost final, her complexion pale and tired, and it did not take long for the truth to come out.

"It's mum, isn't it?"

It was Isabel who spoke, the young girl standing on the threshold clutching her school bag to her chest now as though it was her thumping heart. Her voice was quiet and shaking, fearing that the anguish that was about to come would snatch it from her altogether and leave her with nothing but deathly silence.

Aunt Cassie had no reason to lie, and returned a shallow nod.

"Her condition has worsened, honey," she explained slowly, pushing her long brown hair away from her face with a thin weak hand. Her straggled locks tumbled back almost immediately but she seemed not to notice, or even to care, continuing with the terrible news that she bore. "Her illness, well, it's taking what little strength she has left. The doctor came to see her again today and, well, he doesn't expect her to stay with us much longer."

The statement demanded a question, and it came swiftly from Isabel.

"How much longer?"

Aunt Cassie took a deep haggard breath.

"A week. Maybe two."

Isabel felt herself sway inside and staggered back a step as though she was going to fall. Her hand went to her head as though to keep what few coherent thoughts she had there in place. Her mother was going to be gone soon, away from the house, away from her. She had been told as much for the last year or so, but this news just seemed so unexpected with its finality. Dr Walton had said so. There was just no way to drag out the words her aunt had given her.

"Is she still here?" she breathed eventually.

"Yes, Isabel," Cassie replied with another shallow nod, but as the girl turned to head for the stairs, her aunt quickly held her back with some urgent words.

"Leave her to rest," she said. "She's sleeping now, and will be for some time. You can see her later, love. Perhaps before you go to bed."

Isabel stared at her in silence for a few moments after that, not knowing what to say, not knowing whether to listen or to just charge straight up to her mother's bedroom regardless. She so desperately wanted to throw her arms around her and make her better, now more than ever, but her arms had seemed horribly ineffective as a healing touch, and the mysterious illness had continued to worsen.

In the uneasy silence, her brother's footfalls across the hard wooden floor tapped an irregular beat as he stepped across the room towards his mother's sister. She watched him come, saw his dark eyes burning, his face flushed, and expected the question before it had even come from his lips.

"And dad?" he asked in a quiet voice. "Has there been any news of him?"

Aunt Cassie reached a hand out for him to take but he refused it, and simply gazed at her waiting for her to answer his question.

"I'm sorry, honey," she said, attempting a tender smile. "Nobody knows where he is."

"Somebody must know," he persisted.

She tried to comfort him with that smile, but what could she do?

"I can't tell you anything. I'm sorry."

Kyle stared at her for a moment longer, his eyes narrowing with something that could almost have been suspicion, or even, at a push, contempt. It was a tough time for them all, and strained emotions were obviously to be expected, and yet Cassie felt slightly unnerved being in his presence when he was like this. She knew how close he and his father had been, and she kept her smile as steady as she could for her ten year old nephew, telling him that she was sure everything would be okay.

"You would say that," he said with sneer. "Mum's upstairs. Dad's gone. You're fine to say that."

"Kyle -"

"It's true. You don't care whether dad comes back or not."

"That's not true."

"Yes it is. He's not your father, he's not even part

55

of your family. I wouldn't be surprised if you and her upstairs planned this all along."

It was Isabel's turn to shout his name this time, and she yelled it as she came running across the room after him.

"You're horrible to say such things," she cried, taking hold of his shirt with both hands and shaking him. "Take it back. Take it back."

Kyle wrestled out of her grip with ease, and took hold of her wrists in return and squeezed them hard until it hurt. She let out a squeal of pain, and stepped back sobbing as he released her.

"You're in on this too," he shouted at her. "All of you. You drove dad away, you forced him out of this house."

"It's not true, Kyle," Aunt Cassie tried reasoning again. "He just left, that's the plain truth of it. Sometimes marriages don't work out as we'd want them, sometimes parents leave. It's just a fact of life."

Kyle glared back at her, and that same look came back to his face - suspicion, contempt - but this time she could see a barely concealed snarl of angered teeth behind his thin lips. He would not be told the truth, at least not at the moment, and Cassie chose not to push him any further. It seemed his outburst had pretty much run its course, and she loosed a haggard breath of relief when he finally shoved past his sister and stormed out of the house and back into the late afternoon sunshine.

"I'm sorry, Izzie," Aunt Cassie said to her, as the tears started to run down the young girl's cheeks. "He doesn't mean it. Not really."

"Yes he does," Isabel retaliated, sniffing back her tears as best she could. "He's changing, all the time. He seems to be hating mum the sicker she gets."

"That's not true," Cass hushed her, stretching her arms wide and beckoning for her niece to come into her embrace.

Isabel looked at her for a moment and then went to her.

"I think he blames her, maybe," Cassie continued, "for your father going away, but that's not true either."

"How do you know?"

"I know more about your mother and father than you do, sweet one, and they decided that it was best for him to go away. I know it doesn't seem like it, but it was really the only way."

Isabel gazed up into her eyes from inside her aunt's embrace, her eyes wide with both helplessness and tears. Cassie reached round and held her tiny face in both hands, cupping it gently before pressing a kiss delicately against her forehead.

"This isn't the first time things like this have happened, and one day when you're older and able to understand them, I'll explain them to you, I promise."

"He blames me too. Blames me because I love her."

"Kyle's angry, Isabel. He was very close to his father, just as you are very close to your mother. Give him time. He'll calm down sooner or later, you wait and see."

Her smile was warm, but Isabel felt only the chill of certainty that her mother would soon be gone from her, and what would she do without her then? The doctor knew little about her illness, mystified she'd overheard him say once, and all that he could prescribe - apart from the half dozen brown pill bottles on her bedside cabinet - was plenty of rest, rest that was supposed to keep her energy levels up. But she got plenty of rest. She slept for much of the day as well as throughout the night, and yet she grew progressively weaker and weaker. Her energy levels never stayed the same, let alone improved, and there were becoming less and less waking moments to be able to speak to her in. It was getting hopeless, and with each day that passed, she began to grow more and more worried that it would be the final day, the day that brought the heavy black cloud down upon her, the cloud her own heart kept fearing, and take her away from her forever.

Kyle was sitting on the wall overlooking the lane when Isabel finally went outside. He seemed to be just staring up at the woods on top of the hill, his eyes barely moving as though he was utterly transfixed by the densely packed trees. She knew he liked to go there, perhaps more so since dad had gone, but she just couldn't excuse the way he kept treating mum, like their father's going was all her fault. Isabel started as a crow suddenly cawed raucously from one of the trees at the edge of the garden, before taking to the skies in a vast flapping frenzy of wings as black as coal. The sight of it scared her. It reminded her of death, and it seemed to her as though it was lurking, simply waiting for her mother to die. The fear turned into a shudder of cold and she had to wrap her arms around herself to warm her. Perhaps it was that movement that caused her brother to speak.

"Been bad-mouthing me, have you?" he asked her quietly, without turning round.

"Not everything's about you, Kyle."

"Not everything, no, but a lot of things."

"You think the world revolves around you, don't you?"

"Not yet, Izz, but it will do soon, just you wait and see."

Isabel moved a little closer to the wall so that she could see more of his face. His cheeks seemed flushed and red, and it looked as though he'd been crying too. Perhaps he was just as scared about mum dying as she was after all, just as Aunt Cass had said. But he didn't turn to look at her, though; he just kept gazing out at the dark matted depths of the wood.

"I wish you'd grow up," she said to him finally. "You're meant to be the older one."

He turned to look at her with that comment, and although it wasn't meant to anger him, she saw that his face was flushed not with sadness, but with rage.

"This isn't about you or me," he growled, his voice low and guttural. "It's about mum and dad. She drove him away, Izzie, don't you see that? She treated him so badly that he couldn't stand to be around her any more, any of us."

"That's not true -"

"Yes it is. You're probably too young to remember, but I'm not. I used to hear them when they argued. I used to hear them when they hissed at each other in the middle of the night. They probably didn't think I heard them, but I did. Enough to know what forced him out of here."

Isabel could do nothing but stand and stare at him. Her eyes were stinging with the threat of tears, painful tears, but she was not going to cry in front of him, or because of him. But his words kept coming, words that hurt their mother, words that hurt herself deep inside, and before she knew what she was doing, those tears were running down her cheeks, her throat scratched dry with anguish.

"It's not true," she gasped, clutching her throat as

though her words had grown barbs and become lodged there. "It's not true."

"Yes it is. It's all true. It's mum's fault that dad's gone, and you'd better not side with her. The sooner she's dead the better we'll all be."

Isabel couldn't stand it any more. Her tears were blinding her, but she stumbled away from him regardless and back in the direction of the house, her world a dizzying blur. She knew Aunt Cassie had told her to leave her mother to rest until later, but she wanted to be with her, now more than ever, before death dragged her away from her altogether and into the cruel black soil of the village churchyard where the rest of the dead lay.

## TWO

_____

### WHAT LURKS BEYOND THE DARKNESS

The sky had started to darken before Kyle had even entered the woods. It was quiet beneath its shroud-like canopy, an unearthly quiet as though nothing lived there, or rather everything that had once lived there had died and rotted into the black earth that squelched beneath his feet. The wind barely whispered through the needled boughs of the pines above him, just breaths against his skin, touches that glanced his cheek as if to encourage him further, to entice him in and explore this place more fully.

Almost as soon as he set foot inside the wood, it seemed eager to pull him towards its dark heart, like a tide snatching at his heels, its current dragging him inward. But it was not a fearful pull, however, far from it; Kyle wanted it to take him, wanted it to usher him away from a world that no longer had room for him and into some other place, and if that other place was oblivion then so be it. His father had brought him here often. It felt more like home than home. And it was all he had left now.

The cottage, when his father had lived there, had been his home once. But without him it had simply become a building in which his sister and mother had made their own. His aunt too seemed to spend less time in her own home, and more time at the cottage. He didn't want to be anywhere near any of them, not with things the way they were, not with Cassandra trying to take things over, with the stench of death hanging in every corner of every room, and with his father's name extinguished from every conversation.

It had been so long since his father had gone away, an unannounced departure out of his life. There had been arguments between his parents, he'd heard them through his bedroom wall late at night, but there'd been nothing said to him, nothing that his father had confided, until one day he'd woken to find him gone. There had been no word from him in that time - no letter, no phone call - just a deathly void that shrouded the house, leaving it as empty as a bleached skull.

The caw of a crow suddenly broke the silence up ahead, jerking him from his thoughts. It took a few moments to realise just what was wrong with that, and then it struck him. The wood had seemed dead; a deathly silence had hung in the air like a leaden weight since he had entered, and yet here was a creature to defy that, a crow that broke the poisonous stillness. He gazed out through the low-hanging branches and heavy grey trunks to try and discern its shape, but so dark was the entire canopy of the wood above him, like a solid dark mass that stole all promise of sunlight, that it was impossible to find such a creature in its knotted woven layers. The crow let out a second cry, as if to urge him to keep looking for it, but he could not locate it, and inevitably the wood fell once more into eerie silence.

He'd always been proud in his father's shadow, whether it had been with him amongst these trees or in the church congregation or even at the local village shops. He would do everything with bravery and strength and the other people from the village would know that and respect him utterly. And to have him just disappear out of his life was too much to bear.

It pained his chest to be so alone, to not have him hold his hand or ruffle his hair, or haul him high up onto his shoulders when his legs grew too weak to carry him. Images lurked inside his head, longing to be set free, of his father waiting just around the next tree, or sitting upon an unseen grassed bank, and his eyes would lift from whatever he was busying himself with, and he would hold out his great hands, and he would call out for Kyle to come running into them. But to tempt such longing invited only more pain. His face was already creasing with despair, he could feel the sobs waiting to come, but he suspected that once started, they might never stop, and he would wash himself out of existence in a flood of tears.

He painfully swallowed the huge weight that had lodged itself in his throat, and felt it rasp its awkward passage all the way down. It festered in his belly, writhing like a fist made of maggots, making him feel sick and unsteady, but he did not want to start crying. Not here in his father's wood.

The path thinned and came to a steep incline, and Kyle stood in front of it for a few moments, wondering whether to scale it or simply skirt its perimeter. The energy was not in his bones, but he suddenly wanted to harm them, wanted to force them to work, to haul his weight up to the top and see how much he could make them groan. Coarse grass grew in tufts up its slope and offered slick but firm handholds, and erratically he scrabbled up the steep bank, mud plastering his knees and shoes. He glanced down only once and briefly, wondering what might happen if he threw himself back down, what pain might come, what pain might be ended. But then that image in the dark place inside his skull threatened once again, the image of his father waiting somewhere to be found if only his son had the wit and will to find him, and he turned with a barely stifled sob to continue onward.

He put his fingers to his eyes as his sight blurred and they came away wet with tears. He sniffed back hard but it made no difference. He was crying, it had come at last, and try as he might to continue like a man, he staggered once and fell into a heap, clawing his arms up over his head as he wept long and hard.

His chest heaved and hurt, his sobs wracking his body as if he was getting beaten by some unseen aggressor, his tears coming on stronger. He clenched his hair inside two great fists until his scalp hurt, but still the tears raged. Even the dirt, as he kneeled over and pressed his face down into it and took it up into mouth, could not stem the tears now that they had come. It ground between his teeth, crunching as though his own teeth had cracked and splintered, adding to this filthy meal, but still the pain inside his body would not subside.

Only eventually, once his eyes began to dry, did his heart begin to slow. His cheeks were wet, his lips slick with snot and grit, but there was at least respite.

Slumping back onto his heels, he rocked slowly back and forth, pushing his fingers deep into the black earth, soiling his skin as fully as he could, feeling the black rot in his pores and beneath his nails. The pain in his chest was agony, hurting more than he could ever have thought possible, and his throat felt as if it had been scratched raw with burning nettles. His eyes lifted to take in the sight of the wood once again, searching between the trees, but there was no revelation, no angel come to offer him salvation; just the same trees, the same wood, just as it had been before. And yet his eyes found and settled upon a black shape just ahead of him through the trees, the crow that had goaded him to find it earlier.

Here it was, looking for him through the dense layers, returning his watchful gaze. Its eyes were blacker than holes in a night's sky, its feathers slick and shimmering like polished marble, and its beak, hard and pointed like some long lethal knife, seemed eager to stab at flesh, or to poke out eyes too curious for their own good.

But the menace was not for him, Kyle could somehow sense that as they stared at each other. No, there was something else in the way that this creature regarded him, something different. There was nothing to be scared of here, it seemed to say, we are brothers, part of the same communion, part of the same order of things. You belong here. Stay here and learn our secrets, and then you will become a prince of this dark place.

Pushing himself to his feet, Kyle forced himself on deeper into the dark wood, towards the crow still perched inside its tower of branches, cradled like a beacon inside the ribcage of some vast black beast, his mind losing itself once again to images stirred up amongst the mire of rot and illusion.

His father was there in his old long coat, clambering through this very wood, his gloved hands lifting heavy branches out of his way, forging paths to places he'd not yet visited. There were hollows inside thick trees, big enough to hide a man, and ravines sunk into the ground deep enough to hide whole cities. The boughs above his head were homes for shifting creatures, their translucent figures lifting skyward like veils on an indifferent breeze. All this Kyle saw keenly, the sights wondrous and inviting, but they were not memories that he knew of, and nor were they places that he had visited either with his father or alone or even in dreams.

And then the pictures soured as his mind turned to conjure his father in the village, out walking along the high street, taking in air; but there was no pleasure on his face, no smiles on the faces of those that passed him either. The villagers' eyes burned with loathing and wished him gone or dead, their hands crossing in front of them as they cursed his father in the name of God. It repulsed Kyle to see these memories that were not memories, pictures that were not of his making or even of his desire, and his stomach turned with sickness. He wanted his father back with him now, wanted him to pull him into that great coat of his, to tell him that they would never be away from each other again. Tears threatened once again, his chest hurting madly, but all he could do was stare at the crow.

It continued to look back at him, cocking its head from side to side as if taking in every movement of this young boy. Kyle could feel the weight of its scrutiny, could feel the utter blackness of its eyes as though they were like two tiny soulless mirrors, reflecting all that it could see right back to him. For just a moment, he almost thought he could see himself, a small boy standing amongst a densely-packed circle of trees, lost in a world that had no place for him left. Was this the bird's vision, he thought distantly to himself? Is this what the crow sees?

He started towards it slowly, to examine this creature more closely, this icon of dark fables and superstition, to see its feathers and claws in detail, and stare into its hollow eyes. Kyle was surprised to see that it remained where it was, its head still jerking from side to side, allowing his hesitant approach. And then a breeze picked up from the depths of the breathless wood.

There had been nothing so much as a touch against his cheek since he had entered, no wind finding its way between the deathly-still trees, no life, no movement. He froze momentarily as it lifted the hair from his forehead, and he felt its coolness upon his brow. His eyes flickered closed, thoughts already beginning to stir once more inside his head, and then he heard what sounded like words on the back of that unnatural breeze.

*Become my prince*, it seemed to say. *You belong here. You've always known that.*

His eyes shot open, scanning the wood all around him. He was alone, and yet he was sure that someone had spoken, a whisper somewhere inside his ear. His flesh crawled, his hands began to shake, and yet already the wood was moving to comfort him. It kissed his cheek, caressing his flesh as it embraced him tenderly. He stood motionless as the wood seemed to focus its attention solely on him. It wanted him here, that seemed certain to him, and he let it attend to him.

But then the voice came again on the back of the breeze, delicate but insistent, as the wood cradled him to its message.

*You belong here*, it said again. *Stay here and learn the secrets behind the world.*

The images sought to solidify in the darkness behind his eyes once again, memories that were not his fighting to be seen, to be remembered; his father hunched awkwardly at the back of the church, cowering in the shadows where he would not be seen;

moving from shop to shop in the local village with his collar tugged high, ashamed and shunned by others. It was too much to cope with, too much pain sown inside his own head, and he clenched his eyes shut against it, wishing for it all to go away. All he wanted was to go out and find him, no matter where he'd gone, and tell him that he'd had to live with mum all these years without him. And his dad would scoop him up into his arms and tell him how proud he was that he'd come looking for him and found him.

But no matter how hard he wished for his fantasy, he knew somewhere deep inside, a place where truth nagged cruelly, that he might never find him, and what was worse, that perhaps his father did not want to be found. His mother had seen to that, driven him out with her hate and her loathing. He tried to keep that cruel place hidden, tried to push it way down into his body where he didn't have to go, but it was always there, stinging him like burning acid.

His eyes opened and found the crow once again. It had not moved, and still stood inside its cradle of branches looking down at him. The connection between them seemed almost physical somehow, and despite the distance between himself and the crow, it almost felt as though he could actually touch it.

Reaching out his fingertips towards it, it felt as though he could feel the fabric of its inky black feathers, could feel the warmth of its body against his skin. It was a strange feeling, even though he was sure that it wasn't real, and as he turned his hand in the air, so it seemed as though he could touch the rest of its body; its black underbelly, its claws, its long beak that had seemed so lethal. And all the while he did this, he had that same image of himself, a view of a young boy stood amongst the overhanging trees of the wood; the view that the crow had of him.

But then he saw something else, something strange and disfigured, a flash of raw scarlet and splintered timber, like a tree half-absorbed by blistered human flesh. His heart lurched wildly as he caught only this brief snatch of the monster in the wood watching him. A chill swept swiftly across his body like the clammy palm of a zombie, but the glimpse was fleeting, gone a second later, and yet the memory of it burned itself upon his eyes like the echoes of a searing flame.

He clenched his eyes shut against the vision and turned away from the crow, severing the connection between them, and disconnecting any further horrors that this bird might force upon him. He suddenly wished that his father was here with him now, now that he had seen those unnatural eyes upon him, the horrible eyes of the darkening wood, so that he could take it away and destroy it. But as he opened his eyes again, all he could see was the crow staring back at him with its chilling black eyes, wishing for that long razored beak that promised destruction, to peck at his eyes until he could see no more.

# THREE

## PREPARING FOR THE WORLD ALONE

Aunt Cassie had lied to her. When she'd gone up to her mother's room, Isabel had found her awake and staring half-lidded through the bedroom window, watching the clouds track slowly across the darkening summer's sky. She rolled her head on the pillow towards her as she entered, holding up a limp hand for her daughter to take. Her smile came quickly, glad to see her youngest child come to visit her, and for a moment Isabel hated her aunt for not allowing her to come upstairs earlier.

"Are you okay?" Isabel wanted to know, as she took a tentative seat on the edge of her mother's bed.

"Tired mostly," she told her, wetting her dry lips with a slow pink tongue. "How was school?"

"Fine," Isabel murmured, gazing round at the shadows of the room as if they were shifting themselves uneasily.

For some reason, now that she was finally here with her dying mother, she could barely bring herself to look at her. Her eyes wandered across the bedspread to the cabinet on which sat her spread of brown pill bottles and then back to the white embroidered shawl draped across her mother's shoulders. The whole room smelt of sickness, of staleness, of a rapidly approaching death. Her stomach knotted.

This was it, was all she could think.

This was the end.

Valentine, their aging black cat, appeared at the door, circling Isabel's legs once before wandering to the window to look out, indifferent to her mother's condition. Isabel watched the cat for a moment, studying his shiny black fur, the tufts of grey that tipped his ears, his apparent nonchalance. Witches had black cats, she thought; witches put spells on people too. She glanced back to look at her mother lying back in her pillows, her eyes half-open, ringed with darkness, with secret pain.

"Can I get you anything?" Isabel asked her.

Her eyes flickered wider and settled upon her.

"Only some time with you," she said, squeezing her tiny hand with what little strength she had.

Isabel tried to smile but it was difficult.

"You've been crying, child," she exclaimed suddenly, raising her hand to wipe the dampness from the corners of her eyes.

"It's Kyle," Isabel said, as though that explained everything.

"He's been giving you a hard time about your father again, has he?"

Isabel nodded, and gazed down at her mother's hand still holding hers.

"He says you drove dad out, but I keep telling him that it's not true."

Her mother's grip tightened a little.

"That's not completely true," she said quietly. "I'm not completely innocent. I did have something to do with his going. But Kyle doesn't know as much as he

71

thinks he does."

Isabel looked up at her now, the threat of tears returning quickly.

"Kyle said you were arguing, years ago."

"Arguing, yes, but not for the reasons either you or Kyle probably think."

"He said he heard you. He said you didn't know that he heard you."

"If he did, then he would have misunderstood, whatever he heard. It's a long story, Isabel, and one that I'll have to tell you later."

"But what if..?"

Her mother raised an eyebrow.

"What if I die first?"

Isabel stared at her, terrified. What should she say? Yes or no. She couldn't decide, and simply stared at her.

"I know what the doctor thinks, honey, and I knew this day would come. There's no escape for me, no way to be healed. I know what my illness is, more that he does. And before you ask, no, there's no cure. We both knew that, your father and I. In some ways, that's why he left."

"Because he knew you were going to die?"

"It's not as callous as you think, love. We just thought it would be easier if we separated, that's all. For the good of you and Kyle more than anything. We didn't want you seeing us going through what was to come."

"But daddy should be here. He should be with you now. With all of us."

"No, honey, he shouldn't. That's the worst place he could be. Believe me, it's better this way."

She suddenly snatched her hand back from Isabel's as she began to cough violently, her hands clutched in front of her face as though she was trying to grab the spittle as it came flying. It lasted perhaps only half a dozen seconds, but it seemed like forever, and the exertion took its toll.

When the heaving of her chest finally relented she seemed utterly drained; her face was livid like the colour of beetroot, the rest of her exposed skin as pale and yellowed as curdled milk. Her train of thought had ceased altogether, and all she could do was ask for her sister to be sent up on breaths sucked in through thin raw lips.

Isabel told her that she would, and left the room feeling more hollow and numb than she had upon entering. So this was it, was it, she thought? A week, possibly two, of watching her mother cough herself into exhaustion, before she finally coughed herself into the ground.

# FOUR

## THE RAPTURE OF BLOOD

His hands were literally caught red when a huge roughened hand took hold of his shoulder. The blood dripped from his hands like hot molasses and he had no excuse to give, not that he even cared to give one. The carcass lay in front of him with its head twisted to one side and its body carved open to the point where it was nearly inside out. At his side lay the kitchen knife, its keen edge glinting in the sunlight in the places where the congealing blood did not mire it.

"You little bastard," Oates growled through his clenched teeth, hauling the boy away from the grotesquely butchered sheep. "I'll see you get what's coming to you for this."

"Get off me, or you'll be sorry," Kyle yelled back, scrabbling at the hold Oates had upon him. His hands were slick and could gain no purchase, which only infuriated the farmer more as he plastered them both in the blood of the dead animal.

"Your mother's going to hear of this, and she's going to pay me for this here sheep too."

"She's in no condition to see anyone -"

"She'll see me, boy. I know of her illness, and I

know she'll agree with me. You're a sick little shit, that's what you are, and you're going to get a hiding."

Kyle struggled afresh at the threat, not wanting those two huge spade-like hands to rough him up on the way home. But they were as unrelenting as they were oversized, and they had a hold on him that would not let go.

Oates hauled him to his muddied boots by his shirt collar, and almost danced him around by his clothes as he steered him back in the direction of the old forester's cottage. Kyle began kicking now, lashing out at the farmer with as much strength and accuracy as he could. But with little balance, and a view that whirled as Oates bundled him along, his resistance had little success.

It was only after a few minutes respite, breathing hard to regain what strength he'd lost, that the boy suddenly started up afresh, shouting and thrashing, his tiny fists flying, as though he'd suddenly realised what the farmer had said to him.

"You take back what you said," he yelled. "I'm not a bastard, I'm not."

"Steady down there, boy," Oates said to him, a glint of cruelty overtaking his anger. "We all know about your father running off. And with a boy like you under his roof, who could blame him."

"Take it back," the boy continued, at the top of his voice. "Take it back."

Oates grinned to himself, half with the exertion of dragging this boy off home and half with the satisfaction that he was finally giving some torment back to this kid who'd done untold damage to his livestock over the past few months, even if it was emotionally callous.

He'd found dead chickens tied up with twine,

dead rats sliced in two, even a pigeon stripped of its feathers with its eyes gouged out. He'd caught him close-by on a couple of occasions but it was certain that he'd performed them all. It staggered him sideways to think of anyone being sick enough to do such things, especially a ten year old boy, but the sudden departure of his father had obviously snapped something vital in his head.

"I'll get you for what you said, just see if I don't."

Kyle was still bawling, twisting and circling beneath Oates' mighty fist.

"You'll get nothing," the farmer growled down at him, "except what's coming to *you*. That's what you need the most. Knock some sanity back into you."

"And who's going to do that? You? You haven't got the guts to hit me."

The boy's insolence was rapidly outweighing his past deeds, and with the thought now planted in his mind - and how many times had he thought that same thing? - he found himself wondering why not? Why shouldn't he give the boy a whack? He knew damned well that nobody was going to do it once he got him home. His mother, Irene Rider, was certainly in no state to admonish him in any shape or form, so close to death's door was she. And her elder sister Cassandra wasn't likely to lay a hand on her nephew either. It was the father's job to beat him, and he'd skipped town.

"For Christ's sake, let me go," the boy squealed, reeling beneath his clenched fist.

It was getting too much to take. It would be at least a fifteen minute walk to his mother's house, twenty at this ragged rate. There were some trees coming up, overhanging the roadway, no one would see, not as though there was anyone in sight around these parts anymore anyway.

"Get off, you shit, get off."

Oates could feel his fist tightening even more, his knuckles beginning to ache with the strain of just holding on to him, the cloth of the boy's shirt wet now with his own sweat. No one would see him. And the kid deserved it too.

"Get off me. Get -"

His eye twitched down to the scrawling brat whirling beneath him, arms flinging against his leg. *It was the father's job but he'd skipped town* - that phrase kept circling in his head. And come to join it was - *it would do everyone a favour, the kid included, bring him back to reality.*

"You fucking shit. Get off."

That was it.

Oates swung him round, hard enough so that his legs came off the ground a couple of inches, and for a moment there was a lull of uneasy silence between them. Everything stopped; the birds in the hedgerows, the sheep in the fields. Everything. Even the boy froze momentarily, his arms halted, his face expressionless and afraid now.

And then the blow came.

It came down from a great height, swinging down out of a limbo that almost felt unnatural. Oates didn't even feel the stinging of his hand until it had finished its arc and come to rest on the other side of the boy's face. He stood there with the kid still grasped in one fist, only loosely now, while his great grey eyes took in the swiftly changing shape of the boy's face.

The fear contorted swiftly into disbelief, and then as the fierce pain came to his cheek, tears erupted only moments before the red handprint began to glow vividly on his lightly freckled skin. The sheer volume of the shriek startled Oates more than anything else, wailing fiercely out his throat like a demented police siren, alerting the rest of the village to come see this outrageous assault.

For a few seconds Oates didn't know whether to hush him quickly with the flat of his hand over his spit-flecked mouth or simply jerk him into silence by shaking his shoulders. He had deserved it, anyone would have agreed with him, anyone, and yet...

And yet he had just struck someone else's child. Hard. He thought it would've felt good, but it didn't. *Shit, it didn't.*

"Shit," he muttered, out loud this time, staring at the boy whose face was glowing as loud as his screams. Then the reasoning came, swiftly, as much to justify the action to himself as to the kid.

"You had it coming. You fucking had it coming. Just try telling me you didn't."

The kid's wails went on, blubbing now as his hand came up to his stinging cheek.

"You've done some sick shit around here. It's about time you stopped. Learn from this, kid. And don't you ever come back."

The screams went on and on, and all the time the boy just stood there, his hand pressed against the side of his face. He never moved a muscle. Just stood there with his mouth wide open and that goddamn awful howling coming out.

Oates wavered for a moment, not knowing whether to leave him there or escort him home after all. But what would he say to his mother now? His anger had vaporised, leaving nothing but a guilt that festered and buzzed inside his belly like a hive of bees. Why the hell should he feel guilty, he demanded of himself? The kid had been killing his animals for

Christ's sake, butchering them for his own sick fun.

No, the kid had needed a smack and he'd given it to him. But then, as he turned and started his retreat, leaving the boy to bawl alone in the middle of the rutted track, he hoped he'd never see that weird kid on his property again, and hoped even more he'd never run into his mother or aunt either. But he knew that to hope for that was crazy, as crazy as that damned kid himself.

## FIVE

## WHO STANDS WITH WHO

Isabel waited in the kitchen until her aunt came back. She said nothing, just put some dishes into the sink and then stood and stared out through the kitchen window. Isabel watched her for a moment, but when it became clear that she was not going to say anything about her mother, she decided to go back upstairs and see for herself.

"Is everything alright?" she asked quietly around the bedroom door.

Her mother looked up at her with unbelievably tired eyes, ringed with smudged black circles and lines like cracked paint. She looked older now too, older than her forty one years, older than when she had left her just twenty minutes ago. Her dry lips parted slowly, and only so far, and the few words that tumbled out of them were as delicate as the petals of her favourite roses in the garden just outside her window.

"Just tired, love," was all she said.

"Should I go?"

Her mother creased a tiny smile as she tried to shake her head.

"No," she said, running her tongue across lips as

dry as parchment. "Stay with me. Is Cass looking after you okay?"

Isabel nodded, and looked around her mother's bedroom again. It seemed as though nothing had changed in this room for years, as though time had stopped while its occupant had declined further towards nothingness. The wallpaper seemed grey, the curtains brown, and even the air that hung so listlessly seemed to have a yellow pallor to it. When finally her eyes came back to settle upon her mother, she found that she was studying her.

"You're going to have to make your own decisions, Isabel," she said to her. "You know that, don't you?"

"About what?"

"About your future, your life, who you're going to be."

"What do you mean?"

"I'm not going to be here forever, and there are some things that I've been wanting to say to you, both you and Kyle."

"Kyle doesn't want to come and see you. He spends all his time outside. I've tried telling him but -"

"It's okay, Isabel," she hushed her, "he'll come in his own time."

"He keeps saying horrible things."

Her mother placed her hand over hers again and squeezed it weakly.

"I'm only interested in you at the moment. You're strong, Isabel, stronger than I think you realise, and you're going to need that soon."

"No, mum -"

"Please, honey, listen to me. I want you to promise me some things, promise me that you'll do them no matter what."

Isabel stared at her. Her throat was beginning to tighten into knots again, restricting like painful burning ropes that threatened to hang her up like one of her cloth dolls. She wanted this all to be over, to have her mother back the way she was, with her father living with them again and taking them to school in the morning, cooking porridge in the kitchen, hanging stockings over the fireplace at Christmas, netting minnows in the stream, watching sparrows at the feeder. She wanted it all.

Her mother's voice came again, disjointing her fantasy, startling her with what was real, and what was not.

"You have to go on with your life," she said to her. "Be yourself, be who you are, no matter what happens. Promise me that."

She tried to squeeze her hand more firmly as if to persuade her, and Isabel could see the yearning in those tired black-ringed eyes, and all she could do was nod, once, slowly up and down.

"I promise," she said finally.

"Aunt Cassie will be here to look after you, you know that, don't you?"

Isabel nodded again. Her feet had gone numb, her legs too. All she kept thinking was that this couldn't really be happening.

There had been talk of death in the house for the past couple of months and she still only had the vaguest of ideas about what that meant. All she really knew was that her mother was going away and wouldn't be coming back. That was all she needed to know. What else mattered? Her chest hurt and her throat choked her, her entire body knotted up like the old rope of the tree-house at the bottom of the garden.

Valentine had left a tiny brown bird on their

kitchen floor once, and that had been dead, its motionless body tucked up into a useless bundle, its feathers matted with blood and spittle. She had cried over it at the time, thinking about how it might have left a nest of baby birds alone, and now those thoughts and memories returned. She was going to be one of those baby birds herself now, left alone without her mother to protect her. But she wanted to be as strong as her mother thought she was, and she didn't want to cry in front of her. Not now anyway. But she couldn't help herself. Her mother was still looking at her, studying her face. It seemed she might have tears of her own, and neither of them wanted to show them in front of the other. All Isabel knew was that she didn't want to lose her mother to death. Not now. Not ever.

"Isn't there any other way?" she began to plead, desperately trying to hold back the tears that were threatening to come.

Her mother slowly shook her head.

"You'll have to be brave, my love."

"I can't," she cried, the tears coming now. "Something will come to save you. God will save you. He can perform miracles."

"God cannot help me now. Nothing can. There will be no miracles, not for me."

Isabel began to tremble, her shoulders hunching and shaking, disbelieving everything around her, yet still her mother continued to speak the horrible truth.

"Things have run their path. Aunt Cassie will look after you now. But I will always love you, you must always remember that. I don't want to leave you but my body is weak. Promise me that you will do as Cassie tells you. Keep up your schoolwork, and your table manners. You mustn't let anything slip, do you understand me?"

Isabel could barely stifle her tears as she stared in shuddering horror at her mother. This was a hopeless conversation. Her mother was adamant that she would be leaving her, never to return or to speak to her again, and there was nothing she could do to stop it. It was horrible, all of it.

"I want you to have something," her mother said to her, reaching to unfasten the gold chain and locket that hung around her neck. "Something to remember us by."

Isabel hesitantly opened her hands. She didn't want this finality, her mother handing over cherished possessions. But once she felt its warm weight against her skin, she felt compelled to open the locket, curious by her mother's words; something to remember *us* by.

In each half was a photograph, one of her mother, the other of her father, kept together forever. She looked up at her mother then and saw the truth in her eyes. There was still love there, her mother's gaze was proof of that. Isabel tried to smile, but it was difficult. This was an end, not a wonderful beginning. She didn't want her mother gone.

From the corner of her eye she noticed a dark shape, silken through the shadows of the room. She turned her head, and saw Valentine leap up onto the sill of the open window, looking at them, almost as if she had been following the exchange between them. His black face was reassuring, something familiar in a horribly distorting world, and she got up from the edge of her mother's bed to go pick him up. Perhaps mum would want to stroke him, she thought, maybe it would make her feel better or even change her mind about going away.

As she neared the window sill, however, Valentine suddenly raised his hackles, arching his back as he glared back at her with burning feral eyes. Isabel faltered briefly, hushing the cat, telling him that it was alright and that everything was okay, but he just hissed back at her. Reaching to scoop up the creature in her arms regardless, she yelped in pain as Valentine suddenly lashed out at her, catching her hand with one of his claws and bringing tracks of blood swiftly to the surface.

Isabel sucked at the wound instantly, staggering back away from the window sill as she went to call out to her mother. But the cat was swifter than she, and had already leapt across and onto the bed before any real alarm could be voiced.

Like a spear of blackness, he pounced swiftly onto the pillow, lashing out at her mother's face, and opening a two inch gash across her curdled white cheek. She cried out as she raised her hands weakly to push him away, but she was too slow and frail to avoid the second blow, and Valentine's claws caught her forehead several times before Isabel could take hold of him and hurl him awkwardly towards the bedroom door.

The attack had opened her pale flesh in a number of places, blood running freely between her bony-knuckled fingers from gashes at her temple and above her right eye.

Irene began to sob with pain as her hands slipped across her blood-slick skin, tears mingling with the red and staining her cheeks like a scarlet map. Isabel cast one final look towards the door before Aunt Cassie came bounding up the stairs, but there was no sign of Valentine any more.

The sight of seeing her mother so injured and distraught was almost too much to bear, and once Aunt Cass had appeared at her bedside and began to frantically tend to her, Isabel staggered away from her, unable to bring herself to touch her or see her any more in such a state.

Staggering away from the bed, Isabel held her own wounded hand tightly in the unsteady grasp of her other hand. Just what had gotten into Valentine, she wanted to know? Why would he attack her or her mother like that?

She staggered back towards the open window where Valentine had leapt up and gazed out at the world that seemed so unchanged, and yet so utterly different. The sun still shone and the clouds still crept slowly across the sky. The fields were green and the sheep still grazed in them. But down in the garden, partially obscured by the old apple tree, she saw a shape, a figure, the silhouette of Kyle lurking below in the shadows.

She saw him clearly now, standing with his hands pressed against the bark as he looked back up at her. There was something about his eyes that scared her - a hollowness, a vacancy, she wasn't quite sure - but his face was plain, he wore no expression, and all she could do was stare down at him through the open window as though it was all somehow his fault.

She cursed herself almost immediately for thinking such things about her own brother, but then just as she was about to turn away from the sight of him and see if Aunt Cassie needed any help tending to her mother's injuries, she caught sight of Valentine slinking out from beneath the rose bushes before slithering slickly around Kyle's ankles.

Isabel could not help but shudder with fear as Kyle remained beside the tree, keeping his vigil upon their mother's bedroom window, without moving, without blinking it almost seemed. A chill crept over her body like a cold wet blanket, and she had to force herself to step away from the glass, away from the sight of him, even as the heat of her own piss startled her as it ran down the insides of her legs.

She didn't tell her mother, or even her aunt, about wetting herself or about Kyle standing out in the garden with Valentine at his heels. What would have been the point anyway? Nothing made sense any more, nothing in the world, and soon she was about to be left alone in it to work that senselessness out for herself.

## SIX

### ISABEL IN THE LAIR OF DARKNESS

There was something in those woods, that's all Isabel could think, something that drew Kyle into them, something that made his brain become twisted, unravelled.

There was a darkness there, of that there was no doubt; she could sense it in the knotted depths between the trees and the unnatural shadows that hung like wraiths between their heavy boughs. She could taste it in the thickness of the air that drifted around its perimeter, like a taint encircling it, a manifestation of evil, and it scared her.

Kyle spent so much of his time here - had that taint taken him over, possessed him, and in turn allowed him possession over the creatures around him (the cat and the crows) for his own deeds, his own sick motives? There had been incidents before, some slight, some unimaginable, but after Valentine she could come to no other conclusion; everything had its own possibility now.

Their father was gone, their mother now lay dying, and all Kyle had seemed to do was almost will her away from them more quickly than was natural.

Something was changing inside him, and for the

worse. There was something here that accepted him but kept her out; she wasn't welcome in this place, there was harm for her here, but Kyle was her brother, and she had to try and save him before he was consumed completely.

The air had seemed almost to sour as she'd stepped out of the sunshine and into the shadow of the canopy of the tall pines, the wind dropping to a deathly calm. A chill had crept over her skin too as she'd wandered cautiously between the trees, the darkness thrown down by the overhanging branches almost crawling across her flesh like cold clammy hands reaching down for her. She hugged herself, rubbing her hands up and down her forearms in an attempt to bring some warmth back to them, trying to reassure herself that once she'd made her way through and seen what there was to see and made it out the other side, she would make her way steadily home. Kyle had already entered, she'd followed him from the house, and this was the only way to find out what became of him here.

She'd obviously lost sight of him once he'd entered, but she'd arrived at the same point and searched the shadows for him, but had already lost him. Stealthily, she made her way in, keeping low amongst the undergrowth, scanning the tall trees all the time.

She knew that her father used to come here often, especially with Kyle, and wanted to think that that was the only reason for him to spend so much time here. But something had taken him over, she could feel it in the way he behaved around their mother, in the vacancy of his stares, always gazing out towards this wood from his bedroom window, and now his domination of Valentine. Even now Isabel could feel the oppressive weight of the wood pressing against her, clammy but firm against her face, snagging at her hair; it wanted her gone, and she could not helpfeeling afraid.

But then just up ahead, she thought she could see him in the distant shadows, standing like a partially silhouetted ghost, one foot upon a tree-stump, pointing out towards something as if he'd spied a nesting bird or a patch of bluebells. Something slipped inside her head, like pieces of a child's game slotting into place, a memory, it was familiar somehow. And then it came to her. Her father. He'd stood like that when he'd taken her out on nature walks, showing her the animals that lived here.

The memory rapidly sharpened, her mind pasting a half-made mask of her father's face over the figure, making it real. She gasped aloud, the sound startling her, so unaware was she of having made it. He seemed to turn to look at her in that moment, but his eyes were as hollow as deep pits, his face horrifically transparent and showing the twisted branches of the trees behind him through his ethereal skull. She'd not made him right. He looked like a half-rotted corpse. She had loved her father, still did, but the way her mind conjured this horrible version of him, this hideous distorted memory, shocked her utterly.

She turned away, shuddering at the thought of those unmade eyes bearing down upon her. Her throat tightened and she suddenly wanted to run home. But she had come here for a reason, and she forced herself to look back, returning her gaze to where the image of her father had stood. She hesitated momentarily, staring down at her feet amongst the carpet of fallen pine needles, her body trembling as though she was now being watched from all sides. But as her eyes returned and searched the area where she had placed him, his ghostly image was now nowhere to be seen.

With no trace of Kyle's whereabouts, Isabel had no idea which direction she was even going in, nor any real clue at just how deep the wood actually went. What little light there was that managed to penetrate the canopy overhead was beginning swiftly to fade as the pine trees became denser, cultivating that dank darkness into something that felt almost as though it wanted to fall down and smother her.

The coarse branches and needles began to reach for her as she moved between them, snagging at her dress and scratching at her arms. The carpet of fallen needles slid beneath her feet suddenly as she clambered across the uneven ground, and she loosed a shriek as she half-stumbled down onto one knee as though the wood wanted to keep her back, or bury her beneath its black earth. Her eyes were wide now as she gazed around her in all directions, her heart thumping hard inside her chest, scared that she had no idea where she was, or even how to get out of the wood, but there were trees everywhere she looked and no sign of daylight.

She reasoned distantly that whatever route she took would come out somewhere, but that notion of security evaporated almost immediately even as her mind formed it. From somewhere up above her the raucous caw of a crow sliced the air in two. Isabel loosed another cry as she gazed above her head in panic, tears flowing freely now as she stumbled back to her feet and staggered onward, her hands up over her face as the branches snatched to grab at her again.

The crow cawed again, its biting din just yards above her head. She half-turned her head to look for it, to beat it away with her flailing arms, but there was too much darkness to decipher the black mass of the bird as it chased her. Her feet slid again on the wet matter beneath her, but she managed to keep herself upright this time, but the coarse branches of the pines found her skin and eagerly brought blood to her forearms in sharp narrow tracks.

Her tears were blinding her, but through the densely-packed trees to her right, she made out the shape of that same ghostly figure. She couldn't be certain if it was Kyle or not, but she was sure that whoever it was saw her, and returned her fearful gaze with those same hollow blank sockets.

She was sobbing with uncontrollable terror now, running headlong through a mass of branches that reached from impossible angles to grab at her. The crow cawed again, she could feel its claws already on her back, needle sharp talons sinking into the meat of her shoulder, raising blood, its jagged beak tearing at her hair. But then somewhere up ahead of her, through the blur of her tears, the world suddenly began to grow lighter. It threw spears of bright hope towards her, guiding her from this clutch of darkness, until the blue of the sky and the green of the fields beyond became vivid through the near-black silhouettes of the pine trees.

Gasping for breath and half-blind with tears, she stumbled sobbing from the restricting wood and out into the fresh air of the afternoon. She ran on, however, out of the reach of the shadows cast by the trees and out into the sunlight, until its warmth touched every part of her upturned face and hands, and she could breathe more evenly. It wasn't until she had confirmed that she was completely out of the wood - with the sky unbroken overhead, and the fields rolling to the hills on the horizon - that she dared glance back over her shoulder.

The wood stood relentless and tall, its depths receding into total darkness for as far as she could see. A rutted track ran along the edge of the wood, and she followed it, hoping it would soon deliver her home.

The wind picked up a little as she walked, dancing dust and leaves across her path, but she paid little attention to it, not realising that there had not been a single breath of wind inside the wood before, and yet here it seemed to be its source.

It brushed against her cheek, cooling the tears still wet there, and lifted her hair from her forehead like a delicate hand. It traced around the hem of her dress, caressing the skin of her legs, before rising back up her body. When it found her ear, however, it seemed to dance in tiny patterns, tickling her lobe, before planting barely audible words inside.

Isabel froze, her skin raising hard gooseflesh instantly. The words were there to be heard, weren't they?

Her eyes shot back into the wood, flickering through the blackest of the shadows, praying that she would not see the thing with the hollow eyes.

The words came again, delicate like the breaths on which they were carried.

*Isabel*, it seemed to say. *Come inside and play*.

Her neck bristled instantly. She wanted to run, to dash crying down the rutted track all the way home. But something inside her did not want to let the wood know that it had scared her. The words her mother had said to her leapt up out of her mind: *you must be strong, you are stronger than you realise*. She wanted to be strong for her mother, and she did not want the wood to see her run away from it in fear. Part of her told herself that it was just Kyle playing a trick on her, whispering unseen from behind a tree stump. But she had seen that thing, that eyeless monster from the heart of wood, and that had not been her brother.

So on she went, her arms hugged tight around her, as the wood breathed her name into her ear. The view of Manor Farm appeared as the track bent round, and her heart calmed just a little, knowing that if she could make her way there then she would be safe. Her friend Emily would be there, so too would her father Mr Oates, but as she continued on, her eyes set upon this goal of old corrugated barns and tractor sheds, she barely noticed the cricking sounds coming from behind a fallen tree at the edge of the wood.

It was only once she had passed it and the wind almost changed direction to bring the sound of the chirping back to her, that she stopped and turned to look. She could discern no recognisable shapes in the leaf-litter and debris surrounding the moss-covered tree, but her curiosity had been sparked and if there was an injured animal or bird in trouble, then she did not want to leave it to die, or worse yet, become prey to a scavenging beast like that crow.

Keeping one eye on the depths of the wood, she crept cautiously forward until she began gently parting the tall grasses aside, searching for the source of the distress. It was not easy to find, but once her eyes had settled upon its scarlet mass, she wished immediately that she had never found it.

Two shining black eyes stared unblinkingly up at her from a pulp of bloodied feathers and raw stripped bone. Lying huddled on its back, one wing outstretched and quivering, the other nestled awkwardly and unmoving at its side, the poor bird's beak croaked slowly open and closed as its pathetic chirp rose up into the sky. It almost looked as if it had been tugged inside out, its innards chewed or ripped before being thrust roughly back in. Her heart suddenly felt as crushed as its body, and all she wanted to do was take care of it and see it perched on a branch again and singing its song. But as she had parted the grasses around it and stared down at its wretched condition, wondering just what kind of animal could have done such a thing without actually devouring it, she hadn't kept her watchful vigil on the woods to her side.

She had failed to watch the trees begin to stir, failed to notice the air growing agitated once more, or the voices of the boughs form syllables once again. The wood that had seemed almost to be watching her, now broke its silence again, and spoke to her in eerie breathless whispers, calling her name, and reaching for her cheek with sighs and creaking moans.

*Isabel*, it sighed. *Come closer. Come to me.*

Suddenly the young girl deciphered the words floating around her, and she gazed up and into its contorting depths. The darkness shrouded her sight almost everywhere she looked, dumbfounding her focus, making nonsense of what she saw. Her arms broke gooseflesh again and her hair suddenly lifted off her brow as though a chilling hand had reached out from between the trees and brushed it away from her forehead. She fell back, a hand pressed down into the dirt to steady herself, and with one final glance down at the bloodied bird at her feet, she scooped its warm sickly body up out of the muck and swept it away before the horrors in the wood could do anything else.

She was crying as she ran, sobbing relentlessly with anguish as she dashed headlong and blind over the rutted track that led down towards the farm where Emily lived. She glanced over her shoulder only briefly as she held the trembling thing tightly to her breast, its sharp ebony eyes piercing her own scrutiny, its wet body pliant where her fingertips dug into where the meat was thin and raw. But with tears filling her vision she could discern little but blurred shapes. If there had been something chasing her, she would not have seen it.

Only when she reached the front door of the farmhouse did she look down at the ragged shape of the bird again, and saw that where she had held it, the flesh had regained some of its resilience, the tiniest of downy feathers shooting forth as if they'd somehow managed to re-grow.

She stared down at its tiny broken frame clutched in her trembling hands as she lingered on the doorstep, half wanting to knock on the door and ask Emily's father to please drive her home, half wanting to just look down at this tiny creature and wait for it to heal simply by her touch.

It was crazy to think that it was even possible, and yet she reasoned to herself that she had probably just not seen the true condition of the bird in the ill-light beneath the overhanging trees. But it felt good to have this poor savaged creature at least a little better, albeit moderately, and if it had been by her touch then all the better.

It gave her a glimmer of hope, as she knocked on the farmhouse door, that she might be able to rear it back to health, to steal it away from the brink of death that the wood had bestowed upon it. And perhaps one day she might even see it perched atop a branch, singing its own brilliant song in the brilliant sunlight of a new day, and she would know that she had been the one that had saved it.

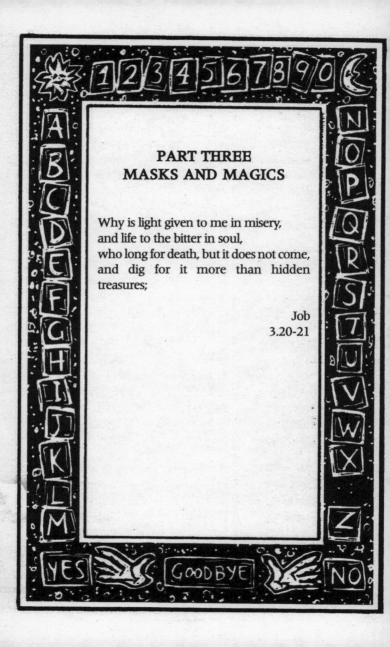

## PART THREE
## MASKS AND MAGICS

Why is light given to me in misery,
and life to the bitter in soul,
who long for death, but it does not come,
and dig for it more than hidden
treasures;

Job
3.20-21

# ONE

## STRANGER IN THE CROWD

It was almost a relief for her to see the kid bounce off the bonnet and turn full circle in the air. The sickly thud of his head against the car was one thing, but the sound it made when it impacted against the road in front of it was something else. Soggy, dull, wet; like some kind of enormous fruit dropped from a height onto clay floor tiles.

There was no doubt in her mind.

He was dead. And that was that.

The car had rounded the corner way too quickly, its adolescent driver too inexperienced and paying way too little attention to the road ahead. The woman waiting at the side of the road had seen the mobile phone pressed against his ear, his eyes vaguely checking himself out in the tilted rear view mirror. It was a wonder he even made the corner at all.

He hadn't seen the boy stray out across the road, hadn't seen him ducking away from his mother's side in the direction of the ice-cream van, wide eyes illuminated with the promise of a vanilla cone with a stubby flake wedged in it. It took a fleeting moment for the accident to play through, a few moments to have the car skid noisily to an angled halt, and then a few more moments for the boy's mother to turn startled and recognise the tangled mass of pliant limbs lying in the street as her child. But when she did, those screams rose like fire in a fuel depot, and they slashed the air without respite for a good ten minutes or more.

The woman had watched it all from across the street, even before the consoling crowd had begun to gather. She watched the young driver stagger out of the car and puke. She watched the mother tumble awkwardly at her dead son's side. She watched it all with a kind of dull weary gaze that commuters get when they see the same landscapes roll pass over and over again on their way to work each morning. The woman on the edge of the street had this gaze because she'd seen death so many times before; the death of an infant, the death of a grown man, it made little difference - some just screamed more than others. She'd seen it all.

She wondered briefly, even as she crossed the street towards them, whether she should just let the child be, let him wither and decay in the ground like dead people did. But before she had even managed to reach a decision, she was already kneeling beside the bloodied twisted body of the youngster with her hands pressed against two of his snapped ribs.

The buzz of the crowd drifted into an uneasy dirge of whispers at her back as she closed her eyes, and even the mother's unearthly sobs died down somewhat, but the woman persisted at her labours, massaging the bruised meat of the boy's torso, kneading his snapped joints and the shattered bones, feeling the blood, feeling its heat, until the small boy's heart suddenly jerked with the memory of its former pulse and began to beat once again, his wide eyes flickering skyward as though in praise of the God in residence.

The woman tried to get away, oh God how she tried. But there had been a miracle performed in front of their very eyes and they weren't about to let go of her that easily. But once the kid was on his feet and examining the holes made in his school uniform from the thirty yard stretch of bloodied tarmac he'd been thrown across, the crowd relinquished their hold on her to inspect him, to check for wounds and permanent damage beneath his ragged outfit, and it was in that moment that she took her usual chance and slipped away from their attention.

The mother couldn't care less at the time. She'd already snatched up her child and was cradling him to the point of asphyxiation, holding him tight to her breast. The woman, meanwhile, was already back on the other side of the street and heading towards what shadows there were on an otherwise hot summer's day, shying away from the crowd's attention, disappearing out of sight (even as her guilt crawled over her thoughts like a sickness) before the first of the ambulance sirens harried the air.

No one caught up with her for nearly two weeks. The mother stood on the threshold to her flat, her boy at her leg. He had a few remaining traces of cuts on his cheek and chin but that was all. He was well on the mend considering what he had been through. The woman stared at them both without expression from behind the partially open door, her eyes narrowing at this unwanted intrusion.

"Someone told me they had seen you here," the mother said, "and I just wanted to come and say thank you, thank you for saving Ryan's life. I never got a chance to say thanks before because, well, you just seemed to disappear."

Isabel looked her up and down for a few moments, the front door between them still held in her hand. She knew that the mother wanted to come in and bestow even more praise upon her, and maybe there was something in her thoughts about a gift or reward too. But she just wanted silence, that was all, and to be left alone too of course, but they were things too valuable and all too unobtainable. She did, however, relent finally when she cast the boy a look and saw a crooked smile on his face for her, a sanguine mask of uncertain joy upon lips the colour of dead flesh.

"You'd better come in then," she found herself saying, and stepped back to allow them into her home.

"My name's Debbie Fry," the mother said, "and this is Ryan, my youngest."

"You have more children then?"

"One more, a daughter, Sarah. She's getting on for seventeen now."

Isabel Rider stared at her, allowing the uneasy pause to hasten the woman's visit.

"Look, you're probably busy, so I'll just tell you what I came to tell you and then I'll be on my way. I felt so blessed about Ryan and what you did for him that I had to do something to thank you properly."

Isabel's gaze intensified at this. She didn't like the way this was going, nor indeed the way Debbie Fry's thoughts were arranging themselves inside her head, collecting on the back of her tongue like little parcels waiting to be delivered.

"I contacted the local paper," Debbie Fry went on, "and they thought the same as I did that they would love to do an article on you."

Isabel grimaced at this, and even clenched her

teeth at the prospect. It was then that her words changed to match her expression, and they flew from her tongue as bitter as acid.

"I helped your son because I could -"

"Yes, and I thank you for that -"

"Let me finish, will you? I saved him because he was dead. He was gone Mrs Fry, do you understand? I could go one further and say that his life belonged to me. But I didn't want him, and so I gave him back to you. But was this enough? No. You had to go further."

Debbie Fry went to speak again but Isabel silenced her with a hand.

"I don't want your newspaper attention any more than I want your thanks. I want to be left alone, can you understand that? I want to sit here in my flat and listen to the silence. Now I've accepted your thank you's with good grace and now I'd like you to leave with your boy."

Debbie Fry stared at the woman with something close to disbelief, perhaps even outrage. Isabel could almost hear the thoughts build inside her head:

*How dare you not want my son?*

*How dare you not want to be in the paper?*

She voiced out loud her reasoning for the newspaper article, but Isabel had already heard enough and hushed her brusquely before her lips had finished flapping. A moment later and Isabel was on her feet, a knife whipped swiftly from her jacket pocket and clutched tightly in her hand.

"I gave life back to him," Isabel cried as she lunged at him, "and I'm damned sure I can take it back if I want to." And with that she drew the keen edge of the blade swiftly across his throat, spilling a sudden torrent of blood down his small frightened chest. The boy made hardly any movement at all, so deft and sudden did the knife come, but his little fingers still made some attempt to haul back the folds of his throat, his legs tensing and shuddering for only a moment, before he slipped awkwardly to one side and slumped dead in his chair.

Debbie Fry held a silent scream for only a handful of seconds before the shrill sound actually made its way out. Isabel's blade wanted her throat too, wanted to hack it in two and silence it, just as swiftly and neatly as she had done her boy's. But she didn't want two murders, not today.

She dropped the knife to the ground and took hold of Debbie Fry's shoulders, shaking her hard until she could almost hear her teeth rattle. The screaming stopped, but a kind of hyperventilating blubber took its place, and all the woman could do was stare helplessly at the woman who had just butchered her child.

"I don't want the publicity and I don't want to kill people. I just want to be left alone." She wanted her head to be silent too, but so muddy was it with voices and guilt that she'd never tell another living soul about it, let alone this sobbing half-wit in front of her. "I told you your boy's life belongs to me and I'll take it back if I want."

In the bulging staring eyes of Debbie Fry, Isabel could see a glimmer of a nod, but in those eyes she could also see what the mother saw. A lunatic that had just killed a ten year old boy. She'd never wanted to be this way, not even in the beginning, but so heavy was her burden, so bludgeoning... how was she to cope? How was she to cope alone?

Isabel let her grip slacken and watched as the mother stumbled back under her own weight. She looked at her for a few moments, watching the shudders pass through her, watch her eyes glance down at her youngest child in a glistening sticky gown of his own young blood. She followed this unholy gaze, and took in the sight of the boy killed by her own hand. How crazy was this, she thought crazily to herself, even as her own tears started to come? Was this death? Had she even given him life back a fortnight ago?

She turned and went down on one knee beside him. Lifting her hand up towards his exposed throat, slick milk-white cartilage visible between the sliced pulsing muscle still raising blood like a squeezed sponge, she placed her fingers against the ragged meat and watched as the wound slowly began to draw itself together, binding flesh against flesh, joining arteries whole. The blood began to course back through the boy's veins even before she had sealed his skin over her unnatural surgery, and his eyes shot open wide and white, settling open her as they had in the street two weeks ago, as a coarse gasp was sucked hard into his lungs. This wasn't life she was giving him, this was a sick curse. He'd died, the way he was meant to, and she'd stepped in and granted him this obscenity. Twice.

The tears were streaming down her cheeks as she let the boy up out of his seat, ushering him back towards his mother still sobbing behind her. Isabel couldn't even turn to look at her this time, so much had she already inflicted upon her family. All she could do was bow her head towards the floor and utter two short words:

"Just go."

She listened to their feet tramping slowly across the floor, the ghostly quiet returning once more to her living room as soon as the door closed behind them.

Soon it would be as silent as a morgue once again, and then she would be able to rest properly. Perhaps it would have been easier to have simply killed them both and left town. Maybe she wouldn't even have needed to leave. She could have simply taken the corpses out of the flat and dumped them elsewhere like real murderers did.

She ran her tensed fingers hard through her hair, clenching her fists so that it tugged at her scalp. She wanted to rip at her head until all the thoughts that she kept there were gone. She wanted to rip out her heart so that she could watch it beat its very last rhythm. But she knew nothing could ever stop her. Not now. Nothing she could do to harm herself could ever end this horror. She would only heal, whether she wanted to or not. It was inside her, the magic that had grown so deep into her being that she would never be able to be separated from it. It was unnatural, unholy, and it felt as though the very Devil himself seethed inside her veins. Yes, she could bring young boys back from the dead, but for what reason? What was the point of it all? She knew what such deeds did, and she knew what terrible anguish Debbie Fry was soon going to face.

Sure, she thought to herself, as she cast her eyes out through the grimy window at the world outside, you might have a few years of happiness before it starts, but it'll come, oh yes it'll come, and then you'll both be wishing for death. Oh yes, you'll both be wishing for oblivion.

# TWO

_____

## THE POWER OF THE PRESS

Emily Oates sat in her kitchen and stared at the blurred picture on page seventeen of the Hunton and District Gazette. Squinting her eyes against the black dots, she tried to decipher whether it was her old friend or not. She'd not seen her in two decades, not since they were little more than kids. People changed over time, she mused as she began manoeuvring the paper backwards and forwards to change her focus upon the page - different hair, different clothes - but something always remained the same; an essence, if you like. A lot must have changed since they had lost contact. And Isabel had pretty much lost her mind then. Could this madwoman really be her?

The photograph had been taken from down in the street looking up at a partial silhouette in a second floor window. The picture was pretty much indistinct, but the caption beneath, _Is this the new Messiah?_, turned the tables somewhat on just an ordinary joe.

Isabel hadn't been a daughter of God as far as Emily had known, but she'd had more than her fair share of family shit to deal with. A disappearing father, a dead mother, and as for her brother, the less said about that sick bastard the better. Emily physically shook with disgust just at the thought of him, and took a long draw on her coffee to try and distract herself from a hideously grinning face looming out of her own haunted memories. It did little to shroud that face, those teeth that seemed to grin like a rabid dog. She forced her eyes back to the newspaper and started to read the article again, hoping to find some clue as to the new Messiah's whereabouts.

*'This unknown woman has been identified by a local housewife of bringing her child back to life. Mrs Deborah Fry brought her son into Hunton Park Hospital on the 14th June with multiple injuries to his chest and arms, most of which had miraculously been healed by the alleged touch of the woman. Doctors examined ten year old Ryan Fry, and were at a loss to explain the blood-stained tears in his school uniform with the healed injuries beneath. They had no comment when asked if they thought Ryan's saviour could actually be Christ.'*

Emily smiled to herself as she continued to read, sipping on her coffee as she imagined Isabel sitting somewhere reading this same ridiculous article.

*'When we called at this woman's flat, requesting an interview, she too declined to comment, insisting that we just leave her be. But this is one reporter that wouldn't mind getting the first scoop on the second coming here in Hunton. Keep reading these pages. God may pay us a visit yet.'*

Snapping the paper shut, Emily slammed the rag down on the table. How dare that reporter be so patronising? If that was Isabel Rider he was writing his shit about, it wouldn't surprise her if she got hold of a lawyer and sued him. She knew she didn't have any facts about what had happened to this Ryan Fry, but by the sound of it, neither did this reporter. She suddenly realised how much she wanted to go see this woman in the picture, find out if it was her old childhood friend or not. If it wasn't, then the worst that could happen was she'd be told to get lost. But if it was, then she guessed that Izzie could possibly do with a friend, perhaps now more than ever.

Tugging the peak of her baseball cap down and slipping on her sunglasses, Emily slipped out of the front door and hurried quickly down to her car parked at the side of the road. It was about an hour before noon, the day was bright and cloudless, and she glanced briefly about as she unlocked the driver's door. As she took hold of the handle and was about to climb in, she caught sight of a small flock of birds, possibly sparrows, perched on a telephone wire hanging low across the road between the poles. To anyone casually glancing their way, or hearing their chatter so high up, they might have spared a thought for them, enjoying the sight of urban wildlife. But for Emily, it was a constant nightmare, a never-ending vigil.

Were these innocent-looking creatures simply looking out for their next meal, or watching her every move. Sometimes she used to shake at the very thought of what they might be seeing, what they might be thinking in secret.

It hadn't always been that way. She'd once been a sane kid. She could dimly recall having normal thoughts. But things had changed. She'd seen shit and felt shit, enough to warp her mind and twist it inside

109

out until she wanted to scream. And scream she had. Many times. Until it hurt or even bled sometimes. But screaming solved nothing. And the shit always remained in its place.

No, this was all real, and there no way out.

The birds were watching her, not all of them, but enough of them to know that she was leaving the house.

It distantly occurred to her, as she climbed into the driver's seat and turned the key in the ignition, that she didn't know the average flying speed of the common sparrow. Was it more than thirty miles per hour? Was it more than forty? As she pulled away from the kerb and started away, she decided that she didn't have a clue, and guessing was just pointless.

She glanced just once in her rear view mirror before she reached the end of the street, but it was nearly impossible to spot a three inch bird from that far back. Needless to say, she kept a nervous eye on her mirrors the entire journey, until she reached the town centre and parked on one of the dark unlit levels of the multi-storey.

She had no appointment, and it occurred to her as she wandered along the high street, that she hadn't looked to see who had even written the article. She'd also forgotten to bring her copy along with her, just so she could point to the story on page seventeen, outlining her outrage at the disrespect that had been printed. She could only hope that they'd have a copy knocking about in the office, or else be helpful in supplying a name of their so-called reporter.

The Hunton and District Gazette office was near the end of the high street, just before the new library building, and she pushed open the tall glass door and entered the small public area ready for a confrontation. The girl on the front desk looked up at her with a friendly little smile on her face, stealing her thunder almost immediately, killing it completely as she asked if she could help with a voice that could have been lifted straight out of a child's talking doll.

"I wanted to speak to one of your reporters," Emily began, realising that her tone, as soon as her voice came out, sounded more reasonable than she had hoped for in the car.

"They're usually only available by appointment," the girl said, a nametag on her thin blue sweater said Kirsty. That wasn't the name of someone you could get angry at. "Who was it you wanted to speak to?"

Emily stared at her, and at her smile that hadn't once slackened.

"I'm not sure."

She could feel her anger becoming rapidly replaced by self-consciousness. It felt like she was a tiny little boat lost in the ocean of the newspaper's office, her wind of righteousness now breathless. She felt stranded and strangely alone. A heat flushed through her face.

"There was an article about..." she hesitated. Now it seemed like she was the madwoman. "A Messiah. In town."

Kirsty kept up her smile. It wasn't so much that she was amused by the article, the way the reporter had obviously intended, but she seemed genuinely interested and keen to help. It stunned Emily to find someone still like that in the world, and for some reason she almost mistrusted her for it.

"That was Kelly," Kirsty said, picking up a handset next to her. "I'll just call up to the editorial office and see if he's in at the moment."

Emily found herself smiling back at her

courteously, and drummed her fingers on the polished wood of the front desk as Kirsty tapped in some numbers on the handset.

"Hi, it's Kirsty in reception... hello... is Kelly Stafford in the office?" her eyes flashed up towards Emily, and there was even a smile in those two glistening blue orbs. "Is he? Can you ask him if he's got a few minutes to come down and see a young lady. Yes, she's here in reception now. Okay. Thank you."

These last two words she almost sang, and it reminded Emily of the chime of cheap doorbells. The girl's smile came again, broader than ever, and she asked her if she would like to take a seat while she waited. Emily thanked her, and turned to look for a chair. There were three sitting in a neat row opposite the tall glass door that led back out into the street, and she was about to take one when Kirsty asked if she would like a coffee. Emily's throat was dry, but for some reason she couldn't ask the helpful Kirsty to be even more helpful, and simply shook her head with a returning smile before heading for the chair at the end.

She forced her mind to try and wander back to the article, picking out things this Kelly Stafford had said about the woman that may or may not have been Isabel Rider. She recalled now that he hadn't even bothered to find out her name, so what the chances were of him supplying an address she didn't know. And yet a photographer had found her and snapped a quick shot through her second floor flat window. Unless it was all bogus.

She shook her head and gazed out through the glass door at the traffic passing outside. Her head was swimming, drowning, with maybe's and could-be's, and it felt sometimes as thought her mind would simply give in to the inevitable deluge and collapse like a house made of rotted straw. All she had to go on was a blurred photograph, a newspaper-quality blurred photograph no less, of a partially silhouetted woman, taken from below, through an upstairs window. Her head was fucked. She'd come all the way down here for that. This reporter was going to laugh at her, either straight to her face or after she'd gone, but he'd laugh at her. And then he'd probably print a story about her the following week with an equally witty headline like *Mary Magdalen came looking for the second Messiah*, or some other puerile shit.

"Fuck," she whispered under her breath, just as the door behind the quietly-smiling Kirsty opened and a man in a blue shirt and tie stepped through.

He was less than thirty, a few years younger that she, and he was handsome. Not in an innocent way, but in a kind of slick he-knows-he's-handsome kind of way. She felt herself become flushed even as she thought it, and it disgusted her to feel so aroused just by looking at him, and reminded herself that she had made a vow never to go near another man ever again. But then Kirsty directed his gaze in her direction, and when his eyes lifted towards her, Emily felt a wave of shyness pass over her, forcing her own eyes down to the well-trodden carpet between them.

So this was Kelly Stafford.

The reporter she was ready to get mad at.

From the corner of her eye she could see him approach. She glanced up and saw his slick smile creasing his face in two. She remembered how much she had wanted to slap it, but now all she could think was how hot her lips had become. He extended his hand to her and all she could do was stand awkwardly and shake it.

"You wanted to see me about one of my stories?" he said, his teeth a brilliant white and inviting.

Emily nodded, transfixed by them.

"Yes. It seems silly, but I wanted to know who the lady in the photograph was. The madwoman."

"Yes, I remember," the reporter mused, staring into middle distance as though the full recollection hung there. "She brought a young boy back to life."

He laughed, half amused by his own story. "What did you want to know about her?"

"I thought I might know her, from a long time ago."

"Did she cure people then?"

Emily paused.

"Not so much..," she managed to say.

She could see how ridiculous her being here was about to get. He'd already had a good laugh about it, and he still had a smile on his face. What she wanted to say was just going to get her out of his company all the sooner. "I just thought it was an old friend, that's all. Do you have a name, or an address, because there wasn't one in the article."

Kelly shook his head.

"I'm sorry, that's either confidential or not available, I can't remember which. If I did have it upstairs, I probably would have printed it. And then again, I might have had to leave it out for legal reasons."

"Would you be able to check for me?"

"I suppose I could."

"It's just that I haven't seen her for twenty years or so, and it would be nice to find her after all this time."

"That's if it is her."

Emily nodded.

Kelly Stafford seemed to think it over for a

114

moment. She didn't think she was asking too much, but then he probably had more important things to be doing. He gazed into her eyes as she waited, and there must have been something helpless in that look because he finally relented.

"I'll have a look through my desk," he said, "and see if I've still got anything like that lying about. It's not something that's ever likely to need a second story, so it usually gets binned."

"I'd appreciate anything you've got."

She smiled, innocently she hoped, even as she blushed at the double meaning she thought her comment might have had. She'd never been with a man, never had anyone touch her, since... not since she was younger. She consciously tugged down the sleeves of her sweater as she straightened herself to leave.

"Should I call back later, or...?"

"Leave me your number. I'll call you whether I find something or not."

"Promise?"

God, she thought, now you sound desperate.

"I promise," Kelly said with a wide smile.

Emily shook his hand again and ducked out of the office door as yet another flush heated her face. Once out in the street again, she berated herself for how she had acted. She'd vowed never to let another man touch her, and yet there she was, wanting to find her childhood friend, and salivating like a whore.

She muttered to herself all the way back to her car, telling herself that she shouldn't have given that reporter her home number, and that she should have made arrangements to phone him later on in the week, and not once did she look round to see if the sparrows had followed her.

He probably wouldn't have the woman's name or number anyway, she thought. And if that was the case, she told herself that she would simply thank him politely for his time, and say goodbye. The trouble was, when he called her that evening and invited her out for a drink, she became light-headed and in a state of confusion, agreed.

# THREE

## SCARS

K elly Stafford was waiting for her at the bar. She
could seem him through the crowded room,
leaning against the wall beside a cigarette
machine. He wore a dark blue shirt, open to the start
of a dark haired chest, and his eyes roamed the room,
she guessed in search of her. When they settled finally
upon her, still standing in the doorway, they initiated
her going to him. There was something about those
eyes, something oddly familiar about the way he
looked at her, and she navigated her way across the
room until they were close enough to speak.

"I'm glad you came," he said to her, his smile
glistening like the sheen of his neatly combed hair.

"You've got information for me," Emily tried to
say, as flatly as she could. "Of course I came."

Kelly's smile faltered for just a moment, but then
came back with the slick speed of fresh oil.

"Can I get you a drink?"

Emily glanced across the busy bar, but she was not
in the mood for spirits, and asked him simply for a
glass of red wine. He nodded agreeably, and as he
turned and lifted his head to get the attention of the
young girl behind the bar, Emily watched the way his

arms moved beneath his shirt, studying the meat of his muscle as it contorted. She still remembered the vow she'd made so many years ago, to have nothing more to do with men. She'd broken that vow only once, with an ornithology student called Simon back when she was twenty two. That had ended badly, the experience bringing shocking memories from her past back to her, and she had run away from him in a near hysterical fit.

Kelly would probably be no different. Just another regular guy asking her out on a date. It was her, that was the simple truth of it. She'd probably never be able to let another man near her again. She had the scars to prove it, and she knew that they were probably never going to heal.

She started as Kelly handed her a round-bodied wine glass, its deep scarlet fluid lapping thickly near the rim. She took it from him and together they wandered away from the bar towards a small empty table in the corner. It was quieter here, they would be able to talk more about the woman in the photograph, and as she took a seat opposite him, Emily waited for him to give her whatever information she hoped he had.

"You're single, Emily, yes?"

The question caught her offguard for a moment.

"Yes," she murmured.

*What about the woman?*

"I've been single myself for a while too. Just waiting for the right one to come along I guess," he added this last bit with a confederate smile, as though they both shared the same grief of loneliness.

"Kelly," she found herself saying abruptly, "you're probably a great guy, but -"

He sat back slowly in his chair, and she saw

straight away the defensive expression.

"What is it?" Emily asked.

"Here comes the but speech. It's okay, Emily, you don't have to continue. I've heard it more than once."

"It's not that. It's just -"

"It's okay," he said again. "It's not you, it's me. I've had some problems in my life and I'm not ready for a relationship at the moment... We've all been there, Emily. It's nothing new. I guess that's why single people stay single. Because they think they need to be a perfect little package, all gift wrapped and ready to hand to someone."

Emily stared at him. She couldn't think of anything to say. This seemed it exactly, her whole miserable life summed up in a short brief sentence.

"But that's not the way relationships work," he continued. "The more we stay alone, the harder it is to become that perfect little package. We need someone else to work out all our problems with. Do you think I'm a perfect little package?"

Emily's eyes flickered down to where his haired chest crept up to the top of his shirt. It seemed pretty perfect to her. She gazed back up into his eyes. This wasn't her. And her problems were nowhere near what he might think of as normal. He didn't know what he was talking about.

"I've had some terrible things happen to me," he went on, "so has everyone in one way or another, but we can only move on by sharing. I'm not saying we can be total therapists to each other, and come out of this singing like canaries, but anything's better than nothing. Happiness doesn't show itself that often."

His plain straight-talking almost shook her off her chair. She knew he was only speaking about deaths or break-ups, or some other natural occurrence, but not the sort of nightmarish hell she'd seen in her short time alive on this earth. And yet something about its simplicity made her want to try again. She still had the scars on her wrists and on the insides of her thighs, scars that had hardly healed at all, and they were things that she never wanted anyone else alive to ever see again.

"You had information for me," she finally said quietly, staring down at the wine glass clasped tightly in her hands.

Kelly waited a few moments before answering.

Emily couldn't bear to face him now, not after what he had said, and the way she could still not open up. Finally he spoke.

"I couldn't find anything about her," he said, pulling a small folded scrap of paper from his pocket. "But I called the photographer who took the picture, and he gave me the address of where he went. He said Mrs Fry gave it to him. I hope it helps."

Emily took the note from him and pocketed it without even reading it.

"Thank you," she said to him. "I hope it helps too."

They sat in silence for a few minutes after that, taking short delicate sips from their glasses, neither one of them knowing how to continue. It was an awkward situation now, made worse by the bustling din of the bar around them, and Emily could feel herself becoming more and more conscious of the situation that she had put herself in.

"I should go," she said at last, and pushed her chair back with the intention to leave.

"This isn't right," Kelly complained. "Neither of us have done anything wrong. Why can't we just finish tonight and enjoy ourselves? What would be wrong with that?"

Emily looked up at him now, and saw again that

same wonderful face she had felt giddy at in the newspaper office when she had first seen it. A tentative smile came to her own lips now, and she conceded, thinking why not? Simon had scared her with some of the things that he'd said, and then Kelly had made reference, albeit vaguely, to past agonies and painful memories. She'd never be able to forget them, but if she could at least put them out of her mind for one night, then she should be grateful for that.

# FOUR

## WITHOUT A TRACE

She'd parked perhaps a hundred yards further down the street from the flat, and had spent the best part of twenty minutes simply gazing up at the window. It was definitely the place. Emily had held the photograph she'd torn out of the local paper in front of her several times, matching the façade of the apartment building, the brickwork, the white paint of the front door. This was definitely the place.

No one had appeared at that second floor window, no curtains had twitched, and she was not sure whether anyone would even be at home. Emily glanced at her watch again. It was nearly eleven o'clock and the sky was as dark as old lead. If Isabel had been at work, she reasoned that she would have gotten in long ago and was probably cooking dinner. She placed her hand on the door handle at her side, but again let it slip back into her lap. What was she going to say to her? It had been twenty years since she had last seen her. Would she even remember her? Of course she would, Emily told herself, she had to. They couldn't live lives like they had only to forget them. Maybe at the end of their years, when they were bald and toothless, they might have forgotten segments or mistaken the order of events. But in twenty years? Never.

And could she even begin to tell her about her own brother? Emily knew that Isabel had suspected him of a great many deeds, but just how far could she believe him going? And might the truth push the two of them apart for another twenty years, or even forever? Family was stronger than friendship after all.

Once again, Emily's hand strayed to the door handle at her side. She could feel the cool hard plastic against the clammy skin of her fingers. Slowly she squeezed, telling herself that if the car door did click open, then she'd have to get out and approach the flat.

Her fingers held for a moment as her mind continued to whirl. Would they ever be friends again? Would they both have secrets to share, old and new? Emily knew she couldn't keep living her life like this - watching the skies and the shadowed hedgerows in case anyone or anything should be spying on her, searching every personal ad and internet chat room for clues to Isabel's or Kyle's movements. She had to know, one way or another, and this one insignificant story in the tiniest of local papers had proven to be the biggest lead she'd found so far.

The lock clicked and the door swung open. With a deep breath in her lungs, Emily put her weight to it, pushed the door open wider, and clambered unsteadily out of her car.

She hoped she looked sober as she made her way across the road and along the pavement towards the white painted door of the apartment building. Her head was light and her feet felt miles away, as though she was being transported upon a cloud of shifting fog. The night air was cool, and yet her face burned intensely, and she felt totally self conscious of her approach, as though every curtain in the street was suddenly lifting, a thousand different eyes aware of her approach.

The white painted door loomed unnaturally quickly, and Emily found herself in front of it before she was ready. She simply stood on the front step gazing helplessly at the peeling paintwork for what seemed like an hour or more, bewildered as to what to do next, until her eyes finally settled on a short vertical row of door bells beside her. Each buzzer had a little plastic window covering a hand-written nametag. There were three tags for the second floor, but only one had a name, Olivia Cander. The other two simply read Flat Seven, and Flat Eight.

Emily thought she was swaying as she stood on the front step. She thought every neighbour in the street was probably watching her, wondering why it was taking an innocent caller so long to ring a door bell. The only thing she could do, other than turning and hurrying back to her car, was to press each in turn and see who answered. If one was wrong, she'd only have to apologise. And if they were both wrong, well, she could return home with a slower beating heart.

The thought occurred, as she pressed the bell for Flat Seven, that if neither flat answered, she be obliged to come back here another time and go through this all again. When the intercom suddenly clicked, however, and the slow rasp of an old man asked who was there, she breathed a sigh of relief in answer. He asked again who was there, as though his deafness might have made him not catch the name, but Emily said that she was looking for a friend of hers and that she had the wrong apartment.

To her surprise, the old gentleman offered her a token of good luck. He said that a young woman of about thirty had lived for a while in the flat across the hall from him, but that he hadn't seen or heard her for a couple of days.

"Flat Eight?" Emily asked.

The old man told her yes.

"If you want to come up and knock on her door, I can buzz you in," he said.

Emily hesitated a moment. Did she want that? Of course she did, that's why she was here.

"Thank you," she murmured into the intercom. "That would be very helpful."

The intercom clicked off and then a buzzing sound came from the door. Emily stepped forward and put her weight to it, finding that she needed to push quite hard to get through the heavy old door. It swung back under a huge spring on the other side, and Emily found herself in a small communal space. To her right she could see twelve mail boxes screwed to the wall, and as she walked past them on her way to the carpeted stairs, she glanced at the box for number eight but found it empty. What did that even tell her, Emily asked herself as she started to climb? Either Flat Eight was still occupied and they'd collected their mail, or they hadn't had any mail delivered in the last couple of days. She was still no closer.

On the landing of the second floor, she half expected to find the old man waiting for her, a smoking jacket tied around his portly waist and a Sherlock Holmes pipe held snugly in one hand, waiting to help her search for her missing friend. But the landing was empty, quiet too, and slowly she approached the bare wooden door, bare apart from a small brass digit screwed two thirds up, a solitary lonely eight.

Emily reached out and rapped her knuckles on the

wood. The sound seemed to reverberate not just around the flat on the other side, but also around the landing, echoing both up and down the stairwell. She listened intently for the sound of anyone approaching, but there were no footfalls on the other side of the door, no internal doors opening or closing, no sound of any kind. The flat seemed empty.

Suddenly filled with the urge to know for sure, now that she had come all this way, Emily reached down for the handle. The brass knob was cold to her touch, but she turned it with a firm grasp and pushed. With her weight almost fully behind it, and expecting the lock to offer substantial resistance, her surprise at it being unlocked, coupled with her weight falling forward into free air, nearly cast her to the bare wooden floor on the other side of the threshold.

It was dark inside, and her fingers fumbled blindly around the wall just inside the door, switching on the low wattage bulb that hung from the ceiling, and filling the flat with an eerie brown luminescence. Finding herself directly in the living room, Emily stared quickly about her in case somebody was home but unhappy about being called upon. But it was clear that the flat was deserted.

The room was sparsely furnished, poorly furnished even, just two armchairs in one corner, an old wooden chair close-by, and a small portable TV beneath the window in the photograph. The flat was reasonably clean, but it was cramped and looked like something squatters had left behind. Surely if Isabel had lived here, and she hoped she was doing better in life than this, then she prayed that she had left and taken her best possessions with her.

She had those fears confirmed when she wandered through into the small single bedroom. The mattress was bare, stripped of all linen, but discarded on the floor beside it lay a copy of the local newspaper that she had appeared in. Was this why she had left so quickly, she wondered? Because she had been given exposure, her picture printed with a location that could be tracked down as easily as she herself had done.

Emily approached the crumpled paper and perched on the edge of the bed as she picked it up. Flicking through, she found the page on which the woman's photograph appeared, and there, in scrawled handwriting right through the middle, was the word *bitch*. She wasn't sure whether it referred to herself or to Mrs Fry who had instigated the entire story, but it seemed clear that the whole incident had been enough to drive the unnamed Messiah out of her home. The only thing left for Emily to do now, was to try and find out whether this flat had in fact been the last place her childhood friend Isabel Rider had lived.

Dropping the paper back on the floor where she'd found it, Emily got up from the bed and looked around the rest of the small room. The doors to the wardrobe in the darkest corner of the room stood ajar, and inside she could see that there were no clothes inside. Where could Isabel have gone, she wanted to know? Somewhere local? Somewhere new and far away? She suddenly felt hollow inside, and it angered her because it made no sense. She was no nearer to finding her after all. There had been no concrete evidence. No names spoken or written anywhere to confirm her suspicions, and when it all came down to it, the only thing she really had was a slightly better than vague recognition about a badly printed photograph taken from a distance of a girl she had known twenty years ago. How had her life gotten this low?

Her eyes fell upon a door in the ill-lit gloom beside the wardrobe, and realised now why she had not seen it before. The architrave had been pulled off so that the door was level with the wall, and they had both been painted the same dull ochre colour. It seemed like a good disguise, but now that she had seen it, her curiosity had been sparked, and it carried her across the room towards it.

She was certain that the flat was indeed deserted, and slowly she took hold of the handle, painted over with that same lacklustre finish. It turned easily in her hand, surprising her that something so well hidden could be so easy to open, but she had pulled it only a few inches before she stopped herself. What could possibly be inside that it needed hiding, her mind suddenly wanted to know, her imagination conjuring hideous images of serial killings and mutilations? If this had indeed been Isabel's flat then there could be nothing of the sort inside. And yet she had nothing with which to confirm that.

But the wall was brown, and the door was brown; there was something secret inside, she knew it. The hairs on the back of her neck prickled with agitation, but she'd spilled light from the bedroom inside now and she had to continue.

The door creaked open in her hand a little more. There was nothing but darkness inside, but then came a stench on the back of that darkness, a kind of fermenting rot, creeping like an undead creature from its dank graveyard crypt. Her skin chilled suddenly, and a shudder passed swiftly throughout her body, her mind once again conjuring images of death and butchered bodies. Perhaps this hadn't been Isabel's flat...

The door stood open, and with what little light

that spilled in from the ill-lit bedroom, she could see that this tiny annex, possibly something that had once been a walk-in cupboard or even an en-suite, was empty. The stench lingered, however, but at least what had once made that stench was now thankfully gone.

As her eyes became gradually accustomed to the murk of this new box room, Emily noticed a few things lying on the floor that had been left behind. There was a small book lying near the back of the room, along with the remains of candles burned down to the nub. There even seemed to be scraps of something littering much of the bare wooden floor, but she couldn't tell whether they were cloth or bread crusts or even slivers of meat, and she wasn't prepared to go in any further to check just in case the door did slam shut behind her and locked her in. She'd seen those movies the same as everyone else, oh yes, and nothing was about to carry her over that foul threshold, curiosity or not.

Emily took one final look around the flat before she left, but she could find nothing that put a name to the previous tenant. In fact the only thing left of any kind of personal trace was the scrawl across that newspaper article. She briefly considered asking the landlord if he'd been given any forwarding address, but she decided as she closed the door to flat eight behind her that if Isabel had left in such a hurry, and making sure there was no distinguishing trace, (as was certain by what had or had not been left behind), she would have been sure not to let anyone know where she was headed next.

Once Emily was back out in the street, the cool night air circling down the road fresh and bracing after the rank humidity of the flat, she realised that she was still no better off. That photograph in the Hunton and

District Gazette had instigated all of this, but she'd not had one thing confirmed, and now that she'd acted on the only scrap of information gleaned from Kelly Stafford, she was still no further.

She heaved a weary sigh as she gazed back up at the window on the second floor. Was that you in there, she couldn't help wondering to herself? She guessed she might never find out, and wandering back towards her car parked further down along the street, wondered just where she might turn next.

130

# FIVE

## A NAME AND A HEART ARE OFFERED

Emily sat in front of the television with a brandy in her hand. The television was off, the brandy was cheap, but it was gently numbing her senses anyway. She studied her reflection in the dull grey glass of the screen, watched as she lifted the tumbler to her lips and sipped once again. Where had it gone? That's all she could think. She'd once wanted to be a show jumper when she was a kid. Her father, amongst all the other animals that he bred for meat, kept a single horse in a small paddock at the back of their house. Her name had been Diamond, and she had loved it more than anything else. It had been far too big for her to ride alone, but her dad would take her out of a weekend and sit her up on her back, and walk her round the paddock with the horse on a halter, sometimes for hours, just round and round. She loved that horse, loved it dearly, but they were just memories now, memories of a wonderful time spent with a wonderful father that she knew would never come again.

Her father was not dead, no, although she had not been home in a very long time. No, it was the horse that had died. One morning she had wandered down to the paddock simply to stroke her and give her an apple; it was a bright Spring morning, vivid blue sky, not a cloud in sight, larks were singing out in the fields, the breeze was gentle and warm, but Diamond just lay on her side, motionless. She'd never seen a horse lying flat on the ground, and she must have stared at her for a while, maybe even ducking under the fence rail to get a closer look, but she eventually ran inside bawling until her father came out with her to confirm the horrible truth. Emily would never ride Diamond again.

She poured another measure of the cheap brown liquor into her tumbler and set the bottle back down on the coffee table beside her. Where had it all gone? That question had become something of a sickening chant over the years, a chant that brought up the same poisoned memories time and again like foul sludge rising beneath a drain cover. And there had always been just one answer, one name that always returned to that rotten dark surface. Kyle Rider.

The doorbell startled her, and a slick of warm brandy spilled out of her glass across her wrist as she jerked. She'd almost forgotten she even had a doorbell, so rarely did it ring. There were never visitors, no evening callers, and as she glanced at her watch, she saw that it was getting close to nine o'clock.

Her mind seemed disjointed as she fumbled to place her drink on the coffee table, her eyes catching her reflection in the television, stumbling to get up off the sofa as she bent to lick the brandy from her wrist. Who could be calling at this time at night? She knew no one, no one well enough to call unannounced anyway.

She looked through the eyehole in the middle of the door and physically trembled inside when she saw the reporter Kelly Stafford standing on her doorstep gazing idly up at the front of her house. Her hand froze on the door handle. Should she let him in or not? She had no idea. Did she even want to, that was a more important question. She'd not dated a man in years, and it seemed obvious that this was Kelly's intention. She could feel herself shaking now, her skin suddenly both clammy and hot, although when she glanced down at her hand still clasping the handle saw that it at least looked steady. Her heart was pounding though, oh yes, and even as she thought to herself what harm a conversation could do, she was already unbolting the door before her sense of self preservation could answer her own question.

"What are you doing here?" she found herself flatly asking his wide smile.

"That wasn't the greeting I was expecting I must admit," he replied, pulling a bottle of red wine out from behind his back. "I was hoping you'd accept this peace offering."

Emily's eyes flashed down to the bottle he was offering. This was not completely new territory, but it still felt unnatural. When her acceptance didn't come straight away, the reporter added that he'd managed to find something else out about the woman in the photograph.

Emily looked up at him blankly.

"You did? What?"

Kelly Stafford hovered on the doorstep.

"Could I tell you inside? It's a bit chilly out here."

Emily apologised as she stepped back and allowed him inside her home.

"I'm sorry, Kelly, it's been so long since I've done this kind of thing. Please, let me get us some glasses and we can open that bottle of yours."

"Thank you," Kelly said, stepping along the hallway, looking through doors. "I'd like that."

"The kitchen's the last door at the end," Emily told him, closing the front door and replacing the bolts before starting after him. "There's a corkscrew in the top drawer under the sink."

"Way ahead of you," she heard him call from the kitchen.

Emily came through the doorway and pulled open the cupboard door above the refrigerator, retrieving two wine glasses before setting them down on the counter as Kelly began to wind the corkscrew into the neck of the bottle. His eyes were focussed on the job at hand, and she was allowed a few brief moments of scrutiny.

He wore a dark grey shirt, silk it looked like, again unbuttoned enough to show the start of a dark haired chest. The hair on his head was neatly combed back, his face lifted from one of the expensive glossy magazines. She'd hardly had a single romantic thought in the years that she was supposed to have them, but she suddenly couldn't help thinking about what might happen with this man. He was an attractive man, well groomed and educated, and he seemed to have a deep understanding of emotional scars. He wouldn't be so quick to dismiss them, as Simon had done so readily. No, she was sure that he'd listen and understand. Especially if he cared enough for her, as he seemed so ready to do. He glanced up at her suddenly as the cork slipped from the bottle with an almost silent breathless pop. He caught her watching him, but his smile stole any guilt she might have had almost immediately.

"There's a knack," he said to her, setting the corkscrew down on the counter before starting to pour the wine, and for a moment Emily had no idea what he was talking about. "Strong and controlled, that's the key. Then neither the cork nor the bottle slips."

Emily felt herself blush as she took up her glass and sipped. It tasted good, and maybe it was the brandy already in her system, but her head became light as she stood there in the kitchen watching this man in her house.

"Shall we go through into the living room?" she suggested, turning to leave. "You can tell me all about what you've found."

"It's not much," he stated, as he followed her through and took a seat in the armchair, "but I hope it'll help."

Emily was disappointed, but whether it was because he had not sat on the sofa beside her or whether he'd already confessed that his news wasn't much, she wasn't sure. The alcohol from the wine was whizzing through her head now, chasing her thoughts round her head as though it was a hare at a dog track, and she found herself simply nodding at him, bidding for him to continue.

"As I said, I'm not sure if it will help, but I've managed to find her name."

Emily swallowed her mouthful of wine before sitting up.

"Yes?" she said, wiping her mouth with her fingers. "That's all I need. Thank you."

This was the moment she had waited a long time for, when she could finally say whether she was on her friend's trail or not. Her glass was held tightly in her hands, but the alcohol in her body had started to make her fingers go numb, and she could hardly feel it. Especially with this urgent news that was coming.

"I asked around at the council offices, a have a few friends there, and they gave me the name Isabel Rider. Does that mean anything to you?"

Does it, she thought dumbly? That means everything.

"Yes," she breathed aloud now, a huge smile

spreading across her face. "That's all I wanted to know. But unfortunately it seems like she's already left."

"Left?" Kelly seemed genuinely concerned now. "You've been to her flat already?"

Emily paused. She suddenly felt as though he was quizzing her, as though she had somehow broken the law for going.

"I went last night," she confessed. "About eleven."

"And she wasn't there?"

"More than that," Emily said. "The place looked deserted. Not a single personal possession in sight. I couldn't believe it." She took another sip of her wine. "I was a bit depressed that I hadn't found out one way or another."

"But at least you know now."

"Yes," she said. "At least I know now."

Kelly watched her as they both took another sip of the wine. They both seemed happy again just to be there in the same place at the same time.

"Are you going to try and find out where she went?" he asked her at last.

"I guess," she said. "But I don't know where to start. I was so close, but now... I don't know. Back to square one I suppose."

"I've got a few contacts," Kelly said to her. "And I'll do all I can to find something out for you."

"Thank you," she said. "I'd like that."

Kelly pushed himself forward in his seat suddenly and placed his glass down on the coffee table.

"You know, I've been thinking about what we said the other night. I know we both share a lot of emotional concerns -"

Emily went to speak but Kelly raised his hands.

"I know you think yours are too much to bring into a relationship, I respect that, but please hear me out. I really like you, Emily, and if you're willing, I'd

136

like to see you again, take you out on a proper date. We can go at whatever pace you feel comfortable with. I just want to see you, that's all."

Emily stared at him for a moment. She didn't know what to say. It seemed like he understood so much, knew so much about her already, and the layers of loneliness seemed to weaken and shift slightly at the thought of spending time with him, talking, embracing.

Sometimes she so desperately wanted to be with someone, to have someone say that everything was going to be alright, despite what may have happened in the past. But other times, she remembered all the things that had happened to her, and she felt sickened about herself, feeling that she never wanted to bring that filth into anyone else's life.

He was still looking at her, waiting for some kind of answer, but the simple truth was that she had no answer to give him. She'd planned to spend the evening slowly getting drunk, but he had changed all that. Instead he had brought a gift for the two of them to share, had brought news too of her friend Isabel. And perhaps what was most important of all, he had brought a gift of himself, willing to spend time with her, offering her a way to filter out all the disease that she knew riddled her body like a festering black plague.

She couldn't help wondering, as the wine warmed her body, that this might be the new start she needed, and that she'd hate herself for the rest of her life if she turned her back on such an opportunity. And so she smiled as she drank from her glass again, failing to notice just how fully the man in her house had begun to study her.

## SIX

_____

## AT THE PARK

The sky was clear the following day and the air was warm. Emily had taken some time to sit in the park for a few minutes, to get some sun and to think about Kelly. She'd left the house around ten to get some groceries, but with the sunshine warming her through the windscreen as she'd driven to the supermarket, she'd decided to stop off to sit and think things through.

She could see the church spire through the trees and was glad it was there. She was not a religious person, her family had never been particularly sided towards any god, but now and again she liked to know that if there was one, at least he or one of his houses was close by.

There were a lot of trees in the small village park, and she felt reasonably content to hear a steady melody of birdsong colouring the air. A breeze circled gently around her, carrying the warmth of the day, and it was indeed welcome.

Her thoughts were literally filled with the reporter Kelly Stafford. He seemed like a nice guy, and under normal circumstances (what did she know of normal?) she would have accepted his advances readily. But after all that had happened, after all that Kyle Rider had done, she wasn't sure if she was ready, or indeed capable, of sharing herself with him, despite all the understanding he offered.

She was sure that he'd had his heart broken, or that he'd had his affections thrown back at him, that was the emotional baggage he was carrying; but hers? That went so much deeper. It was dark down there, as dark as a sewer, and she still wasn't sure if she wanted him to go down there with her.

A sparrow settled on the grass in front of her, cocking its tiny head in all directions. She smiled as it seemed to see her, but before she could study it too much it was off, a blur of fluttering wings back towards the heavy foliage of one of the trees.

It was strange how much things had changed in just the few days she had known him. Yes, she was still wary about a lot of things, and yet so much of that suddenly seemed less significant. It was as though he had somehow been able to lift a veil off her fears. And the sunshine. It seemed crazy to her, but it felt like she'd hardly ever noticed it before. But now here it was, warming the earth around her and her along with it. To think as much as this could hurt her mind and she knew it, but it was insane how blissful that hurt made her feel. It was a good insanity, an insanity to run towards. If anyone had been looking at her sitting alone on a park bench smiling to herself, and she was sure she was smiling broadly, then they would surely have suspected that madness. She didn't want to tempt anything, but she couldn't help the word happy nudging into her thoughts.

The sparrow returned, hopping about on the grass less than ten yards from her outstretched feet. She wished she'd gone to the supermarket first, then she could've broken some bread for it. But it seemed content to peck amongst the blades of grass anyway, searching for grubs or insects, no doubt, or the remains of someone else's bread.

And then her eye became caught by something else moving, another bird come to rest beneath one of the trees nearby. Her vision fought to find it in the deep shadow beneath the heavy boughs of the sycamore.

But then her heart skipped a sickening beat. Her mind flooded with a deluge of all her old fears and dreads.

A crow stood there, its empty hollow eyes gouging her like meat skewers as it returned her gaze.

The warmth of the sun overhead went from her body.

A creeping chill replaced it.

It was watching her.

From the corner of her eye she could still see the sparrow, but even that had stopped its hopping to stand and look up at her. Her hands were becoming heavy, she could feel her own blood thickening inside them, making her fingers useless. Slowly she pushed herself to her feet, and with one final glance at the ebony-coloured crow still standing motionless beneath the huge dark tree, she took up her handbag beside her and hurried away along the path towards the car park.

She wanted to look back, oh God how she wanted to look back. She could feel the needle eyes of the crow digging into her spine as it watched her leave. But she didn't. She kept her sight fixed firmly on the car park, and even though she comprehended nothing of what she saw as she walked briskly, she kept her eyes forward until she neared her car. Only then, and with her numbed fingers fumbling in her handbag for the keys, did her eyes flicker back towards the bench where she had sat.

But there were no birds in sight now, no crows, no sparrows, nothing. Her heart was still hammering as she climbed hurriedly into the car and slammed the door shut after her, pressing down the central locking button as she did so.

Her hands were awkward as she attempted to turn the key in the ignition. Distracted now as she glanced down to see where the key should go, she didn't notice the crow as it landed in the middle of the bonnet. But once the engine fired and she looked back up, she let out a shuddering yelp as it cawed raucously at her, the inside of its sharp black maw hypnotic and terrible.

Emily sat and stared at this thing as it gazed back at her like a waxwork demon, the engine roaring beneath her right foot. So petrified with fear was she, that she couldn't even move her hands to put the car in gear, or sound the horn to frighten it away. Something told her that nothing would frighten this thing, it would stay until it was done, until it had terrified her enough. But that moment came sooner than she thought. With one final horrid caw, it stretched out its vast black wings, leapt up into the air, and soared up and over the top of the car.

Emily hunched down as she watched it swoop out of sight, turning to look through the back window to make sure that the thing had gone. She saw a flash of black before it disappeared completely, like a gaping slash across the sky, and then she slumped back in her seat with an uneasy relief.

She could feel her blood pumping hard in her chest, could hear it thumping in her head, as she finally put the car into gear and reversed slowly out of the parking space.

The darkness that mired her soul had resurfaced, and with a sickening vengeance. It had swamped her completely, had shrouded all those bright thoughts that she'd had of Kelly, and reconfirmed that no relationship could ever dispel the horrors that lived inside her. She was cursed, she knew it, and as she pulled out of the car park and back onto the main road, she vowed never to unleash that darkness upon anyone else again. Except anyone who knew about it all, that was, anyone who had been there at the start, who could hopefully battle it with her, and destroy that darkness.

That one person she could not find, that same person who had eluded her for years. She so desperately wanted her back, back in her life where she belonged. And that one person was the elusive Isabel Rider.

# SEVEN

## WHAT HAPPENED AFTER DARK

W hy won't you speak to me?" Kelly was outside on the doorstep, yelling up at the front of the house.

Inside, Emily sat perched on the edge of her bed, holding her head in her hands. The window was ajar, letting in more than just the fresh evening breeze. She could hear every word he said, every plea he offered, if only she would come down and listen to him. But what did he have to say that she hadn't already anticipated?

Perhaps in a few minutes he would get tired and go away. His words, however, had resilience, and it seemed he wasn't going to be dissuaded too readily.

"Please, Emily, just open the door and let me talk to you."

Emily looked up towards the window. She could visualise him downstairs, shirt open to that tuft of dark hair, face exquisitely sculpted, eyes longing to gaze upon her. But what could she do? What could she offer?

"I can't stay here all night. Your neighbours are twitching curtains. *Please.*"

Emily broke a smile. This was ridiculous.

Slowly she pushed herself to her feet and went downstairs to the front door. Pausing with her fingers clasping the handle, she took a breath before opening it. Kelly's eyes tracked quickly down and found her looking out at him through the narrow gap. Light from the hallway behind her silhouetted her partially, making it difficult to discern her full expression, but he began to talk, hurriedly in case she closed the door on him for good.

"Emily, I don't know what's happened since I saw you last, but this is insane. You can't shut me out, not when I've professed how much I care about you."

"Kelly, I told you -"

"I know what you told me, but what about the things I told you? We can work through everything together. I care about you deeply."

"We just met."

"It feels like I've known you a lifetime -"

"- a couple of days."

Kelly looked at her for a moment, vexed.

"How have you become so cold so quickly?"

"Like I said, it's only been a couple of days. You don't know me. You don't know anything about me."

Kelly took a breath, a calming breath.

"I can still help you find Isabel," he said.

"Really?" Emily asked, testily. "Have you found anything new?"

"I think so. But please, it's getting cold outside."

Emily looked at him some more, and then opened the door wider to let him in. Going through into the living room, she offered him a seat before he began.

"I've asked around," he started, perching on the edge of the sofa, "and put a few eyes out. But the nearest I've come is an area where she may have been seen."

"Where exactly?" Emily wanted to know, coming to sit beside him.

"There are some old office buildings behind the cinema. It's a long shot, but she may be holding up there for a while."

"It would make sense, seeing how she seemed to have left her flat so quickly."

"As I said, though, she's only been seen there. It doesn't mean she's actually there."

"But it's a start. Thank you, Kelly."

The reporter suddenly reached out and took hold of her hands, raising them to his lips and kissing them gently.

"I've missed you, Emily," he said to her. "And before you say it, yes I know it was only yesterday."

Emily stared at him as he pressed his lips to her hands again. The touch was blissful, romantic, but the moment did not last. His fingers slid down her hands to her wrists, touching the scars that had still not healed, and she let out a yelp as she retracted her hands from his, pulling them back swiftly into her lap.

"What is it?" Kelly wanted to know.

Emily had already turned away from him. There was a story involved, a horrible story, and one that she did not want to start. All she would tell him was that he had to leave.

"Please," Kelly protested again, pressing his hand to the top of her leg and pushing it round to the inside of her thigh.

Emily shot him an icy glance as she took hold of his hand and tried to pry it away. But his grip had strength, and his fingers were pressing into her scars there too. Her thoughts suddenly seemed to leave her for a moment, soaring back through the living room into the hallway. Had she locked the front door? She couldn't remember.

"I only want to be with you."

Her thoughts returned in an instant, and she hauled his hand away from her now, struggling to get to her feet before demanding that he leave her house.

He sat there staring at her, and for one horrid moment she thought he would remain defiant. Her mind conjured all those newspaper reports of how women got themselves into situations like these, and how she had always thought how stupid women like that were. And yet here she was, doing the exact same thing.

She was trembling inside. He was strong, she couldn't fight him. But before anything even went that far, he suddenly stood up, right in front of her.

"Okay," he said quietly. "I'll go. But tonight could have been different. I'm not trying to hurt you, Emily. I'm just trying to be a nice guy. I know you've got problems, we've all got problems, I just want to help put right all that has been done wrong."

Emily said nothing, not even as he walked past her and out into the hallway.

She jumped as the front door slammed behind him, and all she could do was collapse onto the sofa, and hold her head in her hands like she had done earlier.

She was sure he was a nice guy, but he wasn't the problem. The problem was Kyle, that sick little shit Kyle. It always had been. No, the only way to resolve anything was to find his sister. Only then could she ever possibly hope to get over the fears she had inside her, when that one hideous problem was gone for good.

## EIGHT

### WHAT HIDES IN THE DARKNESS

When she finally stood in front of the first of the old office buildings, it was already past midnight. She'd told herself a dozen times or more on the drive into town that it would be far safer to begin the search come morning. Hunton was not the largest of towns, and indeed was not one of the most dangerous, but she was still a solitary woman wandering alone through the ill-lit streets behind the main pedestrian area. Even if she did run into trouble from youths or drunks, there would be no one else around to help her. So it was with a pounding heart that she'd left her car and wandered towards the disused offices.

Kelly had offered her little information. She'd driven past these buildings perhaps only a handful of times, and because of their drab grey exteriors she had never given them much attention. She'd hoped there would be an easy route between them, but as she looked up at their decaying brick facades, it quickly became apparent that a quick search would be impossible. She wondered briefly if it might even be possible to have the owners do a quick look through for her, but she knew if Isabel was hiding out somewhere inside, then she wanted anonymity for a reason.

Her first concern arose as she approached the main door at the front of the building in front of her. Never having broken and entered anywhere in her life, she hadn't anticipated what would be involved. She'd visualised a disused building as being an unlocked one, but it turned out that a disused office was more secure than a used one. Not only was the main door double locked, it also had a security grill bolted to the metal frame, protecting the entire entranceway behind an impenetrable steel mesh. Emily put her hands to it and tested its strength, but it hardly moved, hardly shook beneath her grasp.

She stepped back a little way and glanced along the frontage. Similar grills had been bolted to each of the windows on the ground floor. Only one of the windows she could see had been smashed, but the grill was in place and held the building secure. She wasn't sure if this might have been the first attempt by Isabel to gain entry, or just a passing act of vandalism by some drunken idiot.

She was telling herself, even as she left the first building and went on to the second, that Isabel might very well be inside, and that if she gave up so readily on each, she might as well not bother with any of them.

She stopped in the middle of the street and gazed back up at the unlit windows of the first office building, wondering whether Isabel was behind one of them somewhere, either furtively looking back down at her, or else huddled in a corner sleeping out a draughty night until morning came.

But she knew she couldn't get inside, not without proper tools, or even without the courage to break her way in. Yes they were deserted, but they still belonged to someone.

She was at the entranceway to the second office building, and her heart sank as she saw that it too had the same security measures as the first. She gazed up at the building, so defiant in its defences, and wondered just what the hell she should do. It was useless to keep trudging down the street looking at the others, she knew that already, which would leave only one option. See if there was a back, less secure, way in.

A service yard fed all of the office buildings at the rear, and Emily discovered it by chance. She'd wandered around the block and found it was all part of the same complex. Turning two more corners of the same block, however, she'd come upon an old chain-linked gate, now boarded over so that no one could see inside. Graffiti covered most of the boards, and several layers of band flyers had been pasted across the cracks so that it almost looked like part of the wall. But as Emily peered through the gap where the gate was padlocked, she could see the rears of all the offices, and hoped that this might offer her the break she needed.

It took a great deal of effort for her to scale the gate. With the boards in place there were few footholds, and her arms were barely up to the task of hauling her own body weight up and over. But her shoes found some grip on the brickwork beside the gate, and it had been enough to lever herself up and over and into the service yard.

There was nothing definite that showed evidence of a break in, as she had hoped she would find, just more of what had been put in place at the front. Security grills had been bolted to all of the doorways, and she found herself stepping past each one in turn with despair.

If Isabel had been on the run since their childhood, then she'd undoubtedly be good at concealing her tracks. That knowledge was defeating her as much as the padlocks and steel mesh, but this was the closest she'd been. Kelly had not been wrong about her flat, and all she could hope for was that he wasn't wrong about this either.

And then she saw something.

There at the very end, a delivery door concealed almost entirely by shadow, she saw the padlock holding it shut hanging at an odd angle. Approaching cautiously, her heart already skipping with unpromised hope, she could just make out that the padlock had been cut and then hung back outside of the bracket. Now standing in front of it, Emily could see the scratched metal grooves between the door handle and the steel jamb, as though a crowbar had been used to break the lock inside. The jamb itself was twisted and gouged around the lock, and as Emily put her hand to the cold metal, she took a deep inhale, and then pulled.

The door gave a little, perhaps only an inch at the most, but refused to come further. The door was open, there was no doubt about that, but it just wouldn't come any more.

Pressing her face to the gap between the door and the jamb, she gazed into the gloom inside, but could see very little. There was a staircase to the left, and a long hallway ahead, but much more than that she couldn't see.

But then there, what was that?

Something moved in the uncertain air between her and her focus. The middle distance seemed to shimmer, reverberating in the darkness, and then she realised just what she was looking at.

A rope had been tied from the railings of the staircase to the other end of the door handle. There had been enough slack to pull the door just away from the jamb, but not enough to get inside. And because it was ajar just a crack, there was not enough space to get a knife in and cut it, even if she'd thought of bringing one, which she hadn't. She let the door go and simply stared at it for a moment, her mind suddenly numb with fatigue.

It didn't mean that it was necessarily Isabel inside, that was the nagging doubt that kept flashing through her mind. It could be a squatter, or a gang, or just the remnants of someone who had broken in a long time ago and simply left through a different route.

Emily put her hands to her head and raked her fingers through her hair with exasperation. The sound of smashing glass from back in the street snatched her attention. Her first thought was that it was Isabel. But when the raucous laugh of two men came echoing between the walls, she became aware once again of the danger she was in. She was alone, defenceless, and she was straying where she didn't belong.

She swallowed hard as she stood motionless, her eyes straining through the darkness to where the gate to the service yard stood. The laughing of the two men came again, loud and drunken, and she shuddered afresh as the sound of a third male joined the din. She was shaking with fear now, dreading the sight of them appearing over the boarded gate, but the dirge quietened suddenly as they passed by the gate, but it was a few minutes before she had the courage to move again. When she did, however, it was back away from the shadowed doorway, where she could gaze up at the whole of the back of the office buildings.

*Where are you*, she wanted to cry out, just so that she could see her friend's face appear at one of the grimy windows.

But the silence of the place, hollow and enclosed, seemed to bear down upon her like a leaden weight, suppressing any voice she might have had into little more than a harried breath.

And then a hand took hold of her shoulder.

Emily spun round, the scream in her throat silenced by a forceful palm pressed hard against her mouth before it could even find its way between her lips. Her eyes stared wide and white into the shadowed face that bore down upon her, but she could make out nothing but the terrifying weight of that hollow silhouetted stare.

# NINE

## SECRETS OF THE HIDDEN

Emily wanted to hug her, but Isabel seemed so very different to the girl she once knew. Gone was the lightness she'd had as a child, so too was the trust, or even the warmth. What she now looked at, as she watched this bedraggled woman gaze furtively out of one of the windows, was a shell, a cold hardened husk of something that once resembled her. The woman flashed a glance round at her suddenly, her eyes as icy as her welcome. Did she not remember her properly?

"How did you find me?"

Emily did not know how to begin, despite the many years she had waited for this very moment. She'd always thought that the words would pour out, cascading without order like a waterfall, and yet they would not come, but simply hovered somewhere in an uncertain limbo inside her head, blurred and unmade.

"You do know who I am, don't you?" she said at last.

The woman at the window stared at her in silence, her body unmoving in the half-light. Emily could feel the weight of that stare again and it made her nervous. These were all things she'd never thought she'd feel in her company, and yet here she was, perhaps even fearful for her life.

"I could never forget," Isabel Rider said to her finally. "Many things I could and should, but never that."

"Then why are you like this?"

"Like what?"

Emily got up from her seat, an old office chair set upon awkward castors.

"I've been searching for you a long time, Isabel. I've had things I've needed to share with you."

"I never asked you to come looking, and I can not help you with your problems. You have to go, before you are seen, and never come looking for me again."

"No, Isabel."

"No?" the woman exclaimed.

"I'm not going to be without you, not after all this time, not again."

"You don't belong here."

"You don't think so? You think you're so special, so unique?"

"You couldn't understand -"

"Understand what? Your brother?"

The woman still standing inside the shadows visibly shuddered at the mention of her own brother's name, and stepped now into the vague moonlight coming in through the grimy grey window. Her face became illuminated slightly, like a mask beneath a silver veil, and Emily could only make out that she was agitated.

"What do you know of Kyle?"

"I know what he did to me."

"He hurt you?" Isabel could barely make the words audible.

Very slowly Emily made her way towards the

window, pulling her sleeves back to show Isabel the true extent of her scars. Just past her wrists, her skin almost seemed burned, purple-black at the edges as it crept into flesh that looked like melted wax. To Isabel's eyes, it almost looked as if Emily's skin had been unmade, turned inside out. Her cold exterior broke as her eyes took it all in, and she put a hand to her face, she had to, in horror of what her brother had done to her childhood friend.

"Kyle did this?" she whispered.

Emily nodded.

"He took hold of me and said that he loved me. His touch burned, I could feel his hands around my wrists as he held me to him, but I didn't realise - how could I? - just what he was doing to me."

"I'm so sorry..." Isabel began, as if this was all somehow her fault.

"I told him no, but his hands went down between my legs. The searing continued, his fingers literally burning holes through my dress. I told him to stop, to leave me alone, but his hands still rose. It wasn't until he realised what he had done that he stopped. He gazed down at me and at his open hands, and then he ran."

"Your legs are like that?"

Emily nodded again. She could feel tears coming.

"I could hardly stand, let alone walk home."

"Where was this?"

Emily's lips parted but nothing more would come.

"I'm sorry," was all Isabel could say.

"He isn't normal," Emily continued, wiping tears back with her fingers. "But you were gone before I could tell you. I needed to tell you. You were my only friend."

"And you were mine. I'm sorry I went, Emily, but

I had no choice. I thought it was only me that he'd threatened. I had no idea... I'm so very sorry."

Emily so desperately want to go to her and wrap her arms around her, and she hoped Isabel wanted the same. But when she took a step towards her, Isabel simply turned away and continued her vigil out of the window.

"You have to go," she murmured eventually. "In case you were seen."

But Emily could not let their exchange end so one-sidedly.

"I can only guess what he did to you," she said.

"You could never know or understand the truth of that," Isabel told her, her face still close to the glass.

"Tell me," Emily implored, moving closer to her.

Isabel heaved a huge laboured sigh, her breath fogging a circle in front of her face as she exhaled it slowly. Emily could see that her eyes were clenched shut as if watching her thoughts unravel inside her head.

"I am not normal either," she confessed finally. "He has managed to do things to me also, cursed me, manipulated me. I have wanted to kill myself so many times, but he has robbed me even of that."

"Kill yourself? What are you talking about?"

"It would be difficult to tell you," she told her, turning to look at her now. Her face was drained, pale in the cool light coming in through the window. "Words have little use. I would have to show you, but then you would wish for your own death, and that is not something I could help you with."

Emily stared at her for a long time. Just what was she talking about? Death, suicide, being cursed? This was not the woman she was hoping to find. She'd been searching for someone to hear and understand her problems, and here was her childhood friend, huddled alone in the darkness of a decayed old office building, wishing death upon her own head every single day. What could she say that would make any difference? Isabel was right it seemed. Words did have little use.

"Oh Emily," Isabel said after a while, turning back to look at her. Her face was full of yearning, and even in the half-light she could see how drained and ill she looked. "I've tried my hardest, God knows I've tried, but it's taken its toll. Tenfold. I reached what I thought was Hell so very long ago, and yet my life keeps on going. Nothing ends, and I fear that it never will."

"What can be so bad?" Emily wanted to know, going to her. She placed her hand over her friend's, and in the moment before Isabel snatched it back, she could feel how cold it was.

"You shouldn't touch me. I'm cursed, I know that. I don't what you to suffer in any way like I did."

"Why do you think you're cursed? Because you have to live like this?"

"I choose to live like this. It is the only way to hide from the eyes that search for me."

With this comment, Emily suddenly shivered as though one of the icy drafts that circled throughout the building had wrapped its clinging tendrils around her. This was something that she'd had a fear of for as long as she could remember. Yet again it was Kyle's name that crawled up from the filth stagnating deep in her belly. He'd had those eyes, or rather he'd used other creatures somehow to be his eyes. She'd felt them so many times, birds and cats, dogs and crows, their gaze not drifting or insignificant, but focussed and unblinking. She'd felt Kyle's cold gaze so many times in those eyes, but with no proof other than her unnerving fear, she could tell no one. No one, perhaps, except Isabel. And now it seemed even she was not safe from her own brother.

"It's Kyle isn't it?" Emily said to her. "It's his eyes you're afraid of."

Isabel stared at her with utter disbelief. And then she gave her a shallow nod.

"How did you know?"

"These scars... he professed his love to me on more than one occasion. I felt him watching me wherever I went. That's why I had to go away. But no matter where I went I felt him in the trees and in the hedgerows, always something small, always something insignificant. But I could feel him, feel his roving eyes studying everything I did."

"I'm sorry," Isabel murmured yet again.

"It's not your fault. You're only his sister."

"Only his sister? That's everything, Emily, don't you understand? All this is about family, our mother and father. He's always thought that he was driven out of our home, but it's not true, it's not."

"But Kyle didn't believe that. He told me years ago that he thought it was your mother's fault."

"And he still wants revenge. But there's nothing to get revenge for. Dad simply left us."

A silence descended around them for a while after that, neither one of them offering anything else. Indeed there was nothing new to offer, just the same spiralling descent into darkness with Kyle waiting at the bottom.

It was then that Isabel felt that she did have one thing, something new to offer that she had mentioned earlier.

"Do you want to see the reason why I live like this?" she said, stepping away from the window. "Do you want to see what Kyle has done to me?"

Emily stared at her in silence. She wasn't sure if she wanted to know any more of the Rider family secrets. But she had come this far, and perhaps if she came face to face with Isabel's worst fears, it might help her overcome her own. Very slowly she nodded, and said that she did want to see what had brought so much despair to her friend.

"Very well," Isabel said, "but it's darker upstairs, so keep one hand on my shoulder. I don't want you straying and stumbling unexpectedly on what I've done."

Emily gave her a troubled glance. She didn't like the sound of this at all.

"You will understand everything upstairs. But remember, I doubt if you can take your own life, and I won't be able to do it for you."

Emily shuddered even as she took hold of Isabel's cold clammy hand and allowed her to lead her out of the room towards the stairwell. Their footsteps echoed coldly off the tiled walls as they climbed, resounding up towards the roof and down into the very bowels of the empty chambers below. She felt her own grip tightening as they reached the fifth floor and stepped through a doorway and into a room set in total darkness. She could see nothing but the occasional chink of moonlight creeping in between boards that had been hastily secured across the windows, but she could see nothing of the route ahead. Her eyes refused to become accustomed, so total was the darkness, and as they made their slow progress through the utter blackness, the shapes and swirls that contorted before her vision only sought to confuse her more.

"Be careful," she heard Isabel suddenly whisper from just ahead of her.

"For what?"

But before she could answer, another voice came out of the darkness, a voice that she only distantly recalled, and her legs almost buckled beneath her as the sickening truth dawned on her.

She was glad that her eyes were useless here, but she prayed now for her ears to do the same so that she couldn't hear that voice, as her imagination conjured something surely far worse.

"I remember you, Emily," the decayed rasping voice hissed. "Do you remember me?"

Emily stammered. What was going on?

"Go on, try," the voice sounded parched, its tone sarcastic. "Give up? Why, it's Irene Rider, Isabel's own dearest mother."

# TEN

## CONFESSION

Emily stared out through the window at the dark rooftops of the town, dumbfounded by what she had just seen. It was unimaginable for it to be true, and yet she had seen her with her own eyes, or rather had heard her with her own ears. It could have been someone else, she tried to reason, some impostor, but that would be insane. And that's what made the horrific reality seem so plausible.

"I thought your mother... died," she finally murmured without turning round.

She and Isabel were alone and sitting together on the third floor once again.

"She did," Isabel said from the gloom behind her. "Or rather she should have done. You know about the illness she had, how it was terminal. At the time I didn't know what I was doing, and in a lot of ways I still don't, but all I know is that I didn't want her to die..."

"And so she didn't?"

Emily was incredulous, and had turned from the window to stare into the darkness of the room. It wasn't easy to find Isabel, but she located her eventually, sitting near the back of the room with her head in her hands.

"Isabel, it doesn't work like that. Just because you wanted her to stay alive doesn't mean that she just did."

"If you have a better explanation, I'd be glad to hear it."

Emily stared at her. Of course she didn't have a better explanation, what sane explanation could there be? She wanted to say, *Are you sure it's her?* but this whole situation was too crazy for it to be otherwise; Isabel living like a pariah, hiding from society in a dank disused office building. But there was another question that begged to be asked, something else that made no sense, and Emily could no longer hold it back.

"Why does she hide upstairs in the dark like a criminal if she's been given more time on this earth?"

"Because that's all she's been given," Isabel said. "More time."

"I don't understand."

Isabel got to her feet now and wandered towards the window to join Emily, perhaps for the sake of sharing her emotions, or perhaps only to whisper and be out of earshot of her mother upstairs.

"Thank the Lord, Emily, that you came at night when there was no light for you to see by. I only have that grace a few hours each night. The rest of the time when I go to see her I'm reminded how haunted I am by her."

Emily went to put a hand on Isabel's arm but she moved out of the way before her touch could come near.

"I don't deserve your compassion," she said. "Not after what I've done."

"Tell me," Emily urged her.

"She's dead," Isabel finally confessed bluntly, her

eyes glazing as they went to the window. "That's the truth of it. Mum died in her bed twenty years ago and I was the only one there to witness it. Kyle was out, I hadn't seen him for hours, and Aunt Cassie had gone to pick up a prescription. I wept as I held her motionless body, and all I could remember thinking was, *don't go, don't leave me alone*. I probably even began crying that out loud, I can't remember, but all I do remember is the exhilaration when her hand lifted and fell upon my head."

"So she didn't die?"

"Yes, Emily, she did. She'd been dead ten, maybe fifteen, minutes, before her eyes opened again to see me. I'd prayed aloud pretty much constantly in that time for her to come back, and somehow that prayer was answered."

"God came to you?"

"No," she said solemnly, staring hard at her now. "Not God. Something else. Something cursed. My mother came back, but not to the world of the natural, not to the world of the living."

Emily could not understand just what Isabel was trying to tell her. She hadn't answered her question at all. If her mother was alive, had beaten the illness that was to have claimed her, then why weren't they both celebrating, rejoicing in the extra years she had been blessed with?

"Her heart never beat again, Emily, do you understand? Her eyes saw and her lips spoke, but her heart was dead and her blood was cold. It was shortly after she came back that a crow landed at her bedroom sill; it seemed to be watching us, spying on us, and it was then that I realised that we could no longer stay in the house. For some reason I knew then that Kyle had learned of what I had done. He'd wanted mum gone more than anything and I'd stolen his wish."

"So you were afraid?"

"More than anything."

"And it was then that you took her out of the house?"

"When Aunt Cassie returned, I told her all that had happened. It was a very peculiar evening, and there's still plenty that I can't make sense of myself. In hindsight, I can't even understand why Cass would have believed me, but believe me she did, and we moved on to her house a few miles away for the night."

"What about Kyle? He stayed in the house on his own?"

"I have no idea. I've never seen or spoken to him since. There was just something about that crow landing on mum's window sill. My whole body ran cold, and I knew, I just knew, that something bad was going to happen."

"But that doesn't explain why you're both still hiding?"

"Perhaps I'm not telling you everything properly," Isabel said, pushing her hand through hair that looked like it hadn't been cut properly in years. "My mother is dead, she's been dead for twenty years, but she's upstairs now, seeing and talking and eating. Death is claiming her body as we speak, just as it has been for twenty years. I have to see her every day, a bit more skin decayed or fallen away, a bit more yellowed bone showing through the gap that appeared the day before. So much of her face has already gone, and I can see her brown grin even though she never smiles. I wonder each day how I manage to keep going, and sometimes I just can't. I've left her a few times, slipped away in the silence of the night, but I've never gotten far before the guilt slows my escape. I've done this to her, I've made her a slave, a zombie. I can't leave her to carry on alone while I try and start anew. And what of the people who would eventually find her? No, it would be too much for everyone."

"So you bear this burden on your own?"

"Who else would do it?"

"What about your aunt?"

"She died a long time ago. There's just me. And believe me, I've thought all the options through. The best I came up with was to end it all myself."

"Suicide?"

"But I can't even do that," she said in despair. "If I was to throw myself off this building, do you know what would happen?"

Emily shook her head.

"I'd break a lot of bones, but then they'd heal. I've cut my wrists, pretty deep too, take a look," she offered them out for Emily to see, and they did indeed both have wide tracks of scar tissue across them. "They bled copiously for over an hour, I passed out too, but eventually I awoke with the gashes already on the mend."

"But how?"

"It's got something to do with healing my mother, that's all I know. The trouble is I can't do anything else now. I can't put her out of her misery any more than she can. I can't finish myself either. What will happen over time I can't bear to think. All I can hope for is that some day soon neither of us will wake up ever again. But I've been praying for that for twenty years too."

Emily stared at her as her eyes once again flickered towards the window. The entire town outside was asleep and peaceful. She didn't look at her watch, but it must have been after three in the morning by now. Only the streetlamps offered some partial illumination, but the rest of the buildings in the block screened most of their light, and only faint haloes of yellow glimmered skywards above the roof of the cinema building on the other side of the service yard.

"I'm sorry," Emily whispered, putting her hand on Isabel's arm, her touch connecting this time.

"That doesn't help," she replied bluntly, looking at her.

Some new revelation seemed to dawn in her eyes suddenly, and her head cocked to one side.

"Just how did you find me?"

The question had such a different tone and context to what they had just been talking about that it threw her off balance. Her thoughts struggled to comprehend the accusation in her question, and it wasn't until she stepped back away from Isabel and took in the old office building around them that she was able to tell her.

"You left a copy of the local paper behind in your flat."

Isabel stared at her. That wasn't the reply she was waiting for.

"You couldn't have tracked me here from that."

"No, someone told me that you'd been seen around here?"

"Seen? By who? I haven't gone out in daylight since I found this place."

Emily shrugged.

"Your picture was in the article. It said you were the new Messiah."

"That fucking paper."

"You do seem to be doing something God-like, Isabel."

166

"There's nothing holy about what I can do."

"But you saved that boy's life, didn't you?"

"And that's good, is it? How do you think he or his mother are going to feel when things start to drop off him, his skin, his shrivelled fingers? Do you think they're going to feel blessed if he gets ripped in half but carries on talking? He's dead, Emily, and I saved him from that. I saved him right into his own private hell."

She hung her head now and turned away. Emily wasn't sure if tears were coming and she didn't want to press her any more either. It was clear that what she was saying, although unfathomable, was true. Emily hadn't seen either the boy or his mother for herself, but somehow she knew that Isabel was telling her the truth. What other reason could there be for her hiding from society like she'd been doing for so long?

"You still haven't answered me," Isabel suddenly said, looking back at her. "Who told you I'd been seen here."

The face of the reporter flickered somewhere in the back of Emily's head, and despite how much she had wanted him out of her life, she suddenly couldn't voice his name. Her lips must have parted with indecision, because Isabel took hold of her. She was angry now, furious that someone, even her, had managed to track her down after all the care she had obviously taken in trying to stay hidden. And it seemed just as obvious that she would stop at nothing to have that information.

"Just tell me who's been tracking me down?" she said. "Just give me the name."

## ELEVEN

### THE FACE BEHIND THE SMILE

Kelly's face physically paled when he opened the door to Isabel Rider standing on his doorstep. It was long after dark, and to see the new messiah of his article standing before him with her hands on her hips, seemed to knock him sideways. The shock lasted only a moment, however, and then a slick smile washed over his face. He almost seemed to know why she had come to visit.

"You wrote that article, didn't you?"

"It's had a mixed response. Some people have wanted to know which church you're affiliated with."

"I didn't come here for your shit. I just want to know why you wrote it."

"It was news, that's what I do."

"News? It was shit, all of it, and you know it."

"Mrs Fry came to me and told me all about what you'd done for her boy -"

"I don't want to hear about that. He died, I saved him, it happens all the time."

Kelly raised an eyebrow, his expression turning something close to mischief, and there was something in that expression that made Isabel's stomach turn over.

"It doesn't happen that often on my paper, I can assure you. If you want, I could print a retraction, somewhere near the back."

"You're fucking with me and I don't want it."

"Then what do you want?"

Isabel hesitated for a moment. She'd planned this conversation in her head on her way over, but that look of his had all but destroyed it.

"Where did you get your information from? Not what you got from that Fry woman, the other stuff. The private stuff."

"What do you mean?"

"You know damn well what I mean. The speculation about my childhood, where I came from."

"That was just artistic license. I had to pad the article with something."

That mischievous glint still sparkled in his eyes, patronising her, playing with her as a cat would play with a half-dead mouse, pawing it for further response. Isabel was loathe to continue. All that her gut was telling her was slowly making her nauseous.

"Those things that only a couple of people might know. One is my aunt, and she's dead."

"And the other?"

The question was posed lightly, and yet the answer that it begged she felt sure would drag her right into this sick little game of his. She suddenly didn't want to be there, suddenly didn't want to be standing on this man's doorstep.

This wasn't real, that's all she could keep thinking; a dream, a twisted dream that someone else was having, and she didn't know the rules well enough to escape.

Her lips were tight, her answer pressing hard behind them, squeezing to get out. But she would not say his name, she wouldn't.

"Secrets pop up from all sorts of hidden places," Kelly continued. "Some from relatives we hardly knew were there."

She stared hard at him now, at those eyes of his that glittered like all of Hell's fires combined. She wanted to punch him to the ground, she wanted to run and do what she did best - hide - but her feet remained motionless, and all she could do was stand on the doorstep and stare at him.

This was crazy. She wanted to shout her brother's name to his face, but all she could see was someone else's face. And yet all that he had said, all that he had written in the article, it could only have been known by her immediate family. One had run away, one was dead, one was holed up in an unlit disused office building, rotting away like ancient fruit, and the other -

"Has been looking for you a long time."

Her thoughts jerked.

"What?"

"Has she been looking for you a long time?"

The question was posed lightly the second time and her head struggled to make sense of it.

"Who?" she managed to say.

"Emily Oates. It was she who came to see me asking about your whereabouts. I was simply asking if she's been looking for you a long time. She said you were close once."

"Yes," Isabel stammered, staring at the slick smile that had once again returned. Had she imagined all that she'd seen? She wasn't sure now. Wasn't sure of anything. "We were good friends when we were kids. Only friends we had, really."

"So at least my article has done something good. Brought you two together."

170

Isabel stared at him. Her tongue would not move, or make any attempt to form words. What could she even hope to say to any of this. She'd come here so sure, so fired up about what this little shit had written. And yet -

"Reunions are so very overdue, don't you think?"

Her mouth was open, gaping.

"But I guess that's their nature."

His smile had become a mask now, impenetrable, unmoving. It seemed as though there was going to be no more revelation tonight, no more secrets or veils of mischief. He had become the reporter once again, the reporter that Emily had told her all about. She'd said what a nice guy he had seemed, and that's what she was looking at now. But it was that other stuff, the stuff that guttered behind this mask like an evil fire flickering behind an age-old grate. That had disturbed her, turned her stomach like she had not felt in a very long time. She'd hidden herself well over the years, but now it felt like it had all been for nothing. There'd been things printed about her, and it had led to her being found. Yes, it had been by Emily, a friend, but she'd still been tracked down because of it.

Very slowly she stepped back off the doorstep from where she had not moved or even been invited from. It was only a single step into the darkness of the night, but she already felt more secure to have that wrapped around her than the halo of light escaping this cruel man's house.

Her eyes had not once wandered past him to the hallway behind him, but they did now, and a feeling of cold descended around her as she saw the shape of a dark grey cat lurking in the crack of a door. It was looking at her, and she was surely imagining it, but it seemed to be *studying* her, this woman at the door, with eyes that burned just as brightly as its owner's.

The cold descended once again, a shiver that passed across her body, and somewhere inside her head she made the excuse that it was because of the time of night. She took another retreating step, back into the night and away from the halo.

She said nothing more before she turned and left completely. Half expecting the reporter to call something after her, she kept her focus fixed on the street ahead so that the urge would not rise to look back.

But the man said nothing, not even a goodnight, and that silence chilled her even more, as the suspicion strengthened inside her that she did indeed know him, and had known him for as long as she could remember. In those eyes she could tell that somehow he was family.

# TWELVE

## TO RUN AND RUN

Isabel had never passed a test or even taken a single driving lesson, so Emily had driven her to Kelly Stafford's home, with Isabel insisting on her leaving as soon as they got there so that she could make her own way back. It had been a longer walk back to the office buildings than she had thought but it at least allowed her time to think things through.

The night was dark with the moon hidden somewhere inside a thick overcast sky. The streetlamps of the estate stopped abruptly as the fields of rural Hunton swallowed the road and reduced them to narrow country lanes. But she travelled swiftly as her memory recalled details of her conversation with the reporter.

He'd spoken of reunions and how they were overdue. It hadn't seemed like a threat of intent before, but now that his words echoed around inside her head, they began to disturb her.

She glanced over her shoulder as an icy pang of fear grasped her, her eyes searching the darkness between the hedgerows and the overhanging trees, their hand-like limbs dropping low as if to try and snatch her up, any hidden eyes that might be upon her. But her sight was not acute enough to find creatures used to the night, and all she could do was pick up her pace, hoping that they would not follow her.

But the feeling of being watched crawled beneath her skin as she hurried through the night back towards town. She cursed herself for being distrusting enough of Emily not to have her drive her back to the office building, and only now realised how unprotected she was out amongst the fields away from anyone. But she'd been living on the run for two decades without help, other than the twisted magic that flowed through her veins, and all she could do was hope that it would be enough against whatever unnatural threat her brother might be planning against her.

Her recollection of their conversation began to stir in her mind once again as she reached a main road, a single streetlamp burning at the junction. The sickly yellow glow illuminated the road in four directions, but it was eerie and only served to heighten her fears, thinking that if there was something watching her in the murky darkness, it would only be able to see her more clearly now.

Isabel continued on her way, turning right towards town which was less than a mile away, but on foot and through the unlit countryside she guessed would seem to take a lifetime.

The reporter had padded the article with insights into her childhood that were too accurate for mere speculation. There'd been things, personal unnatural things, that the article had hinted at that no one outside of the family would have known or could even have dreamt up. The nagging crawl in the pit of her stomach lurched once again, telling her that the reporter must have at the very least spoken with her brother. Either that or her aunt, but she was long dead and deep in the ground. No, Kyle was at work here, on her trail and tracking her, undoing all that she'd tried to do since she'd run away twenty years ago. Her anonymity and camouflage had gone in a single night. All she could hope for now was to disappear again, this very night, and smuggle her mother out along with her.

2

When the first of the town's streetlights broke the gloom between the canopy of trees hanging across the road, Isabel breathed a partial sigh of relief that she would soon be out of the smothering night and back into the relative safety of the office building in which her mother was slowly decomposing. She would not be pleased about another move so soon after leaving the flat, but it couldn't be helped. Danger was coming, she was sure of it, and that meant they had to be gone.

But as the sight of the illuminated frontage of the cinema came into view, her heart lightened, glad that she had managed to make it back without incident. She turned the corner to where the boarded-over gates stood, but as she took hold of the railing at the top of the gate and was about to haul herself over, something took hold of her waist with a shocking and sudden force and tugged her back.

Her heart shuddered in her chest as she fell, the ground punching the breath from her lungs as she landed hard on the concrete footpath. White shapes pulsed in the uncertain limbo behind her eyes, but with her breath gone she couldn't even cry out at whatever had taken hold of her.

A dark figure loomed over her, that's all she could be sure of, but her sight was still struggling and her breath was still trapped somewhere beyond her throat, and all she could do was flail vaguely with her arms.

She was aware of a considerable weight holding her down on the ground, and for a few seconds her head could not work out why. But then a punch landed hard and stinging across her face, and then kneading fingers of a hand pressed painfully against her breast and another between her legs.

Her sight cleared through the groggy haze of pain, and made out the clean shaven face of a youth growling just inches from her face. The hand between her legs was already struggling to undo her jeans, but her head had reordered itself now, and the breath had come back into her lungs in a rush. She had no need to cry for help now, but used the strength that had returned to send a punch of her own deep into the belly of this street-roaming rapist.

He spat a stream of obscenities into her face, *fucking bitch, slut,* as his other hand relinquished its hold on her breast and rose to take hold of her throat. With all his weight on her windpipe her consciousness threatened to leave her again, but she raised her hands towards his head and dug her fingernails hard into the flesh beneath his eyes until she could feel it begin to come away.

He howled as he tried to arch away from her hold on him, but she dug her nails in harder, clawing them enough to rip his bloody skin clean from his skull. He landed a blow to her body in weakened desperation, but her attack was effective enough to force him off her so that she could at least get partially to her feet.

The youth had managed to take hold of one of her

hands now and was crushing it in his own. She heard one of her fingers snap even before she felt the pain, and her assault was over before she realised. His expression went suddenly from agony to rage, and she saw his fist appear beside his head, clenched and ready to descend. She saw a scarlet deluge of blood running down the length of his face before his fist blackened her consciousness for a few seconds, and when she came to, he was nowhere to be seen. She could only hear his footfalls as he fled injured somewhere back into the night.

Isabel sat shuddering on the pavement, her eyes trained on the street, hoping that he would not return to finish what he'd started. Now the pain came to her hand, dull and throbbing, and she clamped her other hand to it as nausea began to crawl around her belly. Her own touch was already beginning to warm the broken finger, and she knew that soon the bone would become whole once again. She had the power to heal, oh God how she knew that, and knew too what a curse that was. But it didn't heal the pain or the fear, or give her strength to fend off anything that might bring that pain or fear. She so desperately wanted to die, to crawl away from life and forget it all. But it couldn't be done. It wouldn't let her go. And she had to live with it, with every day that dawned, no prayer of death ever answered.

She hauled herself unsteadily to her feet with the sickness of inevitability still gnawing at her innards, knowing that she had to be off the streets and soon in case other dangers descended upon her. She had to wait until her finger could move more easily, however, before she could attempt to clamber up and over the boarded gate and back into the service yard behind the disused office buildings.

The shadows were deep here where so little light could permeate, and she welcomed them like a shrouding blanket as she hurried towards the door at the far end. Reaching her slim hand between the narrow opening, she worked the rope until it was loose enough to slip over the handle before slipping inside and replacing the knot. The ache in her finger had already subsided considerably, and as she dashed up the stairwell to her mother's floor, she found her head much clearer too and willing to find words that might encourage her mother to move on yet again.

It was totally black on the fifth floor except for the few chinks of lamplight that crept in behind windows that she'd not completely been able to cover with blankets and tape. Her mother hated the light, hated anything that might cast a shadow or worst of all a reflection. Isabel knew that deep down her mother resented her, hated her even, for bringing her back from the dead. There was still a surface love, every mother and daughter had that, but deep down, there was a hatred that came from a longing for the grave. That's where she belonged, they both knew that, but twenty years ago Isabel had somehow brought her back, willed her away from God in order that she stay with her forever. And that's what had happened. She'd come back, but her body had continued to decay.

There was a horror in that that outstripped anything else she'd ever encountered, and she'd encountered plenty over the years. To see her own mother rot a little more day after day, that was too much to bear at times. But what could she do? She could run away, but that would be worse. To abandon her and let her be discovered by people who could never understand her condition. To kill her? That was impossible. She had unnatural life, and how could she bring herself to draw a knife across her throat while she slept anyway? Nothing could take that, not even her. She couldn't even take the cowards way out and take her own life, extinguishing all feelings and terrors. Wherever she stuck a knife, from whatever height she threw herself, the wound would always heal, and her bones would always mend. The pain was very real, oh yes, and she had to live through those agonies too, until her body was whole once again, and then she'd have to deal with everything all over again.

"You've got bad news."

It was her mother's voice, guttering up from the back of the room. It was not a question either, but a statement.

"Your feet were quick on the stairs. I heard you. Something's wrong again, isn't it?"

Isabel stepped carefully across the floor in the direction of the voice. There wasn't a great deal of furniture in the open plan room, but still enough to send her sprawling to the ground.

"Mum, I don't know how to tell you this -"

"But we're moving again."

"Yes," she said hesitantly, "we're moving again."

Isabel waited for her mother to add something else but there was only an uneasy silence. She could only have been ten yards away, but without her voice to follow it was simply impossible to place her in the motionless void. So Isabel simply stood and stared forward into the darkness, deciding how best to explain the proximity of Kyle, or at least the proximity she suspected.

"You really expect us never to be found?" Irene Rider said at last.

"I don't know, mum."

"You don't seem to know very much lately."

"That's not fair. I've been doing what I think is best. That's all I've ever tried to do. I don't know what I'm doing, that's the truth of it. Run blind is all I can do."

Her mother fell silent again. She knew the truth of it too.

"I'm sorry for all of this," Isabel started, taking a tentative step further into the gloom, hoping she might yet find her mother in the darkness somewhere. "You know that I'd have it any other way if I could."

"But you can't."

She was off to her right.

"No, I can't," she said, following the voice. "If I *could* end it all, I would."

"I know that you've tried to do what's best, Isabel, I know that in my heart. But it's not your will that can save either of us. The magic that keeps me living is the same magic that keeps you from dying. It's just a malevolent force, a supernatural abomination, and it will keep going until it makes its own decision to stop. That's if it ever will. And that's all there is."

"But I can't accept that. How can we keep going like this? Running and hiding, day after day. Are you saying that's all there is until one morning when we might wake up lucky?"

"Honey, if I get lucky, I won't wake up at all."

There was horror in those words, more than Isabel suspected she meant. But in the morbid silence that followed, Isabel knew that she was right. Neither of them understood just what the hell had happened twenty years ago, and in those twenty years that had followed, they'd come no closer to finding out. How could they? None of it made any sense.

"Have you stopped to ask yourself what you're running from this time?"

Isabel parted her lips to speak, but held her words

for a moment. She wanted to say aloud Kyle's name, but how much of what had happened could actually be attributed to her brother? How would her mother respond to slander of her son's name? It was true that she knew he was no saint, and that she'd not set her clouded eyes upon him in the last two decades, but she must know how hateful he was of her, how keen he was to have her dead and buried. That vengeful rage was still burning inside him, Isabel knew that more than anything, and despite how much her mother wanted to die, she wasn't about to let Kyle hurry her into her grave. And he'd want her to go into it painfully too, she was certain of that as well.

"I don't want to lose you," Isabel said finally, wanting more than ever to find her mother's hand and take hold of it firmly.

"I don't want that either. But I'm dead. My heart hasn't beaten inside me since we left our home behind. My blood is as cold as this damn floor. My bones ache as though all my joints have rotted away, and with what little feeling I have left in my fingers I can tell how much skin falls away from them each day. I need to die, Isabel. I need to go where I belong. I love you more than anything, but I so desperately want it all to be over. Please, help me to die."

Isabel gazed down into the solid void of black but she could make out nothing of her mother's face. Stifled sobs now guttered somewhere behind a decomposed hand, and she could only imagine the dark sunken eyes too dry to spring tears. The imagined scene in the darkness only brought tears of her own, and she stumbled back away from her with mumbled excuses on her lips.

This was no way to live, no way for her to look after her mother. Look after? The words rattled round inside her head like barbed tennis balls in a steel box. This wasn't how people looked after their relatives. Sure, this was no normal state of affairs. She could hardly trek her down to the nearest old folk's home and bundle her upon the social workers. And what if she did? What would those social workers make of an old woman two decades past her own death? There'd be need for more than weak tea and incontinence pants then.

Isabel's misery had turned into a creeping sickness that threatened to have her heaving over the edge of the banister as she reached the stairwell. She could feel her hands shaking, trembling with helplessness, and with hopelessness. She'd felt this way so many times before. There was no one to help, no one to turn to, no one to watch over her even for one night while she had a restful sleep.

A car horn blared somewhere out in the street, long and agitated, followed by men shouting and then a screeching of car tyres. This was real, so very real. She wanted to scream, to cry enough's enough at the top of her voice. But who would listen anyway? Who would come to her and offer any kind of help?

She was alone, alone with a dead mother and a curse on her head that brought the dead back to life as little more than zombies just waiting to rot. She was diseased, a rancid bringer of living death. Maybe letting Kyle slit their throats would be the best way out, at least that way...

What was that?

There, behind the metal grill over the window.

Eyes, garish and white, staring at her, watching. But that was crazy, she was on the fifth floor.

They were gone, fleeing insanely now that they'd been seen.

Isabel was off and running hard, down the rest of the stairwell two at a time, stumbling down the hall towards the back door. The rope held too well, and she had to struggle with her own knot before she could get out of the building and into the service yard at the back. A lunatic fear crept over her as she dashed across the tarmac - *what if this was the youth that tried to rape you earlier, what if he's come back to finish the job?* Her jaw still ached from the blows he'd given her as if to warn her, but she was running too hard to stop.

Her momentum carried her to the boarded-over gate and she'd not set eyes on anyone. She wondered if perhaps she'd not seen those eyes at all, and even as she scaled the gate and dropped down to the pavement on the other side, wondered just what she would actually do if she did come face to face with her brother. But the pavement was deserted in both directions, the road devoid of all traffic. The town was silent now, eerily silent after the screams and screeches of the drug dealers and vandals that usually pierced the night air.

Then she saw him, standing at the far corner of the next block, half obscured by the old disused building itself. But it wasn't Kyle she was looking at, but the reporter Kelly Stafford.

He was too far away for her to catch up with him, even if she did decide to continue her pursuit, which she didn't now that she had seen him, and so all she could do was stand by the boarded-over gate and exchange this uneasy stare.

And then something happened, something unnatural that flickered across his face like a veil lifting in a breeze. It was hideous, and from such a distance she could not even be sure of what she'd seen. But it *had* been Kelly Stafford standing at the corner, that much she was certain of, and not only had he followed her home, but he was now looking at her in a way that was chilling her bones.

His eyes had *altered*, that's the only word she could think of to describe it. No longer was she exchanging a glance across the street with human eyes, but with two orbs that guttered red one moment like the embers of a fire, and then savage black like a portal into a realm of pure evil. Her body shuddered and a cold swept over her skin like ice water. There was horrific intent in that stare, that's all she knew, and only when his silhouetted body turned the corner completely and went out of sight, could she dare to move again.

Her heart was hammering with fear, and she fell back hard against the boarded-over gate with one hand clutched to her chest. All she could think was that this was the end. Kelly had found the place where she and her mother were hiding. They had been found.

But was it Kelly? That was the elusive question that kept circling around her fears. Or was it Kyle? Was he hiding just as she was, she in an old office building, he behind a mask?

Only one thing was certain now: he knew where she was.

But then one more question came to join the others already tumbling around inside her head, fighting for her attention like savage dogs after scraps of fresh bloody meat. If he knew where she was, then why had he left? What was he going back to get?

Her fears began to shake her even harder as she clambered back over the gate, and scrambling quickly back across the service yard she wanted to know just what he might be coming back with, and just what he might be capable of after so many years of planning.

# THIRTEEN

## BEHIND THE EYES OF THE WORLD

It was difficult to tell whether the room itself was moving with insects like one of his hallucinations or whether the body parts that littered it were writhing with the echoes of preternaturally ended life. So many creatures had been taken apart in this room, some with knifes, others with bare hands, others still with the supernatural magic that came from his head more focussed and intense with each act of exploration.

Leftover furless limbs had been left to rot alongside eyeless skulls; broken feathered wings had been discarded beside blood-caked skeletons, both whole and dismembered; in the air hung a dull abhorrent stench, of blood and of premature death; but to the room's sole human occupant, it mattered little because for the most part it was a part of his existence that largely went unnoticed.

There was only one item of furniture in the room, a single armchair on the bare grimy floor boards, set in its centre facing the single curtainless window. Seated in this chair and gazing out through the filth-blackened glass was Kyle Rider.

His eyes were heavy lidded, the pupils behind

them rolled upward so that a mostly white gaze looked blankly out. What few clothes he wore were soiled, dark patches of sweat beneath his armpits, encrusted patches of shit and urine at his groin. A slick of saliva hung from his chin, glistening at the front of his shirt where it had collected and pooled, and the smell that lifted from his body was matched only by the decay that rose all around him. Insects crawled across his body, beneath his clothes, feasting on his fluids, but he noticed none of them.

To say that he was gazing out through the single window could only be said as a passing comment by an observer glancing back in. Had that observer slowed his pace for a moment and taken a closer look, he would have seen that this man's eyes were half-lidded and semi-vacant, as though he was using them to look in the opposite direction, back into his skull. Something else that would have become quickly apparent was that he did not move either. His hands remained on the arms of his chair, his legs set evenly before him, like the vast stone statues carved into the living rock of Ancient Egypt.

His heart beat an unnaturally slow rhythm, like an animal in hibernation, or a trauma patient in deep coma, but other than that, there was very little to distinguish him from an abandoned corpse, left to sit upright until the authorities stumbled upon him and took him away.

Occasionally his lips would part and a thin tongue would wet them as if in a dream, or his fingers would tense or contract as though his brain was causing slight impulses from the depths of disturbing thoughts locked hidden away deep inside his head.

To the casual observer he was a basket case, out there, gone. And in some respects, that was exactly what he was. He *was* out there. He *was* gone.

For twenty years he'd had his obsessions, and despite the magics that crawled beneath his skin like the termites beneath the floor, he'd not been able to do much about any of them. People knew how to hide, that was the problem that had always faced him. The world was big and it was tricky, and it offered a hell of a lot of places for people to disappear into. Oh, he'd come close a number of times, right up to a doorstep or an abandoned car. But when it came down to it, when it needed him to act, he'd always come up short.

Frustrating, that's what it was. To be close and to have power, and still come up short: that had been almost too much to bear at times. And with that frustration had come rage, and how many times had death been metered out on those that had not deserved it.

But it was not his fault. None of it. People tested him, they played him like a fool, and he didn't like that. He had power, for Christ's sake. Why couldn't people see that?

No, it had all started a long time ago when his mother had forced his father out of their home. It was his mother's fault. Hers and his conniving sister's. She'd been in on it as well, he'd had no doubt about that for a long time too.

But there had been other obsessions along the way too, obsessions that should have taken a lot of that pain away. But even they had turned sour. People were tricky, damned tricky, and sometimes he just wanted to skin them alive and burn them all to Hell.

Too far. The rage wanted him to go to the edge and gaze down into the chasm, down into the very depths of its black heart. It needed holding onto sometimes, that rage, holding onto and clawing back.

They didn't work out how they should, obsessions, that was all. But he could fix them. He'd learned the skills, he'd heard the lessons. It was easy sometimes too, with birds and cats, and other dumb creatures. People were a little harder though. Their brains skipped around sometimes, slippery and rolling around like skinned watermelons on a cold floor. But he'd gotten the hang of it a couple of times. And those that he hadn't? Why, he'd just pushed them out the door and let them go on their way. Something would undo what he'd done; a mental hospital, a heavy truck. Something always put an end to the crazy.

There were other things to Kyle Rider's appearance that would have gone unnoticed under casual scrutiny too. The length of time he spent in his chair for one. The states of waking and sleeping merged to the point where day and night seldom had boundaries. Occasionally he would shit himself while he sat in his chair, his bowels and bladder voiding themselves if he'd been seated without movement for more than a day. The small kitchen through the adjoining door rarely held food, and he'd visited it only fleetingly since he'd first occupied the house three and a half years ago.

During infrequent occasions when he wanted to eat, he'd content himself to simply reach down to the nearest dead animal on the wooden floor. The slick of maggots or the hum of black flies made no difference to him; it was only a way of renewing energies. The majority of the times that he strayed from the house to go outside to the overgrown garden at the back, was to bring whatever creatures he could find there back with him. Mostly they were garden birds - sparrows or magpies - but occasionally he would happen upon a fox in the early hours of the morning, or a cat straying across the boundaries from one garden to the next.

But with all the mutilations and corpses surrounding him, his chair sitting inside this glut of death like some demented satanic altar, the magic crawling around his system sometimes played sick games with him. So many creatures had he examined and explored in this room, remnants of their bodies littering his chair and coating his flesh, that sometimes they became motivated and attempted to fuse themselves to him. His hands were mostly filthy, stained scarlet with the blood that caked his skin. Hacked and furless limbs adhered themselves to his arms and lower legs, some glued with the gum of their blood, others seeming to have literally grafted themselves onto his skin as if they might continue to live. Half-battered skulls protruded from his skin like tribal totems, some with dead eyes or eyeless sockets, while others with living stares watched over their master's world of morbidity.

Insects too lived amongst them, laying eggs and planning colonies, thriving on sweat and dirt, hatching in the heady climate beneath week-old clothes. But they were not disease carriers or unwanted pestilence, they were his sentries and his pets, eyes that could see inside every crevice, every room. Nothing could remain unseen, no event could take place without his knowledge.

These mutations and perversions had taken time to grow, years to evolve, to transform him into a semi-conscious monster that watched the inside of his head more than what was in front of it. Whether it was the magic itself or just his proximity to the death and decay at his feet, Kyle Rider had no idea. But so seldom did he consciously think about himself, about the way that he lived his life, that it was of little relevance. His obsessions were just that. He needed to find what was left of his family, and he needed to find his one true love. Then everything would be as it should and he'd be able to leave all this behind him.

No, Kyle Rider had other things to occupy his time, his obsessions, his plans. He had places he needed to see, places he needed to keep watch over, and all these things he did from this one chair in the middle of this room. Kyle Rider was literally out there. He was literally gone. But he had his eyes on everyone, on everything, and all he was waiting for was that one sight that would bring all those obsessions to fruition. And he'd seen so much of it already.

His tasks were already set in motion, his games already playing out. From somewhere deep inside his head, like one cinema screen in a dizzying maze of other cinema screens, he followed the sight of one of his creations now. One of his more successful efforts, a human being that responded to his will quite readily, had worked out better than he'd ever planned or expected. It had started out as a mere fantasy of setting a trap. He'd seen his dearest sister on one of his other screens, seen by a sparrow high upon a telephone wire, hiding out in a tiny flat. His mother was dead, so too was Cassandra, which left only Isabel, and she was guilty because she'd helped conspire against his father. He wanted to find her, to take her in his arms, and then draw a knife across her throat. It wasn't an involved plan, but it had a certain poetry to it that he liked. The rhythm of the blade. The cadence of the flesh opening. Poetry, beautiful poetry.

But there'd been something else, something he hadn't expected to come out of the darkness with the newspaper article. Emily Oates.

190

Like a shining angel she had appeared, her face adorning yet another cinema screen, the magpie that had seen her perched high in a tree overlooking much of the town. Kyle had watched her until she had disappeared inside her house, and even then he had made the magpie sit outside the house for two days without respite, waiting for her to reappear. But the screen in his head had gone blank in less than that time, the bird tumbling out of the tree dead with hunger and thirst. By the time he had commanded another of his eyes to the street she was gone. He'd caught up with her later, of course, but her appearance had thrown what games he'd had planned into chaos.

But what did any of that matter now? Kelly Stafford would be here soon, ready to take him to Isabel's latest retreat. He'd waited a long time for this moment, a long time to lay his own eyes on his darling sister once more, and he knew that he would have to be swift if he was to get there before little Izzie stole herself away from him again. No, he would be there soon, and then he would end her poor irrelevant life for good.

Out in the hallway, his sentries saw the figure approach before he even heard the front door click open. His eyes rolled back in their sockets, focussed and huge, and swung round towards the door of the room. It opened as his eyes readjusted to the murk of the dismal house, as the shape of Kelly Stafford crossed the threshold, his jacket alive with crawling insects. But neither of them spoke a word; dialogue had become redundant.

It was as though he'd already been to Isabel's hideout; what else was there to be told, he knew it all. Now he just wanted to see her with his own eyes, hear her pleas with his own ears, and feel the heat of her blood flowing freely across his skin.

Kyle had only ever seen Kelly once face to face, and he looked now like a trespasser who had entered his home unannounced. He'd used this reporter several times over the last few weeks, trying to generate leads in the fruitless town of Hunton, setting traps that he'd hoped Isabel would bite upon. The business with the Fry woman and her kid had been a Godsend, and had brought her right out of the woodwork, using the woman's own detective work to track her down. The article had not been his intention at first, but with the Fry woman becoming hysterical over what Isabel had done to her boy, it had paid off.

He'd not been able to view this human puppet that much with his own eyes. He'd looked out through this man's eyes at other people, he'd felt what he'd felt through his touch, but most of what he'd witnessed about his puppet had been the reaction that he'd got from other people.

Women's expressions shifted when he spoke, smiles creeping into the sides of their mouths, blouses becoming loosened, hems lifting. They found him handsome, alluring, and that had helped in setting a lot of his games and traps. But it had been a downfall too. The article had brought this final lead about Isabel, a lead that was almost certainly going to bring him to her, but the other lead, the distraction of Emily, had brought a great discomfort with it as well.

Although he'd seen her a number of times, this girl he had cherished since they were both children, through the eyes of sparrows and crows, he'd never so much as spoken a word to her face in years. Not with his own lips anyway. He'd tried to track her down so that he might offer his love to her again, offer it properly this time so that she'd accept him, but he'd faltered each time. What could he say to her? What could he offer other than his love? He was more powerful than he had been before, more controlled, he could offer her the world. Kelly Stafford had afforded him a way of speaking with her. He'd been able to talk to her without fear of showing his own face. And yet she had been talking with Kelly, not with him. She'd touched Kelly, not him. And the frustration had built.

Kelly had had conversations with her, time spent over wine in her home and in public, and the realisation that he had sent another man to be with her hurt him more and more each time he watched the screens in his head. He tried to blank out that she was not spending time with this other man but with him, but the sickness of that hurt just kept creeping into his gut like the maggots crawling amongst the rotten flesh at his feet.

He wanted to be the one to touch and kiss her. He wanted to be the one to hold her hand and place his fingers upon her skin.

He'd done that just once, when they were little more than children. He'd offered her his love, his devotion to her, and in hindsight it had seemed an immature offering because she had rejected him. He'd do it better next time, oh yes. Next time she'd take him into her heart, and he'd make right everything that was wrong. Oh yes, he'd see to that. She'd have to love him then.

Kelly Stafford bent over the side of the armchair and offered his hand. Kyle stared at him for a moment, lost in his surging thoughts, his shoal of cinema screens still playing inside his head like a hive of bees, all witnessing, all watching, before he finally took hold of it and eased himself forward. A slick of congealed sweat and grime formed stringy webs of filth between his skin and the armchair as he lifted himself out of it, and as he took hold of Kelly's arm, the tendrils of flesh that coiled behind his hand reached out like tentacles and grasped the reporter's jacket sleeve for extra support. The man did not grimace once in disgust as his master's abominations took hold of him one by one, but he simply stood and allowed Kyle to force his weight upon him and drag himself up.

His body oozed dark sweat as he moved, the stains at his pits spreading, the encrusted filth at his groin cracking. He had no time to clean himself for the reunion between himself and his sister, and what would be the point anyway? He didn't give a fuck what Isabel thought of him, he was a force of power and she was so far beneath him. She hadn't cared before and it was clear that she wouldn't now. And besides, why venture out clean when within an hour he would be wearing a gown of her own blood.

His body was more used to sitting motionless rather than standing and walking, and his joints creaked with complaint in rhythm with the increasing tempo of his quickening pulse. His eyes had still not found any trace of his father, but they had discovered his sister, and oh yes, he would destroy her tonight, for loving their mother and forsaking their father.

## FOURTEEN

### WITH WAITING COMES UNCERTAINTY

Isabel had decided to leave her mother be. Waiting a couple of floors below, she kept a vigil on the murky ill-lit street outside. A drizzle had begun to fall, making glittering haloes around the streetlamps, and blurring shadows where before they had been crisp.

The sight of the reporter still troubled her, and she guessed that he would undoubtedly be returning at some point. She had few weapons, but there were so many places inside her that said to her, why bother, why continue to hide? So many times she had wanted to just give up, to raise her hands to her brother that she knew was looking for her and let him do as he wished.

Twenty years she'd been on the run, and sometimes when she had crawled inside a warehouse for the night, or waited out a rainstorm in a dank garden shed, she had wondered just what the hell she was doing. She'd been protecting her mother all this time, protecting her from Kyle, but even that made no sense at times. She had healed her all those years ago, healed her of death it seemed, and as much as her mother wanted to go to the grave where she belonged, part of Isabel, the selfish part, did not want her to have that wish. She loved her mother, even though it hurt beyond measure to simply look at her, even though her mother just wanted to drag herself down into the ground and have an end to her unnatural existence. But that hadn't happened. She'd had an illness that nobody had an explanation for. It had claimed her life. And Isabel had somehow brought her back. That was the story, and it was one hell of a sorry tale.

Was that something moving down in the shadows across the road? Isabel pressed her face to the glass and strained her eyes to see into the uncertain darkness swirling beyond the yellow kaleidoscopic patterns of the streetlamp. It was just so difficult to tell. The darkness seemed to shift beyond her sight, concealing anything that might be inside it. Her eyes checked the brickwork, swept down to the corner of the street and back again. Still nothing moved. Maybe she had imagined it, been distracted by the thought of her brother, the certainty of his coming here destroying what was left of her rational mind.

And what had he been doing all these years, she thought now to herself? She couldn't imagine him with a regular day job, the self-proclaimed prince of the world. The notion suddenly seemed ludicrous, and a lunatic smile spread across her face; Kyle in a kitchen apron, or in dirty blue overalls at a tyre and exhaust centre. Maybe he hadn't been searching for them both all this time after all. Maybe he'd just gotten on with his life, or gone looking for his father like he'd always promised to do.

A sick feeling crawled into the base of her gut at the thought of that, of how she might have been hiding like a panicked fox with the rumour of hounds on her tail for no reason. What if she had been running from a phantom? What if her fear had all been in her head? She tried to shake it away, but the sickness wouldn't go. What if he'd made something of his life while she had wasted hers? She returned her gaze outside, trying to focus on the darkness for anything that might be coming for her, but the terror had already taken hold of her and wouldn't let go.

Kyle wasn't coming. Emily was still haunted by something he had done to her when he was just a kid. And Kelly? He was just some lonely guy that had unfortunately given Emily a case of deja-vu.

The street was still quiet outside. She glanced at her watch and saw that it was getting close to four AM. Tiredness was beginning to creep up on her. She was used to sleeping through the day and keeping watch at night, but the itch of fatigue was making itself known, her eyelids growing as dull and heavy as lead, her senses dumbing down.

Somewhere in her head she reasoned how Kelly couldn't just be some lonely guy offering a case of deja-vu. He'd followed her here, for Christ's sake. He'd stood at the corner of the building across the street and stared back at her. And that had been less than a few hours ago.

Hadn't he?

She could feel the tiredness really taking a hold now, and it was making her head heavy, making her thoughts swim through it as though it was thick with mud. Yes, she *had* seen him, he'd followed her here.

The glittering haloes of yellow light swirled around the streetlamps outside, contorting her thoughts even further. But somewhere beyond it all, her eyes made out the shape of something that had not been there before. It was nearly impossible to see just beyond the light that swirled and glowed through the gently falling drizzle, but she was sure that something was different, a dark shape set amongst the uncertain darkness. And then it moved.

It was a man, standing against the wall, partially obscured by the streetlamp itself. She moved her head to the edge of the window, but she could still make out very little, and it was only then that she realised that she didn't know how long he might have been standing there for.

She swallowed heavily, and realised that she was breathing hard. In that moment of realisation, she realised too that all her fears and paranoia about Kyle had been correct all this time as well. He'd come here to find her, to finish what he had started in their mother's bedroom with the cat. Her heart was thumping in her chest, and she knew then that she had to go and face him, she had to end all the running and hiding. If death was the end, and she had no idea if her healing curse would prevent anything he might do to her, then it would almost be welcome. For her and her mother.

With a forceful breath, she pushed herself away from the glass and hurried quickly across the third floor towards the stairwell. She hoped that she'd be able to get outside through the front entrance and across the street before he left his place at the wall to try and find his own way in, but what she would do when finally she got there and met him face to face she had no idea. She only hoped that by the time their eyes did connect after twenty years apart, she would be able to handle her half of whatever would happen with him on equal terms.

The drizzle was coming down heavier than she had thought it had been from her vantage point at the upstairs window, and it made it difficult for her to discern anything in the uneasy darkness. The glare from the streetlamps whirled in dizzying crescents inside the damping rain, and as she crossed the empty silent street she found the place where Kyle had been standing was now deserted.

She slowed to a halt and gazed round in all directions but he had simply disappeared. She thought briefly that he had outmanoeuvred her, had maybe managed to gain access to the office building already, probably via the loading bays at the back, the same route she herself usually took. Perhaps by her leaving through the front entrance she had missed him. Perhaps even now...

A movement, there, at the back of a short alleyway in the darkest of the shadows. Isabel sensed that there was indeed someone there and that they had seen her too. Her scrutiny must have forced them forward because the darkness now shifted and a figure emerged slowly out of the murk.

There was sufficient light emanating from the streetlamp behind her to illuminate his face before he was even within twenty yards of her. It was indeed a familiar face, but not the face she had expected, not the aged face of her brother. This was someone she had seen only a few hours ago. The stranger in the shadows was the reporter Kelly Stafford.

"What the hell are you doing here?" she demanded to know. "Why are you following me?"

Kelly stood motionless, his hands deep in the pockets of his sodden jacket. There was no polished smile for her, no glimmer in his eyes, and rain simply tracked down his forehead in neat rivulets. Hell, from the vacant expression on his face it didn't even seem as though he recognised her.

"I asked you a question, God damn it," she cried

now. "No, I asked you two. What the fuck are you doing here?"

The man just stood there, the light rain on his shoulders and dark hair reflecting the pallor of the streetlamps, glistening like dew. Still he said nothing, and it didn't look as though he was going to either. His eyes seemed glazed, and although he was looking at her, she didn't feel as though he was actually seeing her.

A chill had already begun to get beneath her skin, and not because of the cold of the foul wet night. Something was not right, not right at all. Here was a man who only hours before was grinning and making unnerving innuendoes. Something had happened to him to turn him into this shell.

"I want to know why you were following me," Isabel said again, but more calmly this time. "Before and now."

His lips remained set, his throat too, and it was certain that he was not about to answer her in any way. Slowly she went towards him, reached out a hand, and placed it gently on his wrist. Almost immediately she jerked her head back as if a bolt of electricity had shot from his body and through her hand, shuddering her entire frame with its sudden burning voltage. She opened her hand to let go but her fingers would not release their grip. The electricity came, knotting her muscles until they felt like they'd snap, contorting her limbs so that she clenched her entire body into a tight mass. Her head pounded with the intensity that shook her, and with the thumping dizziness came a series of images, each one of them disturbing and smeared, like a hand forced across a wet canvas.

Here was a family sitting down to dinner, and here

came a crow rapping its beak against a window pane. A shot of livid blood saturated the scene, only to be replaced by shining silver blades slashing the canvas to shreds. A picture of a man came shrouded in darkness, sprouting limbs of living creatures, a head of wild moss and grasses, before it too was gone in a whirlwind of chaos, of flapping birds and rabid white teeth.

The electricity abated as swiftly as it had begun, and her grip fell away leaving her hand lifeless and dull at her side. Tumbling to her hands and knees, Isabel could hardly lift her head to stare at this man as the echoes of her agony bucked and turned deep inside her body, her arms still twitching, her legs still buckled and useless.

Her focus began to return, and as her eyes eventually lifted and found the face of the reporter, she had even more questions for him, and somehow in the midst of all that, she knew that her brother's name would probably answer every question that she had.

"Who are you?" she asked finally, attempting to push herself back into at least a sitting position.

"My name," he began slowly, "is Kelly Stafford. I am..."

But he got no further.

"I know your name," Isabel said to him. "But I want to know what you are."

It seemed hard for him to speak for some reason, and she could not figure out just why he had become so very different in the space of a few hours. His lips parted again, then closed, and then opened once more. The first few words she didn't catch, so breathlessly were they uttered, but the rest she did, as he began to explain just what he was doing outside in the cold wet rain.

"I can see what I'm doing," he said, "and I can see where I'm going, but I have no idea why. I can see you talking to me, but I don't know who you are. I don't even know why I'm here."

"You followed me here earlier."

The man said nothing to this.

"And now you've come back," she added.

Kelly stared at her for a moment, his lips parted slightly as though he was going to add some more. But then they closed and that seemed to be it once again.

Isabel managed to push herself to her feet, so that she might continue to question him face to face. Her legs were still uncertain, aching with whatever force had burned through them, but she managed to keep herself upright while she talked to him.

"I don't know what happened when I touched you, but I saw a lot of images. I don't know if they're your memories or -"

"Yes," he said suddenly, and for the first time Isabel felt as though he was actually looking at her. "I remember your touch. It felt as though something slipped inside me, like a key turning over in a lock. Something became unlatched, but I can't quite... it's difficult. Something's there, in my head where I can't get to it..."

Slowly Isabel reached out her hand and waited for the jolt of electricity. But it seemed that her first touch had dispelled so much of it already, as though she had perhaps earthed him, and she could now lay her hands on him freely. She placed her other hand on his shoulder, and again a stream of images came into her head just as they had done before. She saw a picture of one of the family members more clearly this time, and as soon as she did, she heard Kelly whisper her name.

"Judith," he said, his voice wavering. "My God, it's Judith."

"Who's she?" Isabel asked. This woman seemed roughly the same age as he, and remembering Emily telling her about how Kelly wanted to be with her, wanted to know just who this other woman was.

"My wife," he said, his voice now stumbling as though he was going to burst into tears of joy. "My God, how long has it been since I've seen her."

"Is she dead?" Isabel asked quietly.

Kelly's eyes were huge now, intent.

"I left our house weeks ago. I haven't been back. She must be sick with worry by now. I have to go, I have to -"

"Wait," Isabel cried, pulling him back to her. "What are you talking about? What's going on?"

"I've been gone from my family," he said to her. "He's taken me away from my wife and my son, don't you see? Oh God, it's all coming back now."

He was visibly shaking, and he was now looking down at himself, taking in every sight, his hands, his clothes.

"Who are you talking about?" Isabel persisted, taking hold of his sleeve now.

"The man with the birds - he had his hands inside me, manipulating me. Oh God..."

Isabel felt the familiar crawl of sickness return to her as she realised just what Kyle had been doing over the years, how he had been learning far sicker stuff than just turning birds inside out. He hadn't gotten himself a job at all, he hadn't been wearing an apron or a greasy set of overalls. He'd been fucking with nature all this time, killing birds, taking people from their families. She felt sickened just to be related to him, and she suddenly thought she was going to throw up.

203

Her focus went back to Kelly, just in time to see him backing away.

"Where are you going?"

"Home," he murmured vaguely into the darkness between them, as he staggered crazily from one side of the pavement to the other.

"Do you know where you're even going?" she called after him.

He raised one hand absently over his head in response, and Isabel didn't know if that meant he knew or not. But then as she watched him go, her attention suddenly returned to Kyle, and all that he was capable of. Her eyes flickered back towards the front of the office building that had been at her back during her exchange with the newly healed Kelly Stafford, now released from the unnatural hold her brother had somehow had upon him. The windows up on the fifth floor were still blacked out, but if her former fears about Kyle were correct, and she suddenly hoped that they weren't, then she may well have missed him on the stairs. She may even have gone out the front as he had slipped in through the back. Even now he might be...

Oh Jesus.

Mum.

## FIFTEEN

## REUNION

It was dark and quiet when he entered, and for a while he thought that perhaps Isabel had slipped away from him yet again. It sometimes seemed like a kind of desperation, this seeking out of his sister, time spent tracking her down, time that could have been better spent trying to find his father.

And he'd looked too; he had devoted so much of his time in trying to locate him, but there had been not one single trace, nothing in twenty years. But when it came down to family, as it inevitably always did, there was only Isabel remaining; surely she knew something, surely their mother had dispensed some shred of truth about his father's whereabouts on her deathbed, some measure for Isabel to carry with her.

But there was something else, of course, that the two of them shared, another reason for his tracking of his sister, and her name was Emily Oates. The only child of his father's employer, as well as Isabel's best friend, he had seen so much of her as a boy that it sometimes hurt. They'd not spoken often, and it was true that even when they had exchanged simple words in passing, she had been curt and dismissive. But he had felt something between them, something special and unique, and he had only wanted that chance to prove it to her.

He'd taken that chance one autumn morning, shortly after his sister's and mother's disappearance. He was still going to school, staying reluctantly with his aunt while a social worker named Heidi looked into his case - *his whole family had abandoned him one by one, poor mite*. Emily had stood near the trees at the side of the school building, talking with one of her friends, and when she started away back to class, he had swept in to offer her his heart.

She'd hardly broken her stride, hardly even looked at him, and all he had wanted to do was touch her and convince her. His fingers had found her wrist with the intent of pulling her back to him, to urge her to listen, but even in that moment he'd felt the heat rising in the strength of that grasp.

He'd known what he had done to her even before she had, the blistering of her wrists, his touch like acid against her soft resilient skin. He'd felt her skin begin to run like liquid even before the pain had reached her, and in those few moments before she had run from him screaming, he already felt a guilt that had never left him.

The memory of that day was still vivid in his head, like a painting that had been brushed with bright oil paints only minutes before, and like the canvas he was able to study intricate details upon its weave. He could recall the tiny elephant badge that she wore on her sweater, grey and plastic with ball eyes that rolled as she moved. She wore a red bow around her pony tail, too, and it was not often that she wore a bow, although she nearly always had a pony tail. Her dress, however, was the usual school uniform, a light blue dress with a subtle check pattern. He could remember the sight of it distinctly, especially the sight of his own hand reaching towards it, how soft the fabric had felt against his touch. There had been a moment's hesitation, a moment when somewhere in his head a voice had said - *no, this is wrong* - but it was fleeting, and it disappeared altogether as his fingers slipped beneath the hem of her dress and found the softer skin of her white fleshy thighs. That was when the heat from his touch had licked into a furnace.

His touch against her smooth white skin had not lasted long, however, certainly not long enough to gain any kind of pleasure from the contact. A flood of guilt had coursed through him as he'd felt the glut of her skin flow between his fingers like molasses, melting and running like some horrid grisly soup. Before those perfect round eyes of hers had widened in alarm, before that scream of hers had pierced the mid-morning air between them, he knew what he had done.

Retracting his fingers cured nothing. The eyes stared stricken at him and the scream slashed the air in two. It had happened.

He'd stood motionless as he'd watched her run stumbling back towards the school building, arms flailing wildly, her pony tail bucking from one side to the other, the red of her bow flashing through the air after her like a trail of blood. His guilt had turned quickly to nausea as he'd stood there, his stomach eating itself as though he'd swallowed an army of ants as he watched her flee from his attentions. Twenty years he'd had to live without Emily at his side, twenty years of loneliness and yearning, and he knew that it would only continue until he had Isabel within his grasp and had managed to make right all that was wrong.

He'd never really known how he'd done what he'd done, only that he had. He'd walked out of the school gates after that and had never returned. He never went back to the cottage or to Aunt Cassie's house, and had never heard what Heidi was going to make of him in her initial report. No, he'd left the life of a normal child behind him after that, left its structure and its routines anyway. He'd remained within the boundaries of the village, though, sleeping in the woods where he felt he belonged, where he could keep a watch over Emily.

From such a distance, however, it was nearly impossible to see with his own eyes just what she was doing or who she spent her time with. But he was beginning to see through the eyes of the creatures of the wood, the crows and the magpies, with a greater accuracy and desire, and he began to use them more and more to keep an eye on both her and the rest of the village too.

At first it was just Emily and Aunt Cassie that he spied upon, watching them through living room windows, and through bedroom windows left open on hot summer nights. But soon he spread his attentions further afield, to the post master's house, the newsagent, to the gossip-mongers that he soon began to know by name. He hoped that here he might perhaps overhear some nugget of information about his father, about his sister, something useful about where they may have disappeared to. But it seemed that the Rider family was no longer significant news, no longer worthy of hushed chat behind turned hands, and all gossip slowly died away to nothing.

A few years rolled by, his web across the region fairly encompassing, but still there was little to keep him going. Emily had grown older and moved away to college, and with him wanting to follow her as well as remain in the woods where he felt safe, he began to dispatch those same birds of the wood after her.

It had been during one of his vigils through her dorm room window that he had heard her speak of something that was later to become one of his biggest obsessions. Emily had been sitting up late with one of her friends, a thin blonde-haired girl named Tammy, and the conversation had turned towards friends that they hadn't seen for a long time. Emily had begun to speak fondly of Isabel, telling Tammy of how she really missed her because one day she had simply left home, something about a family curse, she'd said. But one of the stories that she had relayed had been of an injured bird that Isabel had somehow managed to nurse back to health, a raw and ragged thing that he himself had left behind during his early days of exploration into what had made the world work.

Emily had described this wretched creature in detail, showing Tammy, as she placed her palms together and then splayed them back on themselves, how the bird had been found almost inside out, and how it had seemed a mystery that it was even still alive. Isabel had brought it to her home, she'd gone on, where over the next couple of days she'd managed to help it stand and sing once again.

This was the strange conversation that had changed Kyle's thoughts about his sister. Isabel had seemed to have found some kind of affinity to heal, the same way that he had found his ability to manipulate living flesh, only to a lesser degree. At that point he'd had little control over it, and he even remembered the bird that Isabel had later found. He himself had approached it slowly, curious as to how he could almost see himself through its eyes, and it had been that same curiosity that had forced him to go on to examine it, both inside and out, the same way that he'd tried to examine the different animals of the farm. After his scrutiny of that bird, however, it had become clear to him that it was of no use to him any more, and so he had simply left it to die.

Isabel must have come upon it for some reason shortly afterwards and decided to help it; to help the unhelpable. That's what he'd wanted for Emily. He knew that what he had done to her that day beside the school building had not been anything natural, and that the only way to put right what he had done was to claim the power that now lived inside his sister. He needed her, or rather he needed that power. And now he was in the old disused office building that his puppet had driven him to.

He could smell her scent as he began to climb the stairs, and only hoped that she had not been alerted to his entry. A grin creased his face in two as he imagined her expression as she finally laid eyes upon her brother after so many years apart. Finally he had found her, he thought, as he followed the scent on the air to where it was strongest. The third floor.

The open plan building was deserted, however, but he wandered for a few minutes, just looking at what had been left behind. There was very little, but what did remain seemed to him at least too important to leave behind. He had to think hard about a small bear that was tucked away beneath one of the windows that faced out onto the service yard from where he had entered only moments before. Did the bear even belong to Isabel? He tried to remember, and was only vaguely aware of her having had one as a child, but he wasn't certain. An untidy litter of takeaway cartons spilled over the top of a waste basket nearby, which at least confirmed that someone had indeed been staying here, but as to whether she had deserted the place or not, that question had still not been answered.

The building was deathly quiet and Kyle stood for a few moments just listening to that silence, hoping a footfall or a heavy breath might give his sister's presence away. But the quiet was impenetrable and he could discern little.

The sheen of something metallic caught his attention as he moved around the room, something round and tiny on a wooden desk. It had the scent of Isabel all over it, he could smell that before he had even reached it, and as he stooped to pick it up, he saw that it was a silver locket. He prised open the delicate hinge and stared at the two minute photographs inside. One was of his mother, the other his father.

The sight of seeing his father's face was a shock, and his eyes would not leave the image of it for a long time. It was the same face that he had seen in the wood on the top of the hill, the same face that had called to him and offered him counsel. But then a sound came to shake him back to his purpose, from somewhere above him in the building, a drawn out sigh. Isabel.

Kyle snapped the locket shut and pocketed it. It was his now, and quickly he hurried out to the stairwell and began to climb, his ears searching through the stillness of the old building for any further sounds. He reached the fourth floor and halted, listening to the motionless gloom. His feet were anxious, his hands hovering over the stair rail. And then the sigh came again, long and ghostly, from the floor just above him.

Sweeping up the stairs like a phantom, Kyle glided without a sound into a solid murk that shrouded everything from his sight. All the windows had been taped or boarded over, and although it was going to be difficult for him to see by, at least it would disguise his presence to his sister.

He moved silently across the fifth floor, his eyes barely able to penetrate the gloom, his ears trying to locate his prey. His senses were almost totally useless, and although the urge to call out her name was strong, a grin of pleasure began to creep across his face once again. He did not want to give himself away and lose her again if she became scared and took flight.

Instead, he turned his attention towards something different in the room, tuning out the world of the commonplace, and tuning in the world that he knew so very well. He could hear the scratching of insects crawling beneath the floor and up in the cobwebs in the corners of the room and above his head in the suspended ceiling. He could hear their tiny legs as they scratched in search of food. And where they scuttled, he homed his thoughts in upon them, searching out each individual spider and louse until he could see all that they could see.

Much of it was darkness, but there was a whole spectrum of colours within that darkness which gave him an almost total coverage of the layout of the room. One moment he could see the dull metal of a steel support brace as he crawled beneath it, another moment and he could taste the grain of a wooden desk as his mandibles burrowed inside it. Then he was high on a silken web, watching a moth struggle and entwine itself even further in swathes of sticky strands, and even through the eyes of that moth he could see the view of the floor beneath its flailing velvet wings.

As he stood just inside the threshold, Kyle watched the shape of the room unfold; the desks, the toppled chairs, another litter of takeaway cartons. This last made him furrow his brow. Why would Isabel choose two floors to occupy, especially as the other floor had held her possessions and this floor was so dark and filthy.

He continued his search of the room near the litter of wrappers and boxes, the eyes of the spiders and the woodlice penetrating the murk far more efficiently that he ever could with his simplistic human eyes, until he came upon a shape hidden away beneath what seemed to be blankets. Surely Isabel would not try and hide from him in a dark room by simply tugging a duvet over her head like she'd done as a girl. That just seemed so... childish. After twenty years of hiding, she would surely have found better ways of concealing herself other than that.

With the contents of the fifth floor mapped out with a hundred different images inside his head Kyle made his way swiftly across the room to where the figure lay huddled. Strange that she should be hiding from him like this, he continued to think, so infantile, so expectant of defeat. Kyle reached out a hand towards the blanket as he neared it, his sight guided only by the myriad of insect eyes in his head, and tugged it back with a grin of victory. Finally he would have Isabel. He would take the magic that she had inside her, and use it to cure his Emily. Then she would see how right they were for each other. Then everything would be perfect.

Uncertainty overtook him in a single wave as the spiders crawled forward to offer him a closer look at the face beneath the blanket. That uncertainty grew as the lice scuttled across the floor, their antennae flailing as they sought to learn more, until the dreadful realisation came. This was not Isabel. The truth of that came as he saw two eyes open in the head that was far from being that of a thirty year old woman. Ghoulish in appearance and yellowed around their decaying sockets, the eyes that now regarded him through the murk were far from natural. They were as keen upon him as his were upon her, and for a moment he stared dumbfounded at this hideous and most dreadful sight. Then a mouth opened, a devilish maw that held two uneven rows of crooked rotten teeth. Spit stretched between her jaws like cobwebs, as two words came to rattle them.

"Hello, Kyle," was all this zombie said.

Kyle stood and stared at her with utter disbelief. His arms fell slack at his sides, his head felt sickly thick, and all the powers that he had over the insects of the room faltered, taking his sight of her with them. He may have staggered back a step, he wasn't sure, but as the utter darkness of the room began to swirl and blacken the image of her altogether, so he fought to regain his composure, and bring his view back of this monstrous creature.

"Who are you?" he managed to ask, his mind reeling. This wasn't how he had seen tonight's events unfolding. Not at all.

"Don't tell me you've forgotten your own mother?" she said cruelly.

His mouth dropped open, and drool gathered at the edge of it, dribbling out like slurry.

"What have you done?" he gasped.

But his words were not meant for her, he could barely even acknowledge her, but for Isabel.

"We left suddenly, Kyle, I admit," she went on, "but we thought, or rather Isabel thought, that you

214

might have brought harm to one or both of us if we had stayed behind. Wasn't that foolish of her? Don't you think?"

"Harm?" Kyle managed to stammer. "I would have slit your lying throats."

It was his mother's turn to be silent. He knew his words were strong, but hate rarely softened over time. It simply festered and became more rancid.

"Still angry," she murmured at last.

"What did you expect? That I'd forget about my father, forget how you drove him out."

"Your father was never driven out. It was better for us all -"

"Even now," he cried out, "you still hang on to your lies."

"You don't know the truth, Kyle -"

"I know enough. I know that I didn't have a father from the age of nine onwards. I know it was either you or him that had to go."

"And he chose himself."

"He chose to leave me behind?"

"It wasn't like that. He chose to take himself away, for the good of us all, for you. He didn't want you to see how he was, what he was becoming."

"I didn't even know you were still alive," Kyle murmured, his voice hoarse. "I went looking through the graveyard at St Michael's, but I never found a grave. Found one for Aunt Cassie though. Small headstone, handful of boorish words."

"Cassandra?" his mother whispered.

"Dead," Kyle confirmed bluntly. "Probably shock. Probably killed herself because of the guilt."

The silence that came from his cruel words only brought a grin to his face.

"You didn't know about that?" he asked lightly.

215

Again that silence.

"Your sweet little sister tried to stop me. She knew who I was - what I was becoming, to use your phrase - and she tried to stop me."

It was starting to become a one way conversation. His mother had said nothing to anything he had said for a while, and it was only the map of images still being shown to him by the spiders and the woodlice that he still knew she was sitting huddled in front of him.

"It was a long time ago," Kyle told her, "probably within the first year after you went away. I was still getting used to what I could and couldn't do. I saw Aunt Cass on occasion in the village or through the windows of her house, and she saw me too, furtive glimpses, watching eyes. We never spoke - well, she cried out my name a couple of times but that was all - but I could see something in her eyes, something in the way she looked at me, that told me that she knew. Something had taken hold of me, possessed me if you like, and she wanted it stopped. She met me in a shaded patch of woodland one day and brought out a knife that she'd prepared before her trip out. It was a shocking experience to see your own aunt pin your arms behind your back and drag a knife across your throat. It shocked her too, I saw the expression on her face. But what killed her, I think, was the revelation of what she had done. You see, it wasn't me she'd murdered. It was a boy of the same age that I'd made look like me. Human's are tricky things, but in a shaded copse where light and dark can deceive, it makes that deceit just a little bit easier. But once I'd passed a note beneath her front door, and made myself visible for her to see, standing in the middle of her lawn with my arms outspread, she hanged herself a few days later."

Kyle paused for a moment, hoping to hear a sob of anguish, or even some breath of pain, but still his mother made no sound. His grin fell away, and a rage began to build in him again, a rage for his mother that he hadn't felt in a very long time.

"Knives," he said at last, through clenched teeth. "They're tricky things too. A weapon that's been around since the dawn of man, and yet it's never really gone out of fashion. I wonder why that is. I mean, guns are so much easier, so much swifter in the killing, and yet there's something about holding a foot long weight of metal in your hand, something about it sliding into flesh and slicing it cleanly in two."

His hand was already inside his jacket, clutching the weapon that he had hoped he would be convincing Isabel with tonight. Instead, he had slipped his fingers around its handle with the promise of so much more. It came out into the open with a silent whisper, carving an arc in the darkness between them. Its edge was keen, and Kyle could feel its echoes through his fingers.

"Tricky things," he said again, and with a cry in his throat he plunged it deep into his mother's chest, driving it hard and twisting it against her bones until the hilt halted its progress.

His mother gasped aloud with a sudden agony, and through the eyes of the insects on the fifth floor, Kyle could see her writhing in fits beneath his assault, her rotten mouth gaping, her yellowed eyes stark against the decayed murk around her. His grin faltered as he studied the point where his knife had entered her. There was no blood, no fountain or glut. She simply shuddered and crawled around the knife still clenched in his hand.

Swiftly he drew out the blade, took a breath as he

studied where next to drive it home, and thrust it forward with all his strength into her belly. It broke through with a dry sound like stale bread breaking, but still there was no blood. She should have been sodden with it by now, drowning in a bath of rich scarlet, and then the full horror of the situation, of who and what his own sister had become, finally dawned on him, and he withdrew the knife with a trembling fist as he stumbled back a step.

"It was Isabel, wasn't it?" he stammered, his words almost choking him. The rage was consuming him, and now with no outlet, no murder, his hands were starting to shake. "She did this, didn't she?" He stared down at her, still clutching herself. Then he started yelling. "She did, didn't she?"

"I wish that you could kill me," she finally managed to whisper. "But Isabel has kept me alive."

"You don't bleed."

"I'm as dry inside as a twenty year old corpse, which is what I am. You have something unnatural inside you, and so does she. But they are so very different. It was the same with your father. That was why he went."

Kyle wanted to use his knife again, to slash her to pieces and make her feel every blow until she was dead. But that wasn't going to happen. Not until Isabel gave up her magic, and he would have that from her. For two reasons now. For Emily, and now for their mother.

"Where is she?" he growled.

Once again, his mother fell into silence. It seemed clear that his attack had caused her at least some pain, but nowhere near as much as he wanted.

"Tell me or I'll fucking kill you."

"You know that you can't, not while Isabel keeps me alive."

218

Kyle drove his knife at her again, its blade sinking deep into the grey meat of her flank, opening it wide like the parched flesh of dried fruit. She cried out in agony, her hands clasping the wound, but it was clear that death was not going to claim her.

"Then tell her to come to me," Kyle exclaimed, pressing his face close to hers as great sobs wracked her body. "Tell her to come to the woods near our home. You remember that place, don't you, our home that you defiled all those years ago?"

"Why should I send her to you?" she gasped.

"Because it will be safer for her or for anyone else that gets in my way. I found you this time, and you know that I'll find you again. Aunt Cassie underestimated me, and now she's in the ground."

Then he forced his knife hard against her ribs to emphasise his final point, before leaving her to her pain and sweeping out of the building and back into the night.

# SIXTEEN

## THE BLOODY MESSENGER

When Isabel hurried back inside and climbed the stairs to the fifth floor, she found her mother not in her usual place, but by one of the windows that overlooked the service yard at the back of the building. The entire floor, which was usually shrouded entirely in impenetrable darkness, now had some partial light coming in through the glass in front of which sat her mother. She'd pulled down the layers of cloth that immersed both that window and the two adjacent, and gazed out at the electric-lit world outside, something she had not done in years.

By the dim yellow light illuminating her, Isabel could see that something was wrong. She was sitting awkwardly, her arms clasped around her, but it was only as she approached her that she learned the truth.

Deep gashes had been opened up in her flank and across her belly, and such monstrous wounds would surely have killed her had it not been for her own magic that kept her alive. To see her injured in such a way was beyond words, and even as she stumbled past the office furniture that littered the route towards her, she had already guessed who had done this to her.

"He didn't even know about me," her mother said

weakly to her, without turning away from the window. "He came here for you. He wants your curse."

"Mum, are you alright?"

Isabel had her arms around her now, but her embrace only seemed to cause her further discomfort, her attentions opening wounds that her mother had been holding closed.

"I'm sorry for all that has happened to you, Isabel."

"It's not your fault."

"Yes it is," she told her. "In part at least."

"No, mum, it's Kyle. He -"

"He wants you to go after him."

Isabel stared at her, her eyes wide with trepidation. She had just gone out to face him, hoping to put an end to this once and for all, but that had been her error. She was not sure that she would have the courage to do it again. She did not want to face him at all, after seeing in Kelly just what he was capable of, but it was clear that if he could find them once, he could find them again, if they did choose to run.

"Where is he?"

"It's not important. You can't go, do you understand? He wants what you're not able to give him, and I'm afraid that he'll hurt you like he's hurt me."

Isabel glanced down again at her wounds, and even before she knew what she was doing, her fingers were searching out the deepest of the lacerations and drawing them closed with her will. Her mother jerked from her touch, and she half expected her to tell her to leave her be, to let her die. But then she seemed to realise that her living was inevitable, in spite of everything, and she relented and allowed herself to be tended.

"You know I have to go," Isabel murmured as she worked, her mother's flesh melting beneath her touch and sealing itself like fresh tar on a road.

Her mother remained silent, however, her eyes still cast out through the cold glass of the window.

"It's the only way," Isabel went on.

"He'll kill you."

"He's my brother."

"He's also my son. He had murder in his eyes. He..."

"He what?"

"It's nothing," Irene said quietly.

"Tell me."

"Another time," she murmured, her vigil unfaltering.

"It's always another time, mum. When will you tell me any of these secrets of yours?"

She turned to look at her then, and her eyes, as sunken and decayed as they were, shone wet with tears. Isabel hadn't stopped to think about how all this had been affecting her, losing her husband, having a war between her children, her first born son attempting to kill her and now luring her daughter to a similar fate. The family had its share of secrets, that much was plain, but it seemed that her mother was just not ready to relive them again in order. She'd had enough years ago, and all Isabel had succeeded in doing was forcing her into a miserable unnatural life where all she could do was relive those secrets over and over again in her own head.

"Where do I need to meet him?" Isabel asked her softly.

She looked at her then, and with more certainty than she had in a long time. Her lips parted, dry like stale bread, two crusts left at the end of a loaf.

"The wood on top of the hill," she said, her voice

222

scratched raw with anguish.

Isabel swallowed hard, and realised that her heart was now thrumming a rapid beat inside her chest. The wood, where it had all begun. Why not, she thought to herself? Return to the beginning. Return to where it all began. It all seemed somehow logical, in an hysterically insane kind of way.

"You'll stay here?" Isabel asked as she got up to leave.

"Where do you expect me to go? A hotel?"

"I just thought -"

"Just do what you need to do."

That was all she said, and her words echoed around inside Isabel's head as she made her way back across the fifth floor towards the stairwell. Even once she was stood outside at the back of the building in the service yard, her mother's instruction remained with her with all its finality. She could feel the weight of her mother's watchful gaze upon her as she stood in the darkness, something she had not felt in a very long time, and for that one brief moment before she left it felt good.

There was a sense of conclusion in their returning home, to the place where they had spent so much time as children. But it was not to meet with her brother to discuss terms, it had gone too far for that. No, it was to destroy the dark magic that had plagued both her and Kyle since it had first crept into their lives, and who knew at what age they had been affected? She knew now that Kyle wanted to take her power from her, but what he or their mother didn't know was that she intended to destroy them both, once and for all. There was something evil in those woods, and now she had a chance to wipe that slate clean.

## SEVENTEEN

## THE JOURNEY HOME

She hadn't even thought how she would get back home. Kyle would probably have a car, no doubt expecting to be driven by the hapless Kelly Stafford. How furious he would be when he found him gone, cured of his intent, by her of all people. A smile crept into the sides of her mouth at the thought but it was short-lived. There was no humour to be had from any of this. It all had to end and this was the opportunity.

She'd never had a car, and didn't even know how to drive one. She'd left home with her mother at the age of ten and had been on the run ever since, hiding from the daylight mostly, but hiding from the night too. Where had been the time for such things? Where had been the money? Even now she had next to nothing in her pockets, only what had lasted since her last handout off the street, or her last short stretch of cheap labour cleaning warehouses or stacking supermarket shelves. That was no life, wandering and hiding, slaving midnight hours for greasy takeaway food. All she needed now was bus fare or train fare and she didn't even have that. Not as though there were any buses or trains running at this time of night anyway.

She stared up and down the street. Nothing moved, nothing glimmered, except the dim yellow streetlamps that cast their perpetual glow down at the dirty grey road. Her thoughts went inevitably to Emily, despite how much she'd wanted to keep her out of it all, but she reasoned that it was the only way. She couldn't afford an honest route, and there was no other alternative.

She went to a phone box, dug deep for coins, and the phone rang unanswered for over a minute until it was picked up. Isabel had no idea of the time herself, she needed no watch to click off the hours of her lonely vigils. But Emily informed her that it was nearly four, her voice disjointed and slurred at such an ungodly hour.

"I wouldn't have called except -"

"You were desperate," Emily murmured, stifling a yawn. "What do you need?"

Isabel hesitated a moment.

"I need a lift back home."

The yawn disappeared.

"Are you serious? What the hell for?"

"Kyle wants to see me. There's going to be some kind of face off."

"I'm not taking you there, he'll kill you."

"He only wants what I have -"

"And how are you going to give it to him? You don't even know what it is yourself."

Isabel knew that was true. She didn't really know what it was that flowed through her veins, but she figured that perhaps Kyle might know more, might share some shred of wisdom about the condition that had devastated her life before the end came. He'd taken his power a long way, much further than she; Kelly was proof of that. Perhaps he knew a way to get

225

it out of her once and for all, so that there might not need to be an end for them both. But what if he managed to take it from her? He'd always pronounced himself the prince of the world; what if she was walking straight into his unholy kingdom? What if he possessed the will to do both, to heal and to harm, what then? Could he raise an army of devils to take into battle and heal his own wounded at will? But who was his enemy?

"I need you to take me," Isabel finally said to her, images of an undead legion ransacking her head. "Please, I need you to do this one thing for me."

Emily went quiet on the other end of the line, and Isabel could hear her own blood thumping loudly inside her head as though it was amplified by the earpiece. Eventually Emily relented and said that she would drive her, but only if she promised to try and persuade Kyle to leave them both alone once he got what he wanted.

Isabel said nothing to this, knowing that if their confrontation went at least partially her way, then either one or both of them would be left a charred corpse capable of nothing.

·

Dawn rose while they were on the road, the small clock on the dashboard of Emily's white Escort reading six thirty seven as they finally made their way along the high street that meandered through the centre of the quiet village. There was virtually no other traffic on the road, just a couple of cars passing slowly by, and they gazed out through the windscreen in silence, taking in the sights of the unchanged buildings, the shop-fronts and the church, the village green and the old stone war memorial. It was strange for both of them, so many memories, unchanged by time, as though the whole place had been waiting for them to return.

It took them only another ten minutes to reach the cottage in which Isabel had been born and raised. She'd thought often about the place, about waking up to her parents' faces, about summers spent playing in the garden, about skipping home along the quiet country lanes, and about how wonderful it would be to return one day. After twenty years away, she expected the place to have changed a great deal, and had braced herself for heartache at what new owners might have done to the place. But as Emily pulled up outside, she was glad to see that it had changed as little as the rest of the village.

Memories flooded back as she climbed out of the car and stood to face the cottage that had dominated so many of her dreams. A section of the front lawn had been replaced by a paved driveway, and the rose borders that her mother had so loved to see blossoming had been taken over by a low hedgerow; but its white walls, and its dark slate roof, and the vista of fields that stretched beyond it to the hilltops, proved that although so much of it was different, it was still her home and always would be. This was where she belonged, she felt it inside her.

It even smelt the same, crisp and fragrant, of verdant grass and apple blossom, and she turned in slow circles just taking in the sights and the sounds again after such a long time away from them; the sparrows hidden inside the hedgerows, the swallows that arced overhead in the blue sky, the rustle of the breeze through the boughs of the trees, and the tides that flowed through the tall grass as that same breeze channelled it like some vast green ocean. And then as she turned on her heels, her eyes taking in every wonderful spectacle, she eventually took in the sight of the copse of trees that perched atop the small rising hillock, the rot on the landscape.

It seemed somehow denser than she remembered, more compact. Not with undergrowth, or with fuller thicker trees, just darker, immeasurably darker, as though daylight was forbidden to penetrate its barriers of shadowed foliage. A shiver tracked across her spine as she stood and stared at it now, and even the breeze seemed to suddenly build in strength and bring the promise of ice slivers on its back, now that she had laid eyes upon it once again. It seemed almost to welcome her back with some kind of sick mockery, as if saying, *I dare you to come here, I dare you to venture beneath my death-black canopy* .

Isabel answered its threat with motion, and forced herself to the back of the car, retrieving the two petrol cans that she'd filled before Emily had picked her up. Emily appeared beside her now and the vexed expression on her face forced Isabel to explain her simple but deadly plan.

"This thing with Kyle has gone too far," Isabel told her. "It ends now."

Emily stared at the two cans with horror, shaking her head with utter disbelief.

"You can't be serious," she gasped. "I agree he needs to be stopped, but killing your own brother?"

"He's not my brother any more. Something's taken over him, more fully than I could ever have thought possible."

"I know he's done some horrible things, but murder..."

"You didn't see what he did to my mother -"

"But you can't just set light to the whole wood."

228

"Watch me," Isabel said to her defiantly. "There's something terrible in those woods, and Kyle's stronger than I'll ever be. I'll never be able to talk rationally with him, especially in there."

"But if he's as powerful as I think he is, you don't even know if fire is going to do any good."

"Maybe it will, maybe it won't," Isabel conceded, slamming the boot shut. "But it's the only thing I can think of right now. At the very least, it might make him back off or leave us alone, at least until I can think of something else."

Emily watched helplessly as Isabel took the weight of each can in her hands before starting awkwardly away. Emily went to hurriedly lock the car, fumbling with her keys, but Isabel shot an icy glare over her shoulder before she could follow.

"Where do you think you're going?"

"With you."

"I don't think so. I don't want you getting involved."

"But I am involved."

"No," Isabel exclaimed. "This is family business."

"So what do you expect me to do?"

"Just wait here for me," she said. "And pray."

Emily wanted to say *but what if you don't come back?* but she managed to hold her words before they found the air. It seemed clear to both of them that Isabel might not make it back if she was going up against Kyle, perhaps that was even her intention, Emily couldn't be sure, but the words didn't need to be voiced aloud.

Emily wanted to argue, to say that it would be better with two of them, but she kept her silence knowing that what Isabel had said was true, this was

229

family business, and so she'd let her friend go. She didn't want to go up there any more than she suspected Isabel did, and even though she knew how much she was involved, she knew that there was something far greater happening between brother and sister. So she watched her go, watched her all the way across the field and along the track towards the treeline. But once Isabel broke through, she became enveloped rapidly by the consuming darkness of the wood, disappearing from sight altogether, and Emily was suddenly left in an eerie silent void that soon began crawling beneath her skin.

The morning was already warm, the sky overhead clear and radiant blue, but there was a cold that had grasped her, and there was something in that cold, something that knew her, something that could see her, and taste her.

Hurriedly, she ran back to the car, fighting to unlock the driver's door with fingers that trembled and defied her instruction. She wanted to do as Isabel had instructed, to sit there and wait for her, but how could she with everything else happening all around her? There could be murder going on just a few hundred yards away, there could be something invisible sweeping down off that hill ready to consume her. This place was so very wrong, it wanted death, or something beyond death. Her skin was itching with fear, and with a final look up towards the small wood, which even now seemed to be unnaturally darkening even deeper into shadow, she turned the key in the ignition and reversed back out onto the road, catching the dark copse only once in her rear view mirror, before pressing her foot down hard on the accelerator, and leaving Isabel and the small dark wood behind her.

_____

## EIGHTEEN

## WHAT WAITS BENEATH THE EARTH

Dawn had come and gone, but the heavy canopy overhead seemed almost keen to compete with the night sky just past, so dark was its shade as Isabel made her way beneath it. The petrol cans had doubled their weight as she'd climbed the hill towards the wood, and now with their contents swilling from side to side as she walked, her fingers were beginning to ache painfully with the effort. She'd come here to face her brother, to play her part in the trap that he'd set for her, and although she had seen no sign of him since she'd set foot in his domain, she could still feel the familiar crawl of his sickly gaze upon her skin as though he was somewhere in its midst watching her.

Memories rushed back with sickening clarity as she thought she could hear him whisper her name in the boughs above her head. She could almost feel him trying to take hold of her feet in the undergrowth that moved as she made her progress, and yet she tried to keep her focus ahead of her, always on her purpose. Perhaps Kyle had already guessed her intent, had read her mind or smelt the fumes on the cans, and was even now attempting to reason with her, attempting to persuade her not to murder her own family, her own flesh and blood.

Dark shapes seemed to move and shift in the spaces between the trees, unnatural ethereal formless shapes that defied her scrutiny, and for the first time she dared think that perhaps the evil that moved through these woods was not her brother after all. She'd come here to meet Kyle, to bring this whole nightmare to an end, but it seemed the further she went, the further it was from being over. Kyle obviously did not want an end to it, and nor, it seemed, did whatever presence she could now feel inside the wood. Perhaps she had already lost her brother, she thought as she trod through the undergrowth, perhaps whatever she could feel had already taken him. She swallowed hard as the weight of the cans began to tug her muscles into knots, swallowing her fear down deep into her gut, but it wouldn't go, not all of it. A creeping terror was swiftly taking her over. There was something here with her, and it was not Kyle.

The shapes continued to swirl between the trees, watching her, reaching for the echoes of her movement, and she wanted to cry out and tell them all to stop. She'd come here for her brother, she wanted to confess, nothing more.

But she knew that they wouldn't, or couldn't, listen to her pleas. What if Kyle was amongst these things? What if they had already made him one of their own? How would she recognise him then?

Frantic chills spread across the whole of her body, until the urge to look behind her rose to the point of panic; dark things lurked there too, hugging the trees, kissing the dirt. She needed this to be done with, and done with now.

Isabel suddenly stopped and dropped the cans to the ground with a heavy thud. Quickly she set to, fumbling with the heavy plastic caps with useless fingers and spilling the contents across the thick grey undergrowth all around her. The stench of fumes that drifted up was nauseating, and sought to make her vomit so heavy and acrid were they, but her intention suddenly spread rapidly to the shapes that floated all around her for they became agitated in an instant and started to flit wildly in the shifting uncertain darkness.

Isabel seized the second can and dropped the cap from between her numbed shaking hands. The can felt like a vast slab of rock in her hands and she struggled to tip it as she began her return trek. The fuel spilled wildly as she tried to pour it and run at the same time, but her efforts forced her to slow her escape and she stumbled maddeningly, her feet awkward over every tree stump and root.

The petrol had to be out or else this whole journey would have been wasted. In the car she had planned in her head how she was going to walk a full circle around the wood, dousing the entire perimeter before tossing a match in with casual indifference. But that whole plan had vanished before she had even set foot near the wood. She was here now, and terror had taken her over.

The can dropped from her hands before it was even two-thirds empty, and she half-stumbled backwards with the effort, stretching a hand out to the black earth for support. She tried to go back for the can, but her body rebelled. There was no strength left in it. Her lungs could barely even muster a laboured breath. She was done for.

Tugging the box of matches from her jeans pocket, she started away, but as she did so, the whole wood seemed to cry out with one hoarse shriek. Her fingers scattered the matches at her feet as she jerked open the box, and even as she bent to pick just one of them up, so the wood seemed to reach for her, branches clawing at her hands and face, darkness rising swiftly from the earth as if to smother her.

But she managed to grab just one match through the ghosts that had taken hold of her, and forcing her shaking hands together, struck it hard against the coarse black strip on the side of the box. The stench of fuel had soaked the air like a rag, and as the match sparked, so that air seemed to ignite and blaze like a fierce white cloud.

The touch of the wraiths lifted instantly from her flesh as their screams slashed the fireball that consumed them. In that moment Isabel found her feet and darted blindly away, her eyes clenched shut against the horrors that would soon be coming for her, her arms clamped over her hand to try and protect herself from the fire that had surely already ignited her. The voices shrieked again, howling her name this time, and snatched at her hair and arms, trying to claw her back or rip flesh from her bones in revenge and retaliation. She loosed a single cry as they caught her, but she flailed wildly and spun out of their grasp, but they were not to be so easily defied.

*Isabel*, the wood cried. *Where are you going?*

She threw a half-glance back over her shoulder, through the inferno that had lit everything a furious white, and thought she could make out a single shimmering silhouette of something human standing there as the fire blazed around it.

"Kyle?" she gasped, stumbling against a tree that was already smouldering, and hanging on to it for support.

Her name came again, out of the inferno, but she could still not be sure that it was her brother who was calling her.

*Help me*, it cried. *Come to me.*

Isabel stood frozen for a few seconds as the heat of the fire began to prickle her skin. Perhaps it was him. Perhaps he was in danger. What had she done?

Hesitantly she moved away from the tree, stumbling over branches hidden and beginning to burn in the tangle of undergrowth as she tried to circle around the crackling blaze to where the figure was still standing watching her. She called his name again but he still did not answer, but instead moved away and back into the shadows of the wood.

"Kyle," she cried again, and began to run after him, the sight of him disappearing and reappearing in turns between the burgeoning smoke and the densely packed trees confusing her senses.

But he was elusive, and it became more and more difficult to find him. The fire was growing rapidly, the smoke billowing in great surging clouds, unable to escape through the great heavy canopy of pine needles above her head. Her eyes were stinging, her throat and sinuses burning, but still she managed to stumble a ragged path through the dense undergrowth to where she hoped he would be standing. She continued to call his name, regretting now her intent of burning the entire wood to the ground, hoping that he would still be alive, that they might both still stand a chance of escaping this place intact.

Then the smoke thinned a little, and she looked up to see that she was now standing in a narrow hollow bounded on each side by steep earth and heavy trees. She glanced quickly behind her and saw the fire still raging between the trees, before returning her gaze to the hollow. But something was wrong here. It almost seemed as though she had been led here, and not by Kyle either. And then she realised why this place felt so bad. It was silent and it was dank, and there was almost an oppressive weight in the air that tried to push her down into the ground. She wanted to shake off this sudden weight, that now she had discovered it, seemed to be building into something far heavier. It wanted to drag the clothes off her back, drag the hair out of her scalp, to rip her meat from her bones and haul her right down into Hell with it.

She wanted to take a step back, a single step away from this horrible chasm, but even that had been robbed of her now. She stood in the silent dank hollow unable to move as the fire crackled and hissed at her back, and then the shadow creatures caught sight of her once again and came swiftly through the burning trees to catch up with her.

The wood seemed almost to lift a veil, allowing her to see down into its secret heart, and there amongst the rotting black earth was a far deeper hollow that went straight down into the ground.

Her terror seemed almost to crush her heart in that moment, as it felt as though she was standing at the very edge of some bottomless void. Her feet had not been able to move her backwards, but they began to move now, and not with her own will. With a short shuffle forward, the wood drew her slowly towards its core. Her lips quivered as if to refuse, but her second step had already been taken for her, the third coming immediately after. Her momentum picked up as she suddenly began to panic, and as she shot a glance up at the trees that seemed almost to lean towards her, she could see the faceless shapes of the dark creatures hanging from their twisted branches, vilifying her, goading her to become one of them.

At the threshold to the abyss, her eyes began to make sense of the blackness there, and far from being nothing, she could see a rough stairwell cut into the ground that led down into a chasm beneath the trees of the wood. Cold air rose in stale breaths from that place, lifting the hair from her face like ghostly hands, and she slowly she found herself descending into its depths, its chill replacing the heat of her fire-blackened skin.

The wraiths were eager to seal her inside, and before she could turn and catch one last sight of the partial daylight, they had clamoured to cover the opening, stealing any hope of escape with their veil-like forms. The blackness inside became total, and she stumbled forward now under her own weight, her hands out before her to feel whatever way she was being taken. Whatever had brought her down here still had partial control of her movement, she could still feel the crawl of its presence on her flesh, as though it had already begun to burrow there, but where else could she go now but on? There was no going back.

The dank fetid air of the underground tomb clung to her skin like wet rags, and strange shapes began to contort in the swirling blackness ahead of her, beckoning her forward. But as her eyes continued to struggle to make sense of what little there was to see, a pale luminescence seemed almost to seep out of the earth from somewhere up ahead.

The murky route turned a ragged corner in the rough-hewn passage, and then led down even deeper into the ground, but still the luminescence lit her way.

Then it widened and ushered her out into a low-ceilinged chamber, as heavily laced with tree roots as the route that had brought her here, only at its far end stood a monstrous slope of broken and cracked rock.

The tree roots forced their thick veins and tendrils down between the slabs and crevices of the dominating wall, but there was more here than just roots and tree bark. Most of the rock's surface was alive with dank greenery, moss and lichen, tree bark and leaves, but the rest of the chamber festered with rot and ruin. Her eyes searched the heavy shadows that hung between the leaves and the moss, wondering why this hulking mass should even be down here, or why she had even been brought down to this godforsaken place. But as she gazed at this thing, so she felt the weight of the presence inside the wood return, felt too its unspoken voice not upon the fetid air but somewhere inside her head, murmuring her name. And then she saw its eyes, bulbous and black, returning her stare from the depths of the dark stone.

Her eyes sought out the rest of its shape now, its arms and its legs, she couldn't help it, and once it had started there was stopping the act. She found the rest of its face, disfigured by tree roots and rock, gazing out from its sickening prison. A grin of broken teeth parted as if to speak, but then closed silently. Jagged claws hung from the end of a branch just inches from her face, curved and crooked, but they made no move to tear at her, or even drag her closer to this living monstrosity.

Although mostly humanoid in shape, moss and lichen covered most of its crippled body, but had it not been for the uncertainty of her own eyes in the ill light, she might have sworn that it made its body. A mass of heavy roots circled its contorted legs and lower torso in thick muddied knots, restricting it so that it was surely impossible to move, its arm splayed out to its sides mimicking Jesus on the cross.

It tried to make an awkward move towards her, the vines of its legs partially ravelling and unravelling like sinuous muscle, as it tried to speak inside her head once again. But Isabel could already feel her mind beginning to detach, as though her sanity was slipping away from her. She could see its eyes watching her intently, glistening and old from the depths of its shadowed cell. She staggered back a step, her head becoming light as though she was going to fall, and then the creature let out a ghastly inhale of concern. Its arm tensed as if to reach for her, its tendrilled claws clenching, but Isabel managed to keep herself upright for just one moment longer, to keep herself away from its clutching grasp.

Then the bark that covered much of its face splintered to reveal a hideous gaping maw of broken and yellowed teeth worn down to nubs, as hellish words began to tumble from its raw cracked lips like rocks caught in a landslide.

*Isabel.*

Its voice rasped awkwardly, and as her sanity slipped altogether and she collapsed to the cold black earth, she only barely comprehended its sentence before her consciousness went from her altogether.

*You've.*

*Come.*

*For.*

*Me.*

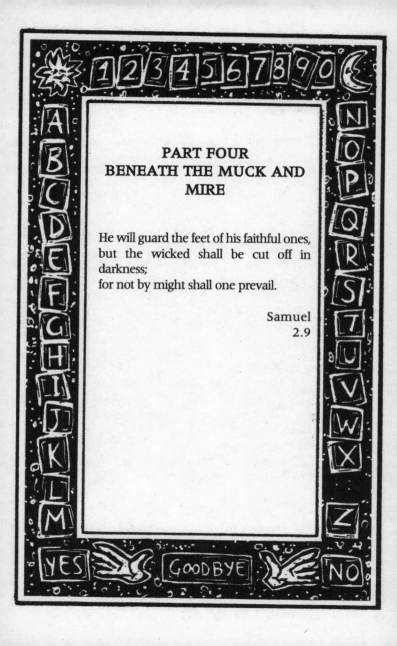

# PART FOUR
## BENEATH THE MUCK AND MIRE

He will guard the feet of his faithful ones,
but the wicked shall be cut off in
darkness;
for not by might shall one prevail.

Samuel
2.9

## PART FOUR

## BENEATH THE MUCK AND MIRE

# ONE

---

## VIEW FROM THE WOOD

To be back in the wood again, that was all that had dominated Kyle's thoughts more than anything else. To stand at the treeline and see sights that had not changed since he'd been a boy overwhelmed him more than he would have thought possible; the fields stretching to the horizon, the trees that crested their peaks and troughs, the cottages and farms and even the village itself, none of it seemed to have changed at all. It was as though the last twenty years had never happened, as though nothing had found its potential. Except for him. He had evolved into something far beyond normal, far beyond greatness. He had felt things surge through him that no one else had ever felt. The common man was beneath him, a puppet, something to destroy at will if he so chose. And as for everything else? It was all a canvas for him to paint upon, clay for him to mould, a populace for him to rule over.

It was getting close to seven, and Isabel had not shown herself. He was sure, after his run-in with their mother, that she would come. She had to. When it all came down to it, there was just the two of them. They shared some kind of influence, some kind of altering

243

what was natural, simply by their will. Isabel had abused that, had kept their lying mother alive. But he would use it properly, he would heal the hurt that he had done to Emily, and put right what he had done wrong at the start of it all.

A smirk had edged into the corner of his mouth as he'd thought about his sister. He'd thought that as she'd be coming here to face him, he should have something special prepared for her, some example of what he could do in case she resisted him. An image then emerged out of the darkness of his childhood memory, of playing with Isabel near the shed at the end of the garden. A rat had appeared out of the long grass and she'd screamed with irrational terror, tugging at her own hair in a fit that must've hurt immeasurably. He'd watched bemused for a few moments as she'd simply stood there bawling at the top of her lungs. He'd smirked then, he recalled. His sister had always been weak.

It had not been easy to find a rat so far from its food source around the barns and farm buildings where they had flourished wildly but he'd found one nesting amongst a litter of dry leaves and grasses less than fifty yards into the wood. It was fat and long, and its teeth had found the flesh of his hand twice, opening deep needle cuts that had dripped blood in copious amounts across the fabric of his jeans. But he'd had plans for that rat, such important plans that made the game with Isabel almost joyless, but he would take his pleasures where he could, and craft the vermin into a messenger. Not everything had gone as he'd expected, and his plans had needed to be changed. Complications had arisen, and he'd seen to them. This was just something to break the tension, and to kill time until his sister showed herself.

His memory conjured another image of its own accord and it placed itself inside his head before he could stop it; his father alive and walking, somewhere in this very wood around him. It came with such speed and intensity that it almost felt as though he was right there beside him. But he tried to placate it, to force it back into the pit of his head where it belonged, and yet parts of that memory would not be gotten rid of so readily.

With the notion planted, Kyle suddenly wanted to surrender his plans with Isabel and go and look for him, to try and find him as though he was still wandering lost somewhere in the small wood, but something was holding him back. He wouldn't be the same, he thought to himself, he'd be different, so very different if only because he'd be older, and he almost hated him for that. Where was the father who had walked with him through this very wood? Where was the father who had told him about the birds and the animals? If ever he found him again, he'd know that he was not that man, even if he named himself, because he had robbed him of twenty years of his existence. He wanted him back, more than anything, but that was beyond anything that flowed through his veins.

He placed his hands across the warm body of the rat and felt the rhythm of its blood as it thudded around its frame. It struggled for its freedom but Kyle had it now, and even as he pressed his fingertips deeper into its sides, he could feel the creak of its ribs. Twenty years ago he would have kept up the pressure until those ribs broke, just to see what would happen, but he'd grown up in that time, matured through exploration and experimentation, and he didn't need to see what would happen. And besides, he reasoned idly, he already knew what pumped and pulsed deep inside its grey jacket.

He could almost hear his father's voice still echoing around the tall dark trees behind him, and it sent a shiver down his spine. The urge grew quickly to look over his shoulder, a childish urge, but he gave into it all the same. His eyes tracked through the shadows of the wood, between the trees and across the undergrowth, in a slow spanning arc, but there was no one there, no one human anyway. He'd skipped town, that was the truth that he couldn't admit to. He knew it as much as anyone, but he just couldn't stand to admit it. He turned back and closed his eyes, listening to his own blood pump around inside his head as the rat continued to struggle inside his grasp.

Other images came into his head, taking over from what hazy memories he had of his father; this was what he knew best. He saw a leaf nest, a litter of tiny twitching rodents, pink and new-born, and a darkness of dry leaves and grasses that covered them all. He saw roots and black earth, and felt panic and terror as a looming monolith towered over it suddenly. This was the rat's memory of him, of course, and as Kyle moved his bloodied hands slowly across the ridged curve of it back and then nearer the base of its skull, so the rat's sight altered to the present - the weave of his jacket, the view of the wood just yards ahead of him. Soon it would become the messenger between human siblings; *oh yes sister, your brother will be reaching out for you soon, and he will want what you have abused.*

Kyle's eyes opened and gazed down at the rat, its body shuddering from the assault he had put upon its mind, and stroked the creature almost lovingly. The blood that it had drawn from him had clotted into raw scabs that cracked open as he moved, but he coaxed it

246

all the same, setting it down gently on the ground and watching as it stood dazed for a few moments before scurrying swiftly into the undergrowth and out of sight.

Glancing back up, Kyle heaved a sigh of weariness at the time it was taking for his sister to appear. He had no watch but he guessed that it must be close to seven. Did she not realise what was at stake? Did she not realise that if he went back and found their mother, which he would do if she gave him no choice, that he would cut her even more? He knew that he couldn't kill her, not with Isabel's magic sustaining her, but he could work some evil of his own upon her, take something apart inside her, force something else in; there was plenty that he could do.

His sight wandered absently as he plotted his deeds inside his head, but his focus suddenly became sparked as his eyes settled upon the farm buildings that he'd gazed down at so many times as a boy.

It was as though nothing had changed, and he was suddenly that same ten year old boy looking out over the fields with wonder and curiosity. But then his thoughts began to change, as though a cloud had formed somewhere in the cortex of his brain and was casting grim shadows across them, as he remembered old man Oates who had lived there, and what he had done to him.

That old man had been Emily's father, of course, and he had slapped him. Kyle couldn't remember the pain, but he could remember how he had felt, and how he had sworn revenge at the time. Having not been home in years, that vengeance had gone unfulfilled, but he was back now, and he had time on his hands. He glanced up briefly to the angular shape of a crow perched up on one of the branches above his head, its inky black feathers glinting like broken glass in the partial sunlight that managed to break the canopy, and moved his sight in behind its eyes. From such a height, he could make out the farm buildings more clearly, and with one final thought about the lateness of his sister's arrival, he launched the crow into the sky and watched the ground disappear far beneath him.

## 2

Eric Oates pulled the farmhouse door slowly open, the old hinges creaking with effort, and laid eyes on the face of his daughter. It took a few moments for the recognition to sink in, Emily not offering him any help, but simply standing there with her hands crossed in front of her, a tentative smile etched upon her face.

"Emily?" he finally asked, taking a step out into the sunlight. "Is that you?"

"Yes, Dad," she told him. "It's me."

The old man gaped, still not willing to believe that his daughter had returned after so many years away. She was well, it seemed, and pretty, and had the eyes of her mother, and oh it was grand to have her back on the farm again. He beckoned her eagerly over the threshold, coaxing her lovingly with one arm crooked around her waist, closing the door behind her before ushering her through into the kitchen.

"Have a cup of tea," he said to her, pulling a chair out for her at the table. "You do drink tea, do you?"

"Yes, dad. I do drink tea."

Oates set to, testing the weight of the kettle before placing it on the stove, giving her a curious glance as he pulled down two mugs from the cupboard in the corner of the room - as though perhaps she might not still be there if he didn't - and continued to give her uneasy glances as he took out tea bags from the larder and milk from the fridge. There was a look about her, he thought, a look she'd had shortly before she left. It hadn't been there when she was younger, and just started about the time the Rider boy went crazy.

"How have you been?" Emily asked him, as he set a packet of biscuits down neatly in front of her.

"The sheep can only look after themselves so much," he said, a wavering smile on his lips.

"It must be hard without help."

"Always was, always will be, that's the nature of things. Was why I chose it, coming out here with your mother."

"You wanted me born and raised in the country, didn't you?"

"That was the thing."

"And I never resented it," she commented with a tentative smile of her own.

Oates looked at her, not sure what to say to her. He mumbled something about the tea and went to keep a look at the kettle on the stove.

He could feel the weight of his daughter's gaze on his back, and because of her sudden reappearance, expected the questions that were likely to come. This wasn't a casual visit, he was smart enough to know that. There had been some weird things going on for some time, most of it, if not all, linked with that fucked up little Rider kid. His father had been a godsend at a time when he'd needed help on a new and growing farm, but the boy had always been bad news, and once he had finally taken his sick little mind away the whole place had settled down somewhat. Not totally, there were always some odd things going on one way or another - disturbances, noises, animals born with defects, and some right terrible happenings in the village itself - but it had all gotten better once he'd left.

"I came back with Isabel," Emily told him, hoping that he would turn round and look at her.

"Yes?" he said noncommittally.

"We both came back because of Kyle."

Her father said nothing this time, just continued labouring over the two mugs.

"Isabel's brother," she prompted.

"I know who he is," her father said, half turning. His eyes would still not fix on her, but hovered in an uncertain limbo between the two of them.

Emily pushed her chair back and got to her feet now.

"We have to have this conversation," she demanded. "You know that we have to have it out."

"Have what -"

"The secrets, the lies, the whole shit that pulled us all apart."

His eyes must have settled upon every damn surface in that kitchen until they finally settled upon her, his only daughter, and she looked so beautiful and perfect standing there in his house after so many years away. He could feel tears starting to well, tears of joy and of guilt, but he knew that this wasn't the time for weakness. He should have told her the truth years ago. But when had been the right time? When had she been old enough? He could have told her, but she would have left all the sooner.

"Dad, I'm waiting."

Oates picked up the kettle as it began to boil and came away from the stove. Steam rose in eager plumes around him as he poured boiling water into the two mugs. After setting the kettle down on the table away from them he took a seat, heaving a long breath as he began to stir the tea in slow lingering circles.

"Michael Rider disappeared, that's all most people knew of. There was gossip, and wild rumours from some of the womenfolk, but no one knew the truth, not even me - at first." He set the tarnished silver spoon down carefully and gazed down into the swirling tea, the brown lines turning in a hypnotic vortex. "I learned more than most about what had happened, but not for a while afterwards, not until the girl and the mother disappeared too."

"But how?"

"Cassandra Craif."

"Isabel's aunt?"

"She was distraught that her family had left her. And without warning too. I know what that was like."

Oates glanced up to see if his daughter's mask would break, but there was no trace of guilt, no sign of her knowing what his loneliness had been like.

"And you met her?" was all she said.

"It's a small village," Oates conceded. "Everyone kind of knows everyone else, them and their business. Sometimes without even meeting." He took up his mug and took a slow noisy sip. "We got to talking. About family, about losing them. About Kyle."

Emily physically stiffened in her seat. Oates noticed but said nothing.

"You want the meat of the story," he went on, "but I really don't know how to tell it."

"Try, dad," Emily said. "I need to know."

He took another sip of tea and then set the mug down.

"Call it what you like," he said. "Witchcraft. Demons. Magic. Voodoo. Take your pick of the names,

251

Emily, because it's all part of the same thing, and that thing is evil. Something claimed and took over the soul of Michael Rider one night and it changed him. Not overnight, but slow, and what it did to him, it took out of poor Irene." He picked up his mug again, stared at it for a moment and then set it back down. "I remember seeing her one day through the window and she looked like death in a shawl. I knew what she looked liked before, a healthy young woman when she first moved here, and to see her like that scared the hell out of me. When she was alive and living in the cottage I only knew what the rest of the town knew, that she was sick. But once Cassandra and me got friendly, she told me the truth, and I was scared in a way like I've never been scared before. And that ain't no shit neither."

He stopped for a moment, a clammy sweat broken on his brow, but more concerned that he had said shit in front of his daughter. There were a few uneasy seconds, and then Emily spoke.

"Kyle was evil, wasn't he?"

Oates stared at her.

"There was something almost beyond evil in that kid. As though his head was vacant, nothing, just a double zero behind his eyes."

"His head wasn't vacant, dad. He had intentions in there."

Oates swallowed. He didn't want to know what intentions that sick little fuck had had for his daughter. He'd wanted to bash his skull in, to wipe that vacancy, that *evil*, out of the world for good. But the guilt had always crept over him, had crawled over him, like bugs in a grave. That boy had been a kid after all, and he wasn't no kid killer.

"There was something in those woods up on the

hill," he went on, "something evil, something that lived in the shadows. Michael Rider found it and it done a number on him. Whatever it was, it unleashed itself upon him and his family."

He looked at his daughter's expression, at her forehead knotted like the boards of an old barn. He didn't want to be telling her any of this, but she'd pried because she knew something, because she knew Isabel, and knowing not to be around this place was the best advice he could give her. At least by scaring her as Cassandra Craif had scared him, she might get out of the village and not come back. As for him, this was his home; he had nowhere else to go.

"She was a witch, Emily," he explained, as he got to his feet and went to the window. "You probably didn't know about that, but that's the truth. A lot of people will tell you there ain't no such thing, and I'd probably have been amongst them, but that woman knowed some things, she'd said a lot of weird things, and I believed that she believed."

He heard his daughter murmur something but he didn't catch what. Truth be known, he didn't want to know either. He turned now to gaze out through the small kitchen window to the back lawn that ran out onto the yard, hulking black-tar barns circumscribing it on three sides. There was no wind today and the sky was fairly clear, he thought, the words coming crazily into his head; good weather for a change.

"Perhaps something could have been done in time if Cassandra had known about what had happened to Isabel's father."

"But she didn't know," Oates told her. "Not until later. Not until it was too late."

"Too late for what?" she asked.

He could see the cattle moving about between the

253

rusted gates of the first barn. He needed to fix the fence in the top paddock before they could go out again. A trip to Sloane's for more barbed wire. More tacks too.

"Too late for what?" she asked again.

His lips were pressed tight. It had come down to it at last, the truth, the meat of the story.

*"Dad,"* she pressed. *"Too late for what?"*

"The evil that possessed Michael Rider," he told her, "went through him and into the boy. Through his seed."

Emily's fingers went to her mouth. He could see the shakes in them.

"But it gets worse," he said, under his breath. "The boy got her."

"What do you mean, got her?"

"Cassandra. Not the official report. They said it was suicide. But I know better."

One of the silver birch trees began to sway outside as a sudden gust passed across the fields, the tones of the leaves shifting as they turned on the branches, grey and white, grey and white, as though the tree was glimmering with a lucid monochrome fire. Something else shifted inside its swirling shape, something dark like a hole in the world, something dark against the light of the glimmering leaf-flames.

Oates could see the crow fold its wings back deftly into its body. Its hard black eyes suddenly found him through the glass of the kitchen window, returning his stare, and for a moment it seemed as though it had been following their conversation. With an eerie chill passing across his flesh, Oates turned to look back at his daughter still sitting at the kitchen table.

"You're here to tell me it's not over, aren't you?" he said, and watched helplessly as her wide eyed gave him his answer.

His eyes had been closed when he'd entered the skull of the crow, and they were closed now as he watched the old man stare out through the paint-peeled windows of his cottage, trapped inside like some pathetic prisoner. Kyle knew that he saw him, and it gave him joy to see the old man emerge from his home, shaking his fists and cursing his name. Sensing that the crow wanted to take flight, he kept it where it was, and waited until the old man was out of safety of retreat back to the cottage before he swooped down and set upon him.

The echoes of the wood distracted him as the crow began ripping at the old man's throat - the wind in the canopy overhead seemed almost to whisper his name, the touch of its breath trying to clasp his hand and coax him back to its shadowed haunts - but he forced his attention back to what was of greater importance, and took glee in seeing with the crow's eyes more of the old man's blood drawn to the surface of his withered grey flesh.

But then the images that came into his head suddenly became disjointed, flashes of livid colours splattering across the backs of his eyes, confusing him, almost dazing him as it bludgeoned the insides of his skull. It berated him to the point where he might almost have lost consciousness, and yet he so desperately wanted to hurt this old fool, wanted to cause him pain, wanted to rip the flesh from his bones until either he or the crow was destroyed.

But the old man had seemed weak, and to see the crow flail so brutally and so unexpectedly caused him great concern. And then he caught sight of another body through the flashes of bruised colours, an extra set of hands that clawed at the creature he controlled. So intense was his scrutiny upon him inside his own home that he hadn't even noticed if he'd been alone. But he now wanted to savage this interloper, wanted to tear at their hands as they in turn sought to take hold of the crow and destroy it.

But in the midst of that maelstrom that was playing out in his head he suddenly saw a face, a woman's face, and he stopped instantly as his heart froze. It was Emily.

It was in that moment that his sight went altogether - the old man, Emily, everything - as though he'd been punched hard from the inside of his head. The blow jarred his thoughts, sending them into a dark chaos, and his blood suddenly thudded loudly, smothering the rest of his senses. It was clear that the crow had been struck or even killed, the attack upon it severing the connection between it and himself. His eyes flickered open as his head jerked wildly, and he reached both hands out blindly to try and keep himself upright as he staggered close to unconsciousness. His fingers went numb, so that he was not even sure if he was keeping himself steady, and his legs threatened to buckle and cast him down into the black dirt. But through it all he somehow managed to struggle to focus on the realisation that he was sure he'd seen. Emily was here. She was home.

He staggered to his feet, his thoughts uncertain and caught somewhere between confusion and delirium. Could it be possible that she was here, once again at home? Yes, yes it was. There she was. She had come after him, to be with him.

His eyes settled on the ground in front of him, focussing on the leaf litter that he had disturbed with his feet. A furious ache had settled somewhere in his brain, buzzing inside his thoughts like a hive of angry bees, and he clamped both hands to his head as if to clamp his skull and deaden it.

His eyes parted between fingers soiled with muck and grime as he took a step towards the treeline, finding the route that he'd used to go down to the farm that had been her home. He had taken that route more times than he could remember, and without another thought, he started off again now with his head still held inside his hands, hoping that she would still be there waiting for him when he arrived.

His memory placed pictures of her behind his eyes as he went, photographs taken from galleries he'd made for her in his imagination, some blurred and creased at the edges, some sharply focussed as though they'd just be taken, but all placed there lovingly and with a knowledge that they would both be together again one day.

And then a snatch of Emily's father lying on the ground, clutching a bloodied hand to his chest, pounded its way into his head, and shattered the tranquillity that had descended around his remembered pictures.

The crow was still alive, still broadcasting sights back from the farm that he was now heading towards. A grin of pleasure parted his lips, replacing the loving smile that had been there, as he saw the old man in agony once again. But then he saw Emily bent over at his side, looking directly back at him, an expression of horror pinching her beautiful face in half as she stared aghast at the crow.

But the bird was dying, Kyle could feel it struggling for life, but he urged it with what fleeting influence he had left inside it to hang on, to keep its black eyes focussed on his beloved Emily.

But the darkness beyond its vision was rapidly becoming more and more insistent, waning one moment, clearing the next. The crow's strength was diminishing swiftly now, and any hope he had of keeping this vision of her suddenly went altogether. Kyle had one last fleeting glimpse of Emily's distraught expression before the sight went altogether, and then he was left alone with his own view of the farm spreading out before him.

## 4

In the middle of the garden sprawled her father, a much older frail-looking man on his back, his limbs held in useless defence against the dusky whirlwind of black feathers beside him, of the crow that was still shuddering with its last rhythms of life. The huge creature had savaged him without mercy or respite, its vast black beak snapping at his face as its great claws had sought to rip at his throat. He had barely been able to get a hold on the monstrous black bird to drag it off him, so furious was its unrelenting assault, and he had only been able to try and shield his eyes from this thing as it tore and gouged at his flesh.

His face was running with free-flowing blood. The crow's caws had been shrill and piercing, and she had staggered dumbfounded for a handful of horrible seconds, not knowing what to do, before she'd finally taken hold of it and fought it off. The bird had lunged at her once, then twice, scoring savage blows that had brought blood welling to vicious wounds on her hands and forearms. She'd looked round quickly, hoping to find any kind of weapon to fight it off with, but there had been nothing within easy reach. The farmyard itself was at least a hundred yards away, the kitchen less than thirty, and she had turned awkwardly on the spot with a whirling mind. What should she get - a knife, a chair? What should she get to beat this thing back with?

But she had only gotten half way back to the kitchen when her frantic eyes had fallen upon a handful of gardening tools, a fork and spade, a trowel, a set of shears, but it was the nearest thing to her, leaning against the wall by the back door that her hands had fallen upon first.

The metal-ended rake had been surprisingly light in her hands as she'd turned back to the melee still raging in the middle of the garden, her father with a wing held violently in one of his clenched fists, holding it as far away from him as possible. Emily's dash had turned into a panicking lunge, and as she'd swung her weight forward, the rake had come down in a swift arc, and before she was even conscious of what she was doing, the metal prongs had found the meat of the crow, spearing it squarely and sending it earthward on the end of the rake in a shower of scarlet blood and shrieking pain.

The weight of the rake unbalanced her as it went back up, and it slipped from her hands, the momentum of its arc taking it soaring to the back of the garden where it landed amongst the flower border. Two vast black wings pounded the colourful blossoms as the bird writhed in agony, its movements constricted by the rake that had skewered it so utterly. Its beak snapped wildly at the air, piercing cries splitting the air so horribly that Emily had to clamp her hands to her head in order to block out its sickening din.

Oates tried to lurch into a sitting position as he held his hands to the deep wounds at his chest.

Coughing violently as he glanced over at the creature - to see if it was dying or preparing itself to come at him again Emily didn't know - he tried to push himself to his feet. But his legs trembled and wouldn't hold his weight, and even as Emily stooped to take hold of his arm to steady him, Oates nearly tumbled back to the ground.

Her eyes went back now to the horrific bird still clawing feebly at the rake that still impaled its frame, as she struggled to support the weight of her father. That bird, that *creature*... to attack a human being like that just couldn't happen.

And then a word popped into her head.

A single name.

Kyle.

"It's already started," her father suddenly rasped, swallowing his terror with deep gulps, his tongue raking across lips as dry as old corn husks. "I can see the boy in its eyes."

Emily tried to hush him, tried to coax his gaze back to hers, but his focus was fierce and wouldn't be swayed from the crow, even as its writhing began to slow to awkward jerks.

"It's the Rider boy," he went on, forcing breaths down into his lungs. "He's back, isn't he? He's here."

"Dad, please -"

His eyes came back to her, intense and wild.

"Kyle Rider," he said, the name seemed almost to physically slap her now that he'd voiced it. "He's back, isn't he? He's sent one of his creatures to kill me."

"There's something in those woods, you said it yourself. It's making him worse. Cassandra knew that."

"What do you know about Cassandra Craif?" her father suddenly demanded to know.

260

There was a tremulous silence after that as the two of them stared at each other. There were secrets here, secrets that were slowly being called like bluffed cards, and Emily only knew the ones in her hand. He'd hinted at things earlier, but now it seemed to run deeper.

"You were up to something with Isabel's aunt," Emily said to him.

"You too it would seem," he said back to her.

He coughed suddenly and doubled in pain, and whatever else that could have been exchanged between them evaporated.

Forcing an arm underneath his shoulder, Emily heaved him awkwardly to his feet before attempting to help him back inside. At least with the door closed behind them, they might be safe from whatever else Kyle might decide to send down from the wood. In the mean time, she would bandage her father's wounds as best she could, drive him to a hospital, but then she'd have to get out of there for a while and try and get some clarity back into her thoughts, somewhere well away from the farm and all the ghosts that haunted its darkest corners.

# TWO

## THINGS THAT CRAWL AND BURROW

With his view of the back of the farm cottage now gone, Kyle picked up his pace, knowing that only he could resolve Emily's pain. As a boy, this well-worn path had taken him thirty minutes to traverse, and now as an adult he didn't think he'd be shaving any significant time off that. But he lengthened his stride regardless and ran until his sides began to ache. He wanted to see Emily now that she was so close, both of them back home once again amongst familiar surroundings, to see her with his own eyes and to smell the sweet fragrance of her hair and skin. He wanted to heal her pain, to take that creased expression from her perfect face and cleanse her like he had wanted to all those years ago. This was his chance, he knew that more than anything, and he wanted only that chance to prove it to her, and to prove to himself that he didn't need his sister's magic; his powers were enough.

When he finally came into view of the cottage and could see the back of it with his own eyes, it was clear that the place was deserted. Kyle slowed his pace as he entered the main yard, the sounds of the animals in the stalls quietening at his approach as if his very presence had become a legend amongst them, their ancestors passing on word of a monster before they themselves had gone off for slaughter. But they were not his target today, and he barely even noticed them as they seemed to shrink back away from the dull metal bars that kept them in. Instead he made his way back round towards the farm cottage, to the back door which now stood closed, his eyes straining to make out anything through the murk inside, his ears sifting the differing sounds of the wind through the trees, the birds overhead, the mice in the hedgerow.

He stood at the back door, his eyes now closed, as he passed his thoughts into the house. There were spiders inside, looking down from webs constructed across light fittings and in corners of infrequently-used rooms. Houseflies buzzed behind closed windows and moths still trapped from the previous night's search for electric light hung from ceilings with their wings folded back. Kyle searched the rooms of the house from behind the eyes of each one in turn, scanning every darkened corner from every different view, in search of his beloved Emily.

The bedrooms were quiet but the kitchen was warm, the air still agitated from where it had been disturbed earlier. But in the front room, where he looked back from a fly now settled upon a grimy window sill, he made out the familiar shape of her father lying back on the sofa as he clutched a bloodied rag to his chest. His soiled scarlet shirt was open and it was difficult to make out the extent of his wounds, but blood had at least been drawn, and copiously.

Kyle grinned mischievously as he sent the fly off the window sill towards him, buzzing round the old man's head so that he had to lift his hands to shoo it away. The pain such agitated movement caused him was clear, his gnarled face creasing as he pulled his hands back to the wounds on his chest that had reopened, and the intruder chuckled with silent mirth about what he could do without really trying.

Kyle opened his eyes now and took hold of the handle of the back door, turning it slowly and quietly as he let himself in to Eric Oates' home. He could smell the old man's blood now with his own senses, could taste it strong on the back of his tongue, but there was no sign of Emily herself. It seemed certain that she had gone.

He wasn't even sure, but he thought he could smell the old man's pain too, viscous and heady, and he made his way towards him now, navigating effortlessly from room to room using the map the spiders and the houseflies had given him from their vantage points overhead, until he stood in the shadowed doorway of the front room and looked down upon Eric Oates with his own eyes for the first time in over twenty years.

His contempt resurfaced more quickly and more readily than he would have thought possible, as the memories came back to him of how this old man had struck him as a child. His teeth ground together as his nose curled with a rabid snarl, and he knew then how much he wanted to cut him open, to see how much he could really make him bleed.

He took a step towards him, and saw Oates lift his head slightly, more from the motion than from the sound of his silent foot upon the threadbare carpet. Kyle wished that he had a weapon, wished that he'd picked up a knife from the kitchen on his way through so that he could just put its edge to the old man's throat and pull it across. That would be easy, to slide a knife across his throat and walk away. But then the face of Emily came back into his head, a remembered smile upon her lips, and he held his desires back. He knew there would have to be conversation first.

"Hurts, does it?" he said lightly, as he moved closer to the old farmer.

Oates turned startled in his seat, his arms flailing to pull himself upright so that he could see this intruder's face. But the swiftness of the motion tore his wounds back open and he creased back into the sofa in agony.

"I wouldn't even bother," Kyle said to him. "You might have been able to lay your hands on a child but you'd never get the best of me now."

He saw Oates turn his head this time, his eyes narrowing to make out his face in the murk of the room. It was clear he didn't recognise him at first, but then horror crept slowly across his face like maggots on a corpse, as his jaw dropped open to silently mouth his name.

"So you do remember then?" Kyle asked, walking round so that they could face each other. "Pretty tough against a kid. Not so tough now though, huh?"

Oates was all eyes and threaded spittle. There was nothing he could do to defend himself, it was clear that they both knew that.

"I don't want to be here any longer than I have to," Kyle began, "so if you just tell me where Emily has gone, I'll be on my way."

"Emily?" Oates mouthed breathlessly.

Kyle rolled his eyes impatiently.

"Yes, Emily, your fucking daughter. You know damn well what I'm talking about. Where is she? I want to know."

Oates stammered, his eyes growing even wider.

"I... I don't know -"

"Don't be starting that shit, you old fucker. I know she was here and you know how I know that, don't you? So just tell me and save yourself a whole lot of pain."

The old man's mouth closed, his eyes just staring, wild and white.

"You know it's coming, don't you? You can't be lying there thinking you haven't got it coming."

"Please..."

"Oh, you're not going to beg now, surely."

"No," he said hoarsely, "I was going to tell you to go fuck yourself. You always were a sick little bastard -"

"Now that ain't going to help you none, now is it?"

"Do your worst. I ain't telling you shit."

Kyle could feel his jaw muscles tense, acid beginning to burn at the back of his throat. He tried to remember Emily's smile, tried to tell himself just how important she was. This old fucker was no good to him dead, at least not until he'd told him where she was.

"Did I ever tell you what I used to do on your farm all those years ago?" Kyle started.

"Yeah, I knew, you sick little fuck. I found what you left behind."

"You couldn't have found all the bodies, surely. You probably found some of the lambs I'd turned inside out, some of the calves I'd cut open. But there were others. Your cat for one."

"Rags?"

"I seem to remember that's what it said on his little blue collar."

"You bastard, I'll kill you," he lurched forward awkwardly, but the attack was useless from the start and Kyle simply lunged forward with his foot and kicked him squarely in the chest, forcing him back hard into the sofa.

"That cat squealed quite a bit, I can tell you, squealed as I pulled the fur off its back."

The old man was gnashing his teeth, his face a mask of agony and fury.

"Terrible sounds from such a small delicate creature," Kyle went on. "And it wasn't a tom for long either."

Oates was spitting his hatred at him now, but Kyle was not done with him, not by a long way.

"Your horse didn't last long either, did it?"

Something snapped inside the old man's body at this, Kyle could almost hear it, as his heart broke in two, his rage folding. Tears glistened at the corners of his eyes and he knew that he'd hit home.

"Yeah, that thing burned from the inside out. Cooked itself like a steak."

"You little... *fucker*," the old man's voice was little more than a whisper, like the frail mew that Rags had let slip before its tiny heart had beat its last.

"Tell me where she is," Kyle demanded. "That's all I want."

But Oates' eyes had fallen now. He was lost somewhere inside his own head.

"Tell me," Kyle yelled, but it was clear that the old man had gone.

And then he felt the presence of a spider in the far corner of the room knitting its silk, and an idea crawled into his head with the same speed as its blotchy legs.

His sight disappeared back inside his skull as he now began to search out all the insects of the room, particularly the spiders. He found them too, most of them small, and he called them all out of their dusty hiding places and darkened homes, and urged them all to congregate at the sofa. He heard the old man mutter

267

something about what he was doing, why his eyes had glazed like they had, but he ignored him. He'd find out soon enough. But it would be sooner than he thought.

Oates let out a frail shriek as the first of the spiders crawled over his bloodied hands. Kyle opened his eyes now and watched as his soldiers did their work. Oates was scrabbling at them now, trying to brush them away as one by one they crested the top of the sofa or rose up from between the cushions, finding their way inside his trousers and shirt. He was screaming now as, not content with being on the surface of his skin, they hungered to move beneath it.

Searching out his ears and nostrils was not enough, they were soon swarming across his chest and belly to his open wounds, crawling beneath his fingers and beneath his torn flesh. He was crying out for them to stop, crying out for Kyle to *please stop them*, his fingertips tearing at them, opening his wounds even further, tearing open his own flesh.

After a few moments of watching the old man's blood flow like hot treacle down the sides of his chest, soaking the fabric of the sofa, he called the spiders to a halt. Their rickety legs stopped in an instant, their blotchy bodies heaving with the momentary respite, eager to continue and bury their way deeper inside the old man's body.

"Should I ask you again?" Kyle said quietly.

Oates was shaking badly, his fingers hooked above his body like claws and trembling as though it was fifty degrees below. His eyes were wide and wild and gouged the air as he stared down at his chest awash with a sea of blood, filled with the bodies of at least a hundred different spiders.

"Should I ask you again?" Kyle repeated impatiently.

"No..." Oates managed to utter, his teeth rattling in his head like stones in an old clay pot. He couldn't take his eyes off the spiders in case they started to burrow into his body again. "I... I don't know where she went," he gasped.

"Now we've been here before..."

One of the spiders suddenly twitched of its own accord and Oates screamed hysterically.

"Your aunt's house," his voice was now as shrill as a schoolgirl's. "But I'm not sure. Please, you've got to believe me."

Kyle felt his teeth begin to grind again.

"Aunt Cassie?" he growled angrily.

Oates nodded a shallow and brief affirmation.

"Thank you," Kyle said politely, as he turned and walked away. "You've been helpful."

And before the front door of the cottage had even slammed shut behind him, he heard the screams of Emily's father start up again as the spiders resumed their feast beneath the surface of the old man's already ragged and bloody flesh.

# THREE

## SECRETS KEPT ACROSS THE YEARS

Emily stood amongst the trees at the back of Cassandra Craif's old house and let the wind lift the hair from her face. So many things had happened inside that house, so many discussions held between herself and Isabel's crazy aunt. Everything had been crazy back then, the farm, her father, what had happened at school with Kyle; she'd stumbled upon Cassandra's knowledge of the family's curse almost by chance, and it was that, perhaps, that had led to her death.

The house looked deserted, run down, as though nobody had dared move into the place once the old witch's body had been cut down and taken away. That's what she'd been called in the village afterwards, her father had told her sadly, by gossips with too much time on their hands. And they'd had plenty of ammunition too, after the house was slowly cleared of its possessions; the books and the charms she'd built up, the crosses and the knives, everything except a smoking cauldron it would seem. She'd taken it seriously too, it seemed, reading battered books that contained information and incantations, rather than the glossy-covered half-novels they sold in the bookshops. She'd wanted to learn whatever she could to protect those she cared about, she'd told her once, and to try and rid her nephew of the evil that had claimed him since before birth.

The house looked empty through the broken windows, their daggers of grimy glass held in wooden frames too rotten and damp to hold their once-white paint. It was a sad sight to see Cassandra's house so shot to ruin, a sad sight indeed, and all she could do was stand at the perimeter of the garden and cast her eyes across the decay.

Emily had first had her suspicions about Cassandra at Isabel's house a month or so before the incident with Kyle. She'd seemed odd then, making comments that almost sounded like questions, and nearly all of them about Kyle; how was she doing at school, how was Kyle doing at school, was she happy, was she nervous around Kyle, did she see animals looking at her? Emily recalled that her answers became rapidly shorter with each question that left the woman's lips, until by the end she could only nod staccato replies or shake her head with bulging fearful eyes.

She'd frightened her a little, that was the truth of it, but only after Kyle's attack did she think about coming to this house without anyone knowing to answer Cassandra's questions more fully.

Yes, she did feel uneasy around him.

No, he wasn't doing well in school.

And yes, the birds in the hedgerows did seem to be looking her way more than usual.

Cassandra Craif had then confessed her own fears about the boy, in-depth concerns about what might be going through that rotten skull of his. She'd already known about the sheep mutilations on her father's farm, but once Emily had explained to her about what had taken place at school and had lifted the hem of her dress for her to see, things had become a whole stack of steps more serious. That was when Cassandra had told her about the occult, and then the witchcraft had started for real for the both of them.

Cassandra had not wanted anyone to know about the spells she had been trying on her very own nephew, attempting to cleanse and refine his soul, but once Emily had joined her, her deeds seemed almost justified, nearly enough to admit to Isabel and her mother just what they had been doing. But Cassandra had convinced her to remain quiet, to keep everything between the two of them until they were sure they were succeeding. It was shortly after that, of course, that she'd mistaken another boy for Kyle, and had killed him before killing herself. Even to this day Emily didn't know if Cassandra had known the truth about the boy's identity; she could have planned to murder her own nephew and then hang herself before her own guilt consumed her. There was no way of knowing the truth now, not with Cassandra long dead and in the ground.

Grass and coarse weeds had grown so high around the house that it disguised the rot of the window sills and showed only the top half of the black-painted back door. Several slates had blown off the roof and were no doubt still littering the property, hidden inside the tangled jungle of what had once been a lovingly-maintained garden. A hefty nest of mud and leaves sprouted from beneath one of the eaves, but even that looked long abandoned, the stain of off-white bird shit soiling the brickwork underneath it like untidy trails of melted wax on a candlestick.

She'd wanted to tell Isabel so many times of her

involvement with her aunt, but how could she have even begun to try? She didn't want to be seen as a freak by anyone, let alone Isabel, and she certainly didn't want her to know the unnatural link between their families. So as much as she had wanted to confide everything with her, she just hadn't been able to; neither the witchcraft with Cassandra nor what had happened with her brother. The only person she had shared her terrible secret with had died because of Kyle, and the weight of that had stayed with her every day since.

She'd found Izzie again, and she felt so blessed because of that, but even now, twenty years on, she still couldn't bring herself to confess the entire truth to her. First there had been her father's disappearance, then her brother's deviance, followed by her mother's death and subsequent rebirth. The only family member she had left she'd thought of as normal. How would she react, then, if she was told the truth, the truth that her aunt had been a practising witch who had died for her magics?

Emily turned away then, the breeze pushing her hair back across her face, with greater concerns for her best friend than when she'd arrived less than twenty minutes before. She put a hand to her face and pushed the hair from her eyes as she made her way back towards the car.

Glancing at her watch, she realised with a sudden immediacy just how long she had left Isabel alone in the wood for, and with that realisation, suddenly gazed in the direction of its jagged black mass.

But there were no plumes of smoke rising from the wood, no inferno of flames or hellfire, but before she could celebrate the avoided holocaust, her worst fears resurfaced with the inevitable and only conclusion: Isabel had failed. She had faced her brother and lost.

Emily fumbled for her keys in her jeans pocket as she hurried down the overgrown path to where she had left her car, tugging open the door with trembling hands. As she clambered inside and slammed the door after her, a huge crow landed squarely on the bonnet and cawed raucously at her. Emily leapt physically in her seat, a scream in her throat, as her hands flailed with panic. Her heart thudded madly in her chest, her eyes unable to focus on anything but the ebony-black crow as it stood and stared at her through the windscreen.

She swallowed painfully and felt a cold sweat break out on her skin, but the crow did nothing but stand and stare. Its eyes glittered like black granite and all she could think of, even knowing that she had killed it, was that this was the same beast that had attacked her father. There was no proof of that, except for the recognition in that creature's hollow eyes.

Very slowly she reached her hand down and inserted the key into the ignition. The crow craned its neck forward as if to try and look inside, to see what she was up to, and she could see its ghastly head in even greater horrific detail. It cocked its head to one side and blinked, taking in all that she was doing, but she knew that it could not get inside, could not break through toughened glass with a beak however hard or sharp, or at least that's what she hoped.

She turned the key, praying that this wouldn't be one of those movie moments where the engine failed to start, but it fired straight away, and she gunned the accelerator hard, more to scare the crow into flight that anything else.

But it remained motionless on the bonnet, its eyes

blinking at her monotonously. But then as her hand reached for the gear stick, she leapt a second time as something moved in the reflection of the rear view mirror. A single dark motion, Emily spun to see the figure sitting upright in the seat behind her, saw too the white of his teeth as he grinned insanely at her.

"Remember me?" he asked, his voice sickeningly saccharine.

Emily shook her head, her mouth gaping with terror.

"Then we shall have a fine time catching up," he said, leaning forward as if to kiss her.

# FOUR

## BENEATH THE BLACK EARTH

As her eyes flickered open through the haze of unconsciousness, Isabel found herself staring up at the monstrous thing in front of her as it spoke her name, its decayed voice crumbling like rotten wood. The earth was dank and cold beneath her, her fingers sinking into its mire as she pushed herself up onto her knees. Her head thudded, the darkness behind her eyes knotted with pain, but through it she tried to concentrate on the hellish monster looming over her from its pyre of grimy rocks.

It seemed as though it could barely move, this thing, as though it was somehow shackled to its throne of stone and mud and roots, as though it had become a part of the earth, and the earth a part of it. She wanted to ask this thing how it knew her name, or even how it came to be, but before her lips could form any coherent words, it spoke again, its confession promising to knock those very thoughts out of her head altogether.

"Dearest daughter," it said. "Do not fear me."

From down amongst the black earth, she gazed up at this horror of flesh fused with roots and bark and fought for some kind of recognition in its eyes, some kind of lie behind its insane words. But as much as she tried to refuse this terrifying revelation, she couldn't dispute how familiar those eyes were that gazed down upon her. The more she stared at them, the more she realised they were not alien to her. These eyes had looked down upon her as a child sleeping in her bed, they had looked across the garden at her as she had played with her dolls. These eyes at least belonged to her father; so how, she tried desperately to think, had the rest of him become so wrong?

"What are you?" Isabel breathed, staring agog at the muck and mire of all that made him.

"It is a long story, Isabel, too long to tell here and now. All that matters is that you finally came to take me home."

"No," she managed to utter.

"Then why?"

"I came here to kill Kyle."

"Your brother?" he gasped. "How could you wish your own brother dead?"

"You haven't seen what he has become. He's... changed." She could barely get the word out, not with her father standing before her in the guise of a hellish beast. "He's become..."

"Like me?" he asked. "Please God let that not be, not my only son."

"Inside he has become as horrible as -"

"- as I am on the outside?"

Slowly Isabel began to nod. She could feel tears begin to well too, but this was not the time to shed them.

Hesitantly she pushed herself to her feet. Her head throbbed with complaint but she no longer wanted to have her touch against the black soil that made this prison.

"Tell me why you went away," she wanted to know. "Was it because of this?"

"Isabel, please -"

"Tell me," she demanded now.

The encrusted tree creature in front of her inhaled a long ragged breath and stared at her for a moment in silence. Vines tightened across his chest and around his arms like constricting snakes as she watched, binding him even harder to his monolithic cell, as though whatever evil inhabited this place did not want him to leave, or even gain any aspiration of escape. And although no part of him - his face, his torso - resembled the loving man who had once tucked her up in bed, or who had read her stories, she could still see him in the eyes that looked at her. There was warmth there, warmth that she had not felt for so many years.

"Not at first," he said to her quietly, "but it started. What it grew in me, it took away from your mother."

"Mum? What has she got to do with this?"

"She knew what was coming, I'd told her what I saw up there," he barely managed a nod upward, indicating the wood above their heads, "the being that confronted me."

Isabel felt a shiver pass over her skin rapidly, and couldn't suppress it as it physically shook her. She'd seen things too, moving between the trees, reaching for her. But she'd escaped them. Hadn't she?

"I'd once liked to walk through this wood," he went on.

"I remember."

"Yes. We used to come here, both of us."

"You used to tell me the names of things, of plants, and birds."

"I remember," he said quietly. "But I came here

278

alone one day. I was walking through a part I hadn't been to before, and I felt the whole wood begin to darken around me. A breeze whipped up from nowhere and it went cold, a chilling cold that managed to find its way beneath my clothes to my skin. I remember becoming anxious, something I'd never felt in this wood before, and as much as I tried to chastise myself for being foolish, my fear increased. That's when I saw that thing moving."

"Shadows?"

"No, they came later, a kind of army that this thing made, moving through the trees and clinging to them like swathes of black silk. No, this first thing was something else, something unutterably dark and ghostly, a terrible evil, a force..."

His eyes intensified for a moment, and then he shuddered as he clenched them shut.

"I cannot describe it, Isabel," he whispered, swallowing hard with the recollection. "It was too hideous to lay eyes upon, but it was real, and its soulless eyes were watching me."

His eyes found her in the gloom, his pupils like pencils stabbed in yellowed paper.

"That evil claimed this wood," he told her. "It claimed the village, and it claimed me too."

The ground seemed almost to shudder then, as though a dull thump or even a sickening demonic heartbeat reverberated through the earth. Motes of soil tumbled from the ceiling like rain, and both Isabel and her father glanced upward in case whatever it was that haunted this place had heard them and was thinking about burying them for good.

It was her father who broke the uneasy silence.

"The world around us wanted a part of me," he whispered, his eyes searching the murky shadows as he spoke. "It let me home that day, but something came with me. I felt it beneath my skin, crawling around inside my head, and all I could think was how do I protect my family?"

"Mum got sick."

"I know, Isabel. The more I grew like this, the worse she became, as though it was drawing the very life right out of her. I wanted to stay, to try and somehow help you all, but we both knew that was impossible."

"She died."

"I know that too."

"You made me what I am as well."

He stared at her, at her face knotted and gnarled.

"What do you mean?"

"I'm not normal either," she said. "I'm different. Cursed."

"Cursed? How?"

"I cured mum. I cured her of death."

"She's alive?"

"Her heart never beat again but she looks out through her skull. That's my curse, to see her every day and see the zombie that she became."

"Oh Irene," he gasped, his eyes yearning with anguish. "Tell me that's not true..."

"You know that it is. After everything that you've become, this is a fairy tale."

"Where is she?"

"Someplace else. She wants to die but I can't help her. Kyle wants to oblige but it's me that's stopping him."

"I know I robbed your mother of everything, that has haunted me as much as losing you and Kyle. All I have is what you see before you, praying of death."

"You don't know how alike we all are," she said to

him, "all wishing our existences to be over, all wanting our lives extinguished."

"Don't say that. You mustn't say that."

"You know it's true, look at you."

"I saw you walk through here a long time ago," he told her, "sometimes it seemed like it was just a dream. I remember calling to you but you couldn't hear me. I wanted so much to talk to you, to explain, to hold you in my arms again, both of you."

Isabel stared at him. Had that been a dream? Had she really seen him in the woods? She remembered something too, a glimpse of him perhaps, a voice on a breeze held amongst the boughs of the trees.

She studied him now, at his form twisted inside the roots and limbs of the trees that grew above them, the moss and lichen growing from what had once been his flesh. It was a hideous sight, repulsive but eerily compelling. His face splintered in two again as he opened his mouth to speak, and her stomach turned over sour acid. It threatened to vomit, but it held somewhere in her throat.

"I came here to kill you," she gasped, cutting him short, her voice hoarse with anguish. "I wanted the magic gone, destroyed."

"I don't think it can be destroyed," he told her.

"How do you know?" she retorted, frustration souring her words. "You don't even know what you are."

He kept his words this time, and his silence pained her.

"But you're found," she relented softly. "At least there is that."

She could see his face begin to splinter again, as though he was perhaps trying to smile. But the effect was cruelly hideous and could not bring her any

281

comfort. All she could do was look at him, try not to see the horror that made him a monster, and try instead to see the man that she had once called daddy a very long time ago.

She knew it was wrong even before she started, but to see him in so much distress and pain was just too much to bear. She laid her hands across his chest, his torso coarse and hard beneath her touch, and felt instantly the unnatural bonds that kept him in this place. So corrupt were these bonds that it surprised even her how many of them there were.

Hundreds of tendrils, some an inch thick, others the width of hair, shackled his feet and ankles to the hard compacted ground. Powerful roots had grown through his spine, spreading out like knotted fists into his organs and grabbing at his ribs. Even the rock had fused itself across and into his flesh, making it one hybrid skin that seemed impossible to undo.

Isabel heard her father's cry of agony as she began to unmake him, severing the roots that kept him prisoner and dissolving his heavy flesh. He was crying for her to leave him, to take herself away before it was too late, but she could not leave him, not now that she had learned the truth.

But her labours had made her blind to the rest of the chamber, left her defenceless to the forms that were already crawling out of the dirt, up out of the soil and out of the walls.

Something grasped her foot, something black and claw-like, and where she looked down, she could see nothing cohesive except movement itself. Slippery shapes ebbed erratically across the floor like a vast seething tide; no, not across it, through it, beneath it - hell, it was the ground itself. She stared at the earth now, her hands still laid upon her father's protean body, and in that moment of scrutiny she saw the dark army begin to raise themselves.

The chamber shook again, earth cascading from the ceiling in torrents, as shadowy forms hauled themselves from the belly of the floor. As though they were made of the earth itself, they clambered to their ill-made feet until they stood in the murk like vast hulking beasts, her eyes barely able to find the expanse of their frames so lost in the darkness were they. She could only sense their eyeless sockets upon her, their oppressive gaze bearing down on her like vast physical weights.

Then they reached for her in turn, their claws of mud taking hold of her, grasping her wrists and arms. She could feel the coarseness of the mud against her skin, rasping like sandpaper as the sentries of this place began to drag her away. She heard her father cry her name in vengeful defiance, she could see his partially-disfigured form writhing to come after her, but she had already been claimed.

She cried out through the bullying assault, but her scream was short lived as a gag of dirt found her mouth and silenced it, pressing hard across her lips and forcing grit between her teeth, compacting inside her throat. Even as she tried to pull away from them, to dig her heels in and force herself back, they tugged harder, taking her feet out from under her so that she was gathered up mid-air and berated with more venom. Finally a cloak of blackness descended to claim her consciousness, as the air went altogether, smothered by the muck and mire of the prison beneath the wood.

## FIVE

## LOCKED DOORS

Emily sat perched on the end of the bed and hugged herself as she stared out through her old bedroom window. The view had changed little, her bedroom not at all, and although the door out onto the landing was not locked, it just as well might have been.

Kyle had brought her back here. Terrified of what he might do to her after years spent watching her, her flesh had crawled as he'd guided her ahead of him up the stairs to the bedrooms. When she was ushered over the threshold into her own room, the desperate desire to escape heightened to the degree where she would have willingly hurled herself out through an upstairs window to be away from his filthy touch. But he had remained at the threshold, and she had turned to see him halted there, as though he dared not enter such a sacred place without permission. But that permission would never come, not from her lips anyway, and after a few horrible moments where she did not know his intentions, all she could do was stare at him with dread.

There had been a terrible smell too when she'd entered, and although there'd been more to worry about than a sour stench at the time, since Kyle had left the house and left her alone, her mind returned to it. It had drifted up the stairs and through the floorboards, a sour almost sickly aroma that turned her stomach as she inhaled it. She couldn't place it to anything, not food or rot, but it hung in the air and with no fresh air she could do little but breathe it in.

Kyle had told her not to leave, and he had done more than hope that she'd behave. She had watched in disbelief as he had stood in the doorway and somehow summoned an army of spiders from between the cracks in the floorboards, from behind picture frames, from the corners of ceilings and beneath furniture. Her skin itched at the sight of them, as the very floor seemed to come alive, moving like a living carpet of scratchy legs and blotchy bodies. They congregated at his feet, pulsing around him as a single mass, some even daring to scale his ankles and shins in order to pay homage there. Kyle's eyes rolled back into place and found her again after that, a hollow gaze that chilled her more than the spiders.

"They will watch you," was all he'd said to her.

Her eyes must have gone to the only other way out then, because he added quickly:

"From the window as well as from the door."

There they still sat, a hundred or more spiders decorating the window frame in quickly-spun silks like tiny wardens protecting their prison bars. She wasn't sure what they could do if she attempted to swipe them out of her way, or even to simply charge at the door, but if Kyle had left them to keep her in, then she was at least sure that they were up to the job. And even if she could get past them without incident, what might he have left outside, or worse still, what beast might be patrolling the rest of the house?

Kyle had stared at her for a while before he'd left her, his dark eyes glazed and hollow, as though he had somehow slipped into a trance. His eyes had flickered back and forth but she had been certain that he was not actually looking at either her or the room. It was as though he was elsewhere, watching some other sight play out somewhere inside his own head.

She'd become scared as she'd watched his teeth clench in anger; she'd seen his jaw muscles tense horribly, seen his clenched fists turn his knuckles white, and she had been in fear for her life. But then he had left, swiftly and with this new and sudden fury inside him. Only once the door to the front of the house had slammed shut did she manage to relax her own muscles, releasing the tension that she had built.

Her thoughts went to her father as she sat on the edge of her bed, and she wondered then why she had not thought about him before. This was his home after all, and she had brought Kyle Rider into it. She only hoped that he was somewhere safe and had escaped anything that Kyle might have intended for him.

Slowly she got to her feet and crossed the room to the door. The spiders at the window tracked her all the way, but they did not move from the place that Kyle had obviously instructed them to guard. Cautiously she pressed her ear against the wood of the door and listened. There was an almost imperceptible sound coming from the other side, a kind of rapid tik-tik-tik. The wood was amplifying it slightly, and as she strained to make out what it could be, she suddenly pushed herself away from the door in both horror and disgust as the realisation came. It was the spiders Kyle had left outside, crawling across the door, no doubt spinning and weaving their own prison bars, keeping her sealed inside.

She wanted to bang on the door and scream for help, but would that cause them to crawl under the door as they had crawled up from between the floorboards?

Her hands went instinctively to her arms as she imagined them crawling across her skin, their tiny stick-legs pattering across her flesh, crawling, burrowing beneath it.

She staggered back to the bed and perched once more on the edge. She started to rock slowly now as she wrapped her arms around herself. What was going to happen? Where was her father?

She could feel tears of anguish and desperation coming, welling behind her eyes like a flood. But she didn't want to spill them. Not for Kyle anyway. Never again for Kyle.

## SIX

## POSSESSOR AND POSSESSION

He had seen her enter the wood from behind the eyes of the rat. Skulking through the undergrowth, Isabel had made her way through his domain, unhindered and without his welcome. Forced to leave Emily alone in order to come back to face his sister, something he had not wanted to do, he had realised that to return to her with a power that could heal all her wounds would be a gift truly worth delivering.

But once he'd left the farmhouse, however, the images that came into his head of his sister making her way through the wood became more and more disturbing. It seemed as though she was following a path, a route between the trees that did not seem random. The sight given him by his creatures of the wood was not clear enough to confirm his suspicions, but he was sure that there were dark forms circling around her, clawing in her wake and ahead of her, leading her onward.

What could possibly be of importance in the wood that she be led there, he wanted to know? What was there that he did not know about?

Kyle's curiosity intensified as his seething fury

burned, but as his borrowed sight saw her descend into a darkened hollow, a sacred place beneath the trees that even he had never set eyes upon, his teeth ground together hard enough to draw blood from his own gums.

By the same route that Isabel had taken he found the hollow easily. In the small clearing he noticed the shape of something floating in the darkness between the trees. He gave it a look that caused it to retreat a short way, but it returned, and seemed almost to beckon him towards the chasm. The ground looked as though it had dropped away, hollowing the ground out into a kind of bunker. He noticed too as he stepped down into it, that it continued further down a short way, or so it seemed, beneath the huge gnarled roots of the overhanging tree. Glancing back up once more at the ghostly shadow as if to threaten it should it be trying to trick him, Kyle continued on down the slope in order to gaze further into the chasm beneath the tree. The darkness seemed not only impenetrable, but unending, and with a final glance back up at the creature still watching him, he ducked down and made his way into the void.

There was a secret to be learnt, that was what lured him in; not the faceless things that hung from the trees, nor the ghost that loomed above him, nor even the fact that he was now somewhere near the heart of the wood. No, there was a greater secret somewhere, and going down into the bowels of the earth, into the darkness where all bad things happened, seeming a fitting place to start.

A long mud-lined corridor awaited the end of his steep descent. The clinging odour of winter rot found his nostrils and he breathed its potency in as he made his way. Something was down here, more than just his sister, he could feel it, prickling the hairs on his skin, tingling inside his teeth and fingertips, chattering in staccato tongues deep inside his head.

Wrought of mud and muck, he followed it to a chamber vaulted with black twisted shapes knitted into its structure of roots and rock. At the far end he found Isabel, her back to him, and it took him only a few moments to realise that, beside the shadows that were crawling down the walls towards her, she was not alone.

Something stood in front of her, and for those few short moments of bewilderment he had thought it was just part of the chamber. Until it moved. And howled her name.

The shadows took hold of her, wrapping around her wrists and ankles, entwining their sinews across her forearms and legs, smothering her utterly. She tried to resist, he could see that she tried, but so swift was their assault, that she was dragged back away from the monster that she faced.

Somewhere in his head, Kyle had distantly named this creature as the face of the wood, the force that had brought him above the level of the normal man. But as he took a step towards it, his eyes found the face that had nurtured him as a boy, the eyes that had watched him, the hands that had held him, and somewhere inside his head something cracked.

So much of him had become unrecognisable, but then so had he; one altered on the inside, the other on the out. He uttered his father's name on a silent breath as he took a second step towards him, and it was then that he saw his father return his incredulous stare. To have that gaze fall upon him was almost too blissful to explain, despite the monstrosity of what he had become, and Kyle felt his thoughts slip with joy. But the rapture was short-lived. His father cried out with alarm as the shadows took hold of Isabel and began to haul her away, constricting around her body like terrible black snakes.

He could see Isabel's eyes white with terror, so intense were their hands upon her, smothering her mouth, starving her of oxygen, and he felt himself storm forward to intercede.

He could feel their number in the darkness, could feel the air thick with them even before he'd stepped amongst them. But by that time they had circled him, a hundred different forms surrounding him with a furious might.

Kyle stared at them for a moment, turning slowly as if to take in every last one of them. They were insolid, most of them, some of them little more than gestures of forms, drifting like fragile mists. Others, however, were made of stronger stuff, hard and sinuous, and manufactured not only from flesh and bone. Some seemed made from the wood itself, bodies of timber and branch, heads of black earth and clay. Others still appeared to be abominations of walking moss or stone, roughly hewn or carved, their maws slowly clamping and clenching into sick lunatic grins. Only when one of them reached for him did he fully understand their intent, and as soon as he felt its cold fleshy palm against his wrist, his thoughts entered through its pores and surged upward throughout its being.

The journey took perhaps only a second or two, but in that brief span of time, Kyle saw everything that made up its presence. There was little that he had not seen amongst natural animals, and he had seen inside so many, and so much of it seemed contradictory, as though this thing should not even be in existence. It fascinated him to see inside this creature, unnatural or supernatural as it obviously was, but he found the intent, the desire to harm him, and he acted immediately, taking it apart with his will as his thoughts returned back through its pores.

He felt the fear ripple swiftly throughout the congregation as the creature that had seized him suddenly shuddered with shock. Its skin slipped effortlessly away to reveal meat the colour and texture of skinned tomatoes. Blood welled swiftly to the surface, but even that dissolved from sight as Kyle saw through it. Its head swung back on a spine suddenly softened, its jaw swinging open before coming away altogether and skittering away into the corners of the black earth.

Kyle watched with keen wonderment as the creature then sank down onto its knees, its innards slumping out through the bottom of its pelvic cavity, suddenly opened as he willed it, its bones melting like candle wax and running away down into the dark floor before sinking completely out of sight.

His eyes rose up once again to view the gathered crowd, but none of them had come advanced any more. He could feel the weight of their presence all around him, but not the weight of a single hand or claw upon his skin. They all seemed to wait to see what would happen next, as if awaiting instruction, holding back momentarily. The hesitation lasted only a moment, and then they descended as a single furious beast.

He'd actually interceded, that was his crime, stepping in to protect his sister from the creatures that had nurtured him. It felt as though he was being torn apart by a thousand different hands now, most of them invisible, but all of them now clutching at him and wanting his throat.

They found their way in too, through his nostrils, his mouth, gouging at his eyes in an attempt to get inside him and take control. His hands twitched in spasms as he fought to keep his actions his own, but amongst such an onslaught it was impossible to resist for long, and soon he was merely watching though his own eyes, a spectator lost alone and defenceless inside his own head, as the wood retook control of him.

# SEVEN

_____

## THE FACES BEHIND THE MASK

Her sight focussed rapidly out of the blackness to see Kyle looming just inches from her face. His expression was like a mask, set in an awkward grimace somewhere between anguish and rage, and even as she wrestled in the grip of her tormentors, she was uncertain of his intent towards either her or their father.

The hands that held her suddenly lifted as Kyle stared at her, and she slipped down into the dirt at his feet. Before she had even struggled to regain her balance, Kyle was looming after her, a grisly grin hacked across his face, his expression flickering like a schizophrenic, torn between masks.

"What do you want?" she cried out at him, but when his voice came, it came buzzing like a hellish turbine, discordant and vile:

"You've changed since you were last here."

"You too," Isabel managed to stammer. "Although I think you've been keeping yourself busy spying on people."

"Spying seems a harsh word."

"You've been tracking me since I left home."

"Don't flatter yourself. I hung around here for a

while, taking a good long look at the world. You should've seen what happened to me. Aunt Cass had me for a while, and social services stuck their noses in, but I did okay."

"And what about mum?" Isabel said. "You wanted to hurt her."

"Oh, I wanted more than that."

"I know exactly what you wanted. I saw what you did to her."

Kyle grinned at this, as though he'd forgotten that he'd actually caught up with her, had opened her up too.

"Your magic," he said now, remembering his track. "I want it. You've had it long enough. Time to hand it over."

Isabel stared at him.

"I'm not sure I could give it to you even if I wanted to."

"I could always try and take it."

He floated this last statement lightly, disguising the intent that Isabel felt in the hardness of his fiercely-focussed eyes. She tried to scrabble back away from him, but almost immediately felt pressure at her back. She turned her head sharply, as if someone was standing there, a foot against her spine, but there was nothing, just the darkness that had seemed to thicken to envelop the space around her.

Her mind went instantly to escape, but the air had texture against what skin was exposed to it, her face and hands. She now felt slender-fingered hands slide up the insides of her legs, beginning to restrict themselves like snakes once more should she try and break away. Isabel swallowed hard, her throat feeling tight as though there were unseen hands inside there yet again, ready to stifle any scream, or perhaps simply to choke her if they so wanted.

She was scared now, more than she had been before, and her eyes ultimately returned to her brother. He hadn't moved, and stood casually with his hands at his side. There was no intent in any way he carried himself now, and Isabel realised that he had no need. Whatever was in the wood with him could despatch her more readily than he could with his own hands. But his eyes still regarded her sharply. He'd offered her his threat. He could take it if he wanted. But then a doubt entered her mind as they remained looking at each other. If he could take it, then why hadn't he?

The snakes were upon her and taut, like the roots that had imprisoned her father, but they weren't tightening. Was this all some empty threat, goading her into handing over what she didn't even want, because Kyle knew that he couldn't take it? She had no idea, but she didn't want to test her theory either. What he'd done to his own mother was unspeakable, and if he could do that to her, then what could he do his sister?

She figured quickly that he didn't know, couldn't know, how to strip her power from her. It gave her an advantage, but she was still alone fighting an army of something that she didn't understand.

"Let me go," she said finally, her voice as strong as she could manage.

Kyle's eyebrows flickered upward, a smile of disbelief creeping into the edges of his mouth.

"Let you go?" he repeated, with a laugh. "Why the fuck would I do that? Would you do that in my circumstances? I don't think so."

"What are your circumstances, Kyle? Are you pissed off that dad left? Are you ashamed because of what you did to Emily?"

His smile dropped instantly at her name.

"Oh, I know all about that, you sick little shit."

"Don't you call me that."

"What should I call you? It doesn't leave much."

Isabel could see his jaw muscles clenching. The unseen hands around her throat tightened a little, not much, but enough for her to tense her body and struggle to swallow. Maybe this wasn't smart, but who the fuck was he anyway, just her twisted older brother.

"Do your worst," she threatened, her voice thin, forced out on a restricted breath.

"Don't tempt me."

"Go on, do it. I've had enough of this life. I've seen death and I've lived with a walking corpse. Do what I can't, and kill me."

The hands around her throat tightened once again. Her eyes bulged painfully as her head turned into a solid mass, thick with blood that had nowhere else to go. Blackness shimmered somewhere inside her skull, pulsing and swirling, and for a moment she thought she saw the grim reaper's mask pasted onto her brother's evil face. The agony lasted only a moment before Kyle relented.

The hands went from her throat, blood pumped swiftly in, and Isabel couldn't help but slump backwards as though she had been held up on wires that had now been severed.

She sat in the black dirt coughing violently, her hands clenched into fists clasped in front of her mouth. Her throat stung and her sinuses burned, but Kyle had not been able to bring himself to kill her.

"So this has been dad's home for over twenty years," she heard him say quietly.

She wanted to say something to that, but the

words just couldn't make their way out. She lifted her eyes up towards him, and saw him standing over her, looking down at her.

"He's... changed."

"I know," Isabel managed to gasp, coughing immediately after. "Roots and stone."

"Your magic could undo what this place has done to him."

"Don't you think I tried?"

"He's my father," Kyle yelled.

"And mine," Isabel yelled back, struggling to push herself to her feet. "But there's too much inside him. The wood's been growing through him for over twenty years. Where do you think he's been all this time? He never left us, Kyle. He never went away. Not ever."

Isabel watched as Kyle shut his eyes, his teeth beginning to grate inside his skull. It was clear that something was going on inside his head. His mask shifted suddenly, recognition swept briefly across his eyes, but then it went all too soon.

"You could take away the roots, the skull, it doesn't have to be like this -"

His voice decayed suddenly into the buzzing cacophony that had scared her before, his eyes clenching as though something was inside and trying to get out.

"He's too far gone, Kyle," she tried to say to him. "There's more wood than man."

Kyle's eyes flickered open then, and a wildness was burning inside them. Isabel staggered back a step, fearful at such proximity to him. His teeth bared into a sickening grin, stained red from his own bloodied gums, and she felt the malevolence inside him before he even played his final game.

"I have Emily," he hissed, his voice guttural like a wild animal.

Isabel stared at him in horror. What was he saying?

"You'll never save her. Only I can save her. Hand over what you possess or I will take her life."

The glimmer of madness was in those eyes. She had suspected him of it a thousand times, but here it was, staring back at her from just inches away.

There was a silence between them for a while, an eerie calm in which they simply stood and stared at each other. But then something seemed to dislodge inside him again, some memory or revelation, and his eyes sparked visibly with utter focus. They terrified her, his eyes, the way that he now looked at her, the way that she could almost see right into his blackened soul. Something was happening to him, even as she watched, but she could not tell what. And then his grin came again, cruel and like that of a rabid beast, as a low thunderous growl resounded throughout the whole chamber like a heartbeat.

"I want your blood," he hissed, his voice guttural and seething from between clenched teeth.

"Kyle?" Isabel murmured, taking a step away from him. "What's wrong with you?"

Her heart was hammering, thudding against her chest, pounding against the inside of her ribs.

"I want it on my hands. I want it on my face."

"Stop it, Kyle. Stop it."

"So sick of your whining. So sick of your breaths desecrating this place."

As these words came, Isabel finally realised why she was suddenly so afraid. She could no longer see her brother in these eyes. Kyle, or who she had thought Kyle was, had gone. Something else had taken over, and its malice was indisputable. There would be no return from it now.

She took another step just as a second growl rumbled at the back of his throat, and then she turned and tried to run. But the ghosts that had lifted their grasp upon her now took hold of her afresh, and she tumbled headlong into their waiting arms. She could feel them clawing at her, fingers raking across her skin, at her clothes, her hair. She tried to scream but they swiftly found their way in once more, filling her mouth, clogging her throat.

Tears began to stream as she struggled uselessly, their grasp around her tightening, always tightening, keeping her fast amongst the black mass of their shadowy forms.

Finally she was spun back, or rather was allowed to spin back, to face her brother, his form now crawling with half-made creatures leering back at their captive.

His figure suddenly loomed over her, his eyes like hollow craters, devoid of any humanity. Something had taken over him utterly, surely the thing that had taken possession of the wood, the entire village, of that there could now be no doubt. And then her eyes found his right hand, stricken in the shape of a talon, as it came up into her, the force of the blow piercing the flesh of her belly, and clasping her innards like a livid fire.

The pain did not come immediately, and for a moment she thought that he had actually somehow missed her. But as she saw this thing in front of her withdraw its talon high above its head, she had only a few seconds to see the deep scarlet that coated it, before it was thrust round and into her belly a second time.

Now the pain came, a sharp agony that seemed to burn deep inside her like acid. Her breathing halted, her lungs became stricken with shock, and she could feel a terrible cold permeate her feet and lower legs. Her hands went numb, her fingers turned dead to the world, and all she could do was stand there as she watched this crooked claw exit her body before plunging into it a third time.

Her eyes closed after that, her torso tensing as her organs were pulled from their place, her ribs cracked and broken. She had no idea how many more times the creature stabbed at her, but she could distantly feel the thuds, as though her body had slipped some way away from her.

And then she toppled backwards, the dull agony coming in pulses now, burning like fires trapped inside a terrifying smothering numbness. All feeling had gone from her arms and legs and her sight could only discern a thick ebbing blackness. But even through that, all her mind could register was the fact that her fears about immortality had been wrong; death had claimed her at last. She had died.

## EIGHT

---

## BEYOND THE EXEUNT

The house was deadly quiet when he returned. Kyle stood outside, his mind numb from what his own hands had done to Isabel, gazing up at the still façade, wondering why even the spiders had disappeared. Nothing moved, nothing made a sound, and with a feeling of dread growing inside him, he went to the front door and pushed it slowly open.

His footsteps echoed off the wall around him as he stepped across the threadbare carpet, and almost immediately he was met by an acrid stench that soured the stale air. He glanced through the doorway into the living room as he passed it, and saw the grey husk of the old man's body lying on the sofa where he'd left him. One arm hung loosely, the hand hooked as though he'd spent his dying moments clutching for mercy. His torso was unkempt and blackened with dried blood from where the spiders had chewed their way inside him. His eyes gaped wide and white, his lips pulled back over his teeth in a silent cry preserved for eternity, his expression cast in a mould of agony.

Kyle had always thought he would've enjoyed such a sight, the death of the man who had struck him many years ago. He'd nurtured revenge for a long time, cherishing what bliss it would be when finally he would kill him, but there was no bliss, there was no contentment, only a sick empty feeling as this horrendous sight met his eyes. Poor old fucker.

He moved away from the doorway and continued on towards the stairs. There was still no sound of movement, no hint of life, and as much as he wanted to search the house with the eyes of its tiny inhabitants, part of him didn't want that, didn't want to see what the wood might have done to his beloved Emily as punishment for attempting to save his sister, how his actions might have hurt her yet again. If something had gone wrong, if she was harmed in any way, he wanted to see it with his own eyes, and not with some unnatural freakish vision lent him by some poison-hearted spirit.

The stairs creaked with protest as Kyle began to climb, his hands disturbing dust on the banister as he leant his weight upon it. His eyes rose upward as he went, looking for signs of the spiders that he had left to guard her, had left to prevent her escape. But there was none; no sound, no sight. Had he done his job too well?

Turning at the top, he hovered for a moment, staring down the length of the landing. The door to the room in which he'd left Emily was vacant of life, but was shrouded by sheaths of white shimmering silk, the webs of the sentries that had sealed the room like some ancient tomb. But where were those sentries, he wanted to know, where had they gone? He forced his feet forward, the empty sickness crawling in his stomach like the spiders that ought to be here.

Reaching out a tremulous hand, Kyle took hold of the thick wadding of silk and dragged it away from the door. Its fibres were sticky but fragile, and did not come away cleanly. They adhered to the door jamb and the wall, looping in strands that glimmered in the half-light coming in through the landing window. But with the process started, he took his other hand to them and began clawing them fully away from the door.

The spiders had found their way in through the cracks between the door and the frame, between the door and the floorboards, even through the keyhole. Kyle took hold of the handle and turned it but the door would not readily open. He pushed at it harder, but it was not locked, just stuck, and with both hands now he grasped the handle and put his weight to it, shouldering the door until it began to give.

With a ripping sound the door finally relented, swinging inward as Kyle stumbled forward through a shroud of cobwebs far denser than what he had pulled away from the landing.

Emily's bedroom was festooned with webs, hanging from the ceiling, the walls, and looped from every visible surface. At first he had trouble finding the bed, so overturned was the furniture in the room, but he saw it nearer the window, and upon it a mound that could only be his beloved.

Like a wanderer in a desert thwarted by the mirage of water, Kyle stumbled numbly towards her. Swathed entirely in blankets of white silk, no part of her was immediately recognisable, but it was clear that she was not moving. He sank onto the edge of the bed, his throat coarse and parched, his chest heaving, as he reached out a shaking hand to pull the webs back away from her face.

They came away like shreds of candy floss, delicate strands sticking to her hair and face, broken fragments floating on the air, but there was no mistaking the horrible truth. Her eyes were mercifully closed, no accusation in the deathly stare like her father in the room below, but she was dead. The wood had used his own sentries to kill Emily.

He turned away, unable to look at her pale skin, her dry blue lips, and saw the window swathed in silk. Had she been eaten from the inside like her father, Kyle wondered numbly, or suffocated by the stale dead air? How long had she survived on her own, how long had she suffered?

Kyle slid off the edge of the bed and onto his knees, folding his head into his hands with utter grief. What had he done?

Tears threatened to come, he willed them to come, but nothing came. Normal people grieved for those that they lost, but he couldn't even manage that.

He wanted to cry, he wanted to bawl like a blameless infant, but nothing took over from the dry rasping anguish that raked the back of his throat and burned deep inside his gut.

What else was there that mattered, now that Emily was gone? They'd all gone now, hadn't they? All those he... loved.

The word didn't flow like he'd thought it would, it hung uneasily in his mind. Did he love them? Of course he did. He'd always thought that, always held onto that, why else would he have searched for them for so long, an unnatural search that had destroyed any hope of any real existence?

He tried to picture his father in his head, but what he remembered as a child was blurred, vague, and defied clarity. There were walks in the woods, he remembered that, but visually it was unclear. Even his face he couldn't picture, not with any real accuracy.

Would love allow that? To not be able to remember your own father's face? And what of the man who'd been imprisoned beneath the wood, who was that? Had that been his father, a man fused with the living earth, a mutation? That face had not been the one he could barely recall either, but something else entirely, something hideous, something different, jarring. And what of his mother, had she been right all along, had she lost her husband through no fault of her own just as he had lost his father?

The thoughts in his head picked up momentum with every question that came, hurting his skull, hurting his eyes as he tried to sift through every one of them. What of Isabel? What of Emily? What of Aunt Cassandra? Too many lives, all poisoned by him. What had he done? What had it all been for?

He glanced back up at the silken shroud that covered the corpse of the beautiful girl he had known as Emily Oates. She was dead because of him. All he'd wanted was to see her happy, to see a smile on her face made by him. And yet here she was, murdered by his actions, killed by what he had thought was a love she couldn't see.

He closed his eyes and watched the whirlwind of images surge through the blackness of his head like a vortex as though they would destroy him. He hurt, and it was more painful than anything else he had ever known. Inside the images he could see flashes of scarlet, livid and rich, flooding the darkness, the soup of his own making. He stared at the red, the blood between the memories, and suddenly despised it, loathed it. He no longer wanted to be the prince of the world; now all he wanted was an end to it all, an end to everything , an end to pain.

He used his vision and gazed inside his own blood,

saw the cells that made it what it was, and sneered with venom at them. He wanted them gone, dead, destroyed, and watched with grim fascination as those cells began to wither.

But as his sight flickered from one to another, so they seemed to spark back to life, regenerating, rejuvenating, the same power that he was using to undo them, making them whole once again.

This maddened him, enraged him, and only multiplied his hatred of what seethed inside his veins. He fought harder to undo the fabric of his own being, destroying the tiny elements that made up its structure, and even as he watched them come apart, he felt the consequences of his actions as a dull blackness began to sweep across him.

He felt it first in his hands and feet, his extremities failing as his body tried once again to maintain its equilibrium. But Kyle tried to focus through the mire that was slowly overtaking him, fighting off his own will to live, trying to kill himself even as his own body fought for survival.

He heard the thud as he slumped to the ground more than he felt it, his limbs numb, his senses distant, but he knew that what he was doing was right. It was no recompense for what he had done, the lives he had broken and ended, but it was all he could think of. Perhaps it was the cowards way out, his thoughts told him from a place beyond where he thought his consciousness lay, escaping the hurt, running away from all the harm that he had caused. But it was all he could think of, all he was good at, and used what last will he had left to undo his own heart, and destroy himself for good.

The rhythm of his decaying blood slowed and then stopped, and for a moment there was a deafening silence the likes of which Kyle had never heard before.

His thoughts clouded over like a grim soup. Death had come, but the void of nothingness into which he thought he would be delivered never came.

A heartbeat thudded in the silent murk, a single unmistakable thump, and his eyes flickered open to see the cobs of white silk still hanging in loops across Emily's bedroom. But as his jaw dropped in surprise and exasperation, the motion caused his body to take a breath, filling his lungs, drawing life back into itself with rapid resilience. He tried to resist, oh God how he tried, but the chain reaction had already begun, and worked faster to repair itself than he could to take it apart again.

Slumping back against the side of the bed, he cried aloud as he threw back his head, running his hands through the unruly mop of his hair, dragging it up and out with clenched fists. There would be no easy escape from what he had done, and the pain inside his chest and throat choked him but would not kill him. He could think of nothing else to live for, and yet it seemed he would have very little choice.

He clenched his eyes shut and thought of what future might await him. His sister lay dead in a place he had once thought of as home. The woman he had loved so dearly lay dead beside him. His father, whose love he had wanted more than anything, lay poisoned and disfigured by a power he had bastardised inside himself. And his mother? He had hurt her irreparably, physically and mentally, sliced her to ribbons with a knife he had carried for the job. What a son he was.

Forcing himself to his feet, he left Emily in her silken tomb and went from the house. Goodbyes - he'd said so many in his life, and yet he would be saying so many more; for those he had loved, for those he had despised.

It was dark when he left, and the night welcomed him into it as he made his way away from the farm, the darkness enveloping him, hiding him from sight, hiding him from judgement. Who, indeed, could deliver justice now other than God? He had found his own self guilty but his punishment had been rejected.

What was left? To live, and resurrect the face of evil in every mirrored glass, or seek the thing that had destroyed his family and take whatever vengeance he could?

# NINE

## THE HOST IS FOUND

Her eyes flickered open to the dark disused office, familiar pain coming instantly as her dry lids scraped across her pupils, heightened as she blinked away the remnants of a few hour's restless sleep. The room had not changed, Isabel had not returned, and the stench of her open wounds still soured the stale air. She lifted herself up onto one elbow, agony creasing her in two as those wounds separated, terrible wounds that her own son had inflicted upon her. They were much healed already, inside at least, but Kyle's knife had gone deep, and her body, under Isabel's hateful influence, had fought to keep her a part of the world a little longer.

She moaned aloud as she pushed herself up into a sitting position, the lonely sound echoing coldly around the fifth floor of the building, before easing herself onto the blankets that made her rudimentary chair on the floor. Perhaps she would not be coming back, she thought to herself. She'd not suspected Kyle of being able to attack her like he had. She knew he blamed her for Michael's going away, and Isabel had always convinced her that his grudge had continued, but she hadn't believed it; not to the extent to which

310

Isabel did, at least. But she'd been proved wrong, and her daughter proved right. Her son had developed into a guiltless murderer. And that hurt her more than anything.

She tried to put the sight of his teeth grinning at her with utter hatred out of her mind, to try and recall his tiny frame nursing in her arms, his delicate kiss against her cheek as she'd tucked him in at night. But this latest sight of him shattered everything that had once filled her head, destroying ten years of motherhood, ten wonderful years before her child had turned bad. He'd wanted her dead. No, worse. He'd wanted her dead by his own hand.

She shivered with cold and ran her hands over the tops of her arms. The room was silent. The whole building was silent. Even out in the street, at whatever time in the early morning it was, nothing moved; no cars, no people, not even an idiot drunk out singing or smashing bottles. She was alone, and as she sat in the corner of the fifth floor of the disused office building and hugged herself, it seemed like she was the last person left alive in the world.

She could feel her throat begin to tighten, begin to burn with the onset of tears, but she choked it back, telling herself that when her daughter came back, they'd do something to change it all, to find a way to make it different. Despite the odds.

But then she noticed something moving at the far end of the room, something black against the blackness, something unseeable. No one living would have spotted it, she was sure, but after living without light for so many years she could see a great deal more than most.

Irene gazed at the doorway in front of the stairs for a few moments, confirming the shifting form, trying to put a face to the figure. Was this Kyle come back? Was this Isabel? But then other dark shapes came to join the first, a dozen more forms twisting and writhing across the walls and floor.

She was already motionless, but she dared not move now, not even as they approached slowly as if exploring every inch of every surface of the room. Then they froze, all hanging like black bed linen, and she could sense that she had been seen.

Almost immediately she felt movement around her, forms knitting themselves across her hands and arms. She tried to pull them free but they were already tightening quickly around her. Panicking now, she tried to clamber to her feet, but unused to such swift motions her limbs refused her, and sent her reeling onto her back instead.

And then something inexplicable happened: words came into her head, not spoken, but their meaning. Something was instructing her, not verbally, but she had the knowledge of what they wanted. There was something about her son, something about him searching for her. This she already knew, had already paid the price for, but then the revelation of his search came. She was wanted not for herself, but for who she was hiding.

The forms held her down as this same phrase kept making itself known inside her head: *I don't come for you but for who you keep hidden.*

So many thoughts rushed through her head, some her own, others placed there - was the message meant for Isabel, hiding her mother; was it meant for her, hiding her daughter? - all conflicting with the unnatural forms that held her to the floor.

She could feel them wanting to crawl inside her skull to explore there, pressing at the soft flesh around her mouth, her ears, her nostrils, ⸎⸎⸎ invading her mind. Her wounds ⸎⸎⸎ advances too, their weight pressing be⸎⸎⸎ meat, searching out her innards, sear⸎⸎⸎ darkest corners.

*For who was hidden?*

The phrase bullied her head, over and over⸎⸎⸎

*I don't come for you but for who you keep hidden.*

A spark of light illuminated the darkness around her, and her eyes flickered open to see it, pained by the sudden brightness. It was gone a moment later, transient in the murk, but so little used to anything but her pit of darkness she was sure she had not imagined it. And then it came again.

Her eyes focussed on one of the dusty strip-lights in the ceiling, its length sparking erratically now. The wraiths that covered her body contorted as burning filaments began to drop downward in bright arcs. A flame caught briefly, flickering weakly, and then died, until the sparking intensified and the dry dust inside the ceiling ignited, sending a cloud of fire billowing from the fitting.

The writhing black forms recoiled as the heat reached them, and Irene rolled awkwardly onto her side, pushing herself to her feet before staggering as quickly as she could towards the main doors that led out to the stairwell. A ghastly scream erupted in the wake of her escape, rising in unison with the blossoming fire, but with the intervention of the fused electrics she had found her means to take flight, and she threw herself down the stairs as she reached them.

There were more forms there to catch her, however, but she staggered through them regardless, their arms clutching at her body, slowing her descent

...e tumbled headlong down the steps. More ...nore of them took hold of her as she made her way down to the door that led out to the service yard, until she could barely take a step forward. But she wanted to reach the outside world, wanted to see the sky one last time, if this would indeed be her last moment alive before these things claimed her.

Her withered hand fell upon the cold metal handle, her strength fading as she tried to turn it. But once the light from the infant dawn fell upon her face, her body weight lent her momentum, and she managed to haul herself out into it.

She turned in the hold the creatures had on her, forcing herself onward, past the windows that lined the ground floor of the building. Her eyes found the mesh-covered glass, and suddenly all strength drained from her body.

She'd not seen her reflection in a very long time, although she had held her crumbling fingers to her face and knew how dried her skull-like face must have looked. But to stand outside the building and see the horrific mask in the reflection of one of the windows, her drawn and hollowed features lit by the early light of the new morning, was almost too much to bear.

She was a monster, a zombie, a thing of walking death that would terrorise people if she were to star in some cheap horror movie. And yet it returned her stare with such intensity that it chilled even her to look at it, and she had to fight to recognise the woman she had once seen in the mirror.

This irregular reflection was enough to roughly show her the face that she actually wore, like a sketch made quickly with crayons, or a hunk of clay hacked with a palette knife. Full daylight would have shown her the true face, a photographic image that hid nothing; semi-darkness disguised so much of her with deep shadow, with utter blackness, and yet it highlighted the angular bone that jutted out over her eyes, the parched and stretched skin across a nose that had withered to almost nothing. Her lips, which she recalled had been soft and known to pout so effectively, were now gone almost entirely to nothing, receding back from her teeth so that they showed little more than a hideous yellow death-grin. Her throat had tightened with grief almost immediately as she'd seen herself, tears welling behind eyes that rolled in decayed sockets as hollow as two rabbit holes. It had taken her a while to finally turn away, so sick was the fascination of seeing herself after so long, but when she did, Irene Rider collapsed onto knees that cracked like dead branches, creaking with protest, before she tumbled into a heap of dry grey flesh on the rough concrete surface of the loading bay.

The black shadow-like forms raced quickly to smother her now that she had defeated herself, as images of her daughter kept tumbling into the blackness behind her eyelids, vying for dominance with what she had just seen. She was helpless now, as they kept crawling over her, kept searching for ways to get beneath her skin. All Irene wanted was to just lie in the gutter and fade away, even though her daughter was surely back home and alive, needing her, needing to know that what the pair of them had endured over two decades would not have been for nothing.

It was perhaps that hope that kept her alive, the resilience to survive beneath an onslaught that would have killed any other. The sight of the office building she never saw again, however, the black forms swarming around her keeping her trapped inside a cocoon of their own making. But she was conscious of motion, conscious of being taken somewhere, and she was sure that that place would be home. Finally she would be going home, she thought numbly inside her own head. Either that or oblivion.

# TEN

## THE OTHER SIDE

The air was busy, lacerated red raw and black, shot through with white noise that scratched at her ears like rusted wire. Her body had abandoned her, leaving only senses to try and keep sanity inside this shuddering defiled limbo, a disembodied consciousness aware only of itself and the hell in which it had been dumped.

The buzzing of the air clawed at her mind as she tried to make sense of where she was, what had happened to her, but against such an influx it was maddening.

Isabel's mind summoned pictures of a claw-like hand running wet with scarlet, of a crescent of teeth cut to needles, of a man fused with trees, eyes gouged from rock and splintered timber. Her senses ached, wracked with the burden of what they had carried for years, what was expected of them even now after death. There was no calm, no peace, just an endless assault of insane shapes and noise.

It battered her as she tried to move through it, her head thick with monstrous calamity, but was she even moving, was motion even a commodity here? With no terrain to cover, no distance to make sense of, how could anything be certain, how could coherent thoughts possibly be made?

Images passed across her mind in rapid succession; memories or fantasies, it was impossible to separate the two. Images of teeth, of claws, of faceless things that swept down from the treetops. Images of death, and graves, of insects and worms that fed on cadavers. Images of light, of redeemed beings, soaring through heavenly constellations. And of running, of hiding, and of the darkest pits in which no one sane would come looking for her.

Then words came fleetingly between those images, barely registered enquiries; questions, answers, and everything in between. Isabel's head swelled with the information that pounded it from inside and out, ransacking her thoughts as they began to slip away from her, elusive beyond even her control.

And yet the words heightened until she was not even sure that she was making them. Some she heard clearly, others not, but those that were insistent seemed planted just beyond her grasp. Her sight attempted to sift through the raging colours of scarlet and ebony, swirling in maddening dervishes, disorientating, diverting. Until a word suddenly came as clear as glass, scything through the flickering muck of senseless matter.

One single name: Cassandra.

There was no opportunity to snatch that moment back, no calm in which to ascertain whether she had even heard it or not, because the howl of the hellish storm snatched it away as soon as it was spoken. And it was spoken too. Pronounced upon a breath planted close to her thoughts.

Isabel went to speak, to call out to her aunt dead

for two decades, but with no throat and no tongue, she was unable to manufacture even the simplest of utterances.

The storm raged on, haranguing the only thing she possessed inside this terrifying maelstrom, a consciousness that seemed ready to slip away from her altogether at any moment, and she feared that she would not hear that name again. And yet it passed by her a second time, so swiftly that she had to grab at it and hang on as though it was something physical. Was Cassandra here, she thought quickly to herself? Yes, she had to be. Why else? Why anything else?

There was no evidence in front of her, no face to clarify her hope, no sight of anything familiar, just a snatch of her name tugged out of the white noise. Isabel tried to communicate, to will her own words out into the storm, but she had no idea how this world worked, no idea of its rules or limitations.

But the words came more readily into her head now, planted there, she hoped, by the spirit of her aunt. She was here with her now, she knew, fighting hard to stay with her.

*Where are you?*

*There are suicides here.*

Isabel could feel herself slipping again, could feel the thoughts that Cassandra planted in her head becoming dimmer, more fragile. Words went altogether, leaving fractured sentences, uncertain meanings.

*Dead...*

*Yes...*

*Killed by their own hand.*

*I can't hear you.*

*Saw the face...*

*Saw the grave a better place.*

319

Shapes began to pulse out of the jagged storm ahead of her, blemishes or bruises too crude to take form, come to gather inside the madness, come to flock to the latest damned soul. Isabel's mind was cavorting now, backing up on itself as it tried to take in so much input. There was no sense to be made out of any of it, and it invited insanity. Madness was a better place. A better place.

*No.*

*I saw the truck coming... Saw its lights flash white.*

It was a different voice; not Cassandra's, but one of the suicides.

Isabel wondered if she had perhaps become the magnet for these poor ghosts - the focus of reason, a conduit, their only hope to escape this hell. More and more of them began to grow bolder in front of her, their shapes becoming more defined, solidifying. Words began to compete over the din of the limbo itself, creating a greater dirge that pounded at her head, craving entry, demanding answers and reason. It was too much to cope with, too much to hang onto, and yet there was no way to block it out, no way to screen the cacophony.

*The farm... Saw the darkness bleed.*

*The truck... The lights.*

*Asylum...*

*Tried to kill her baby... Killed herself.*

*Lizbeth...*

So many cries found their way through, but this last name grabbed at her thoughts. Emily's mother, was she here? Had what she failed to do to her own daughter, been realised in herself? Emily had always been told that her mother had died peacefully in her sleep. Could it be true that she had seen the face of the horror that had decimated her own family, and attempted to take the lives of herself and her daughter? No wonder her father had shielded her from that.

She wanted to confirm the truth, to ratify her own suspicions about this place, about the unholy demon that had destroyed so many people's lives simply by showing its true face to them. But something suddenly jerked inside her mind, a violent tug that sought to rip her head in two. It thickened her consciousness like a soup, dulling her senses to everything that was around her, stamping on her sight, her hearing. A handful of words got through, but there was no meaning in them.

The snag wrenched at her now, crippling her thoughts, and she screamed with madness. It came again, harder than before, but this time it threatened to bludgeon her out of existence, as though her very being was being ripped apart. The suicides around her cried out with a single terror, a uniform fear that found its way through - the beast had come for her.

But Isabel knew the truth, and deep down she understood her condition more fully now than she ever had before; even death could not cleanse her of her curse. Her power to heal was bringing her back from the dead the same way that it had brought her own mother back. She would become a zombie too.

A clutch at her stomach verified the manifestation of her organs, the solidification of her being back to flesh and bone. Pain came quickly from all sides too, her chest and her heart, her abdomen and her groin, all piercing her senses, shattering her nerves as much as the endless blows that had put her here. Her fingers suddenly slipped down between the deep lacerations that slashed her torso, now the memory had been drawn so vividly, her touch feeling the wet organs inside, slick from where they had been punctured.

Tears ran freely down her newly-made cheeks as the agony creased her in two, her eyes flickering open to see her blood staining the very air in front of her. Beyond it she could see the barely-formed faces of the suicides, and of her aunt now strangely clear through the taint of scarlet. Her expression was one of complete dread, torn by what she had to witness, the red-raw meat and brutal lashing together of her own niece.

She saw words mouthed silently upon Cassandra's lips trying to find their way in, disjointed and meaningless, but she could make no sense of them through the disrupted din. Was it a message, perhaps, or pleas for herself, blessings for her safety or safe passage back to the world of the living, she had no idea. But as the hook inside her caught deep and snagged harder still, tugging her sharply backwards, Isabel knew deep down that she would never know.

Something thudded hard and loud inside her skull then, knocking her consciousness out of her, as a hazy numbness claimed her and dragged her headlong out of the hellish limbo, back to the world she had not wanted to be a part of for as long as she could remember.

Her eyes flickered open but found nothing but inky blackness, and for a moment that's all she was aware of. Then she realised that she was lying down, a dullness aching her back from the cold hard earth, but as she tried to lift her arms up, she found that something was restricting her movements. A sudden fit of panic came, her arms trying to flail, but she was lying in some kind of trough, rough earth packed in hard to either side of her, above her body too. She tried to sit upright, but almost immediately hit her head on a ceiling of compacted dirt, motes of grit fluttering down to blind her. She winced and turned her head as she fell back, her hands squirming to clear the fallen muck from her face, but she was trapped inside a hollow; a coffin of earth.

Ice found her body the instant the word came, chilling her utterly. The wood had put her in a grave for finding her father, only this was no casket from a funeral parlour, just a rough-cut hole the size of her body in the ground. She tried to struggle more violently now, rolling her entire body from side to side to an attempt to free her hands, but there was not enough width for her elbows to extend out, or indeed enough room above her to slide her arms beneath her.

She fell back panting, a cold clammy sweat pasting her hair to her forehead. Grit still scratched at one eye, and she tried uselessly to blink it away, only heightening the pain. What she had to do was think. How could she get out of the hole that had been dug for her? She didn't even know how deep it was. How far into the ground had she travelled before she'd stumbled upon her father? How much further might she have been taken? An image of the mud-shadows came rocketing back into her head, and of that sickening grin plastered across the face of her brother. But then a worse fear crept into her head - suppose they hadn't dug down from the surface, but dug up from below. She could be hundreds of feet from the surface; no one would even hear her scream.

This last thought became more and more certain in her mind, and slowly she began to form the idea that she should go down, kick out with her feet and try and force her way down into whatever chamber the wood had begun her grave. Taking a breath, she lifted her leg and struck down at the ground. But so tight was the grave that she raised her legs perhaps only a handful of inches, and managed only to kick dirt up around her ankles. She tried again, in the hope of dislodging something, anything, but there was simply no room, and nothing happened.

Except something did happen. It was only marginal, but in that moment when her feet had connected with the ground, Isabel felt as though it had changed. For a third time, she scuffed her feet against the ground, and the coffin altered yet again. Dirt rained down onto her face, and a sense of dread shrouded whatever hope she might have formed. Her actions with her feet had caused the ceiling to drop; the grave was actually getting smaller.

With the revelation now certain in her mind, Isabel lay as still as she could, holding her breath in her throat in case even that might bring tons of earth down upon her and smother her completely. But then another patter of rain sprinkled across her face, grains of dirt finding the corners of her clenched eyes and mouth. She wanted to spit it away, but what damage might that cause?

Her breath was choking now, desperate to clear her lungs, but before she even had time to expel it, the mountain of earth above her dropped altogether, sending its load downward to bury her body and crush it with its tremendous weight.

She landed hard inside the torrent of dirt as the chamber below collapsed. Isabel's eyes shot open and stared into the impenetrable murk of swirling dust. Her arms flailed around her, desperate to find the walls or smothering ceiling around her, but there was space now, unrestricted space, and she gazed hard all around her as she filled her lungs with ragged breaths.

Clutching herself with the memory of what she had been through, Isabel tried to discern with her fingers what her eyes were barely able to make out on their own. Her injuries were real, the sting of open wounds clogged with detritus was proof of that, and tears of frustration and rage threatened. How many times had she thought that when death finally came, it would answer all her prayers of oblivion?

She had suffered the agony of passing, had travelled the passage through into the next state of being, but to have her curse deliver her back into the hateful world of the living was almost too much to bear. But to know she could do nothing about it chewed at her innards. What was more final than death? What could she possibly hope for that was greater than oblivion?

Looking around her now, Isabel saw that the hard earth floor had given way onto grey slate tiles littered with dirt and debris; the walls were old brick, heavily decayed and worn, but still man-made; and as she began to walk its length, she discovered that it was vaulted by huge brick archways, as though she had found her way out into the forgotten cellars of some huge ancient mansion. But as she came to one of these brick archways, a pile of black earth littered the passageway, and halted her progress.

The sense of not being alone crawled into her stomach with a dreadful swiftness as she gazed up at the ceiling, and saw to her horror that part of it had given way. She was not so concerned for the rest of the ceiling coming down on her so much as how it dragged her nightmare back to the forefront of her mind. Had someone else been buried alive up there? And if so, where was their body now?

Her stomach turned as she heard something next to her right ear, as though something was just a breath away, whispering to her. Her head jerked in the direction of the voice but there was no one there, just the empty corridor, and the clammy moisture pressing once more against her skin.

Isabel ran then, as hard as she could, clambering up over the mound of earth and on along the passage on the other side. A mist rose up from the ground, and even though there was no wind in the chamber, it seemed almost to reach up for her like fog caught on a blustery moor.

She'd wanted to scream before but had managed to hold it back, but it came now, shattering the dank silence ahead of her, echoing off the walls dissonantly with the pattering thud of her footsteps on the litter-strewn stone floor.

What partial light there had been suddenly faded altogether as she skidded round a corner, and as she flailed into a darkness that seemed not only impenetrable but almost alive and reaching for her so dense and yearning was it, that she tumbled headlong into the dirt and landed painfully against the base of one of the stone pillars that supported the heavy archways.

Her hand went to the stabbing pain at her shoulder, but as her eyes opened and settled upon the empty sockets of the eyeless skull just inches in front of her, she screamed again and scrabbled backwards away from it.

Her scream slipped effortlessly into the black void beyond the skull and the rest of the broken corpse twisted behind it, but came back rapidly as something else ungodly. Like a banshee's wail it was almost physical as it seemed to take hold of her and shake her, rattling her teeth in her head. Isabel shuddered with absolute terror, helpless beneath whatever horrors haunted this place, and only once the scream had begun to die down, could she haul herself back onto her feet and hobble away.

The fall had hurt her ankle as well as her shoulder, and it caused immense discomfort to go back the way she'd come. There was no way she could continue past the eyeless corpse, into the blackness of the tunnel where anything could be waiting for her. But she hadn't passed any other corridors on her way here.

She tried to think just what she'd seen as she'd run from whatever had been chasing her, but she couldn't recall anything. She halted as she came upon a junction that offered her three routes, left, right and ahead, but she was sure that she had not passed them before.

Had that corpse been the body that had fallen from the grave in the ceiling? Had they been alive, as she had been, and dropped to the ground only to crawl a handful of broken yards before dying? She knew she would never know, but the chilling thought that came immediately after was how could she be sure that there weren't any more?

Her eyes were stark, and went to each tunnel in turn, searching the emptiness for anything else that might be waiting for her. Were there things watching her even now? Things with no name or form?

She started slowly forward, knowing that she didn't want to stay where she was. But she had not gone more than a hundred yards before the ceiling suddenly crumbled without warning and sent a shower of heavy black earth down upon her.

Isabel flailed wildly with her arms, stumbling back

out of the mire as it sought to cover her. As her eyes came up, however, they were met with more than just an empty hollow this time. Something big was swinging out of the darkness, and her eyes struggled to make sense of what it was. But it was a body, a human body, swinging on the end of a noose, as dead as anything could be.

Isabel let out a yelp as she stepped back away from it, her hands over her mouth in horror. The face belonged to a woman, most of it plastered with thick mud, but it was clear that she had been buried without a casket, just thrown into the wet earth and covered over. Clearly it was not a proper burial. The noose was still in place, and it was from the same rope that had taken her life that she was still swinging. Her eyes bulged like sallow fruit from a mask of black earth and blue-white flesh. Her hands hung lifeless and crooked at the end of arms still swaying like those of a scarecrow filled with straw.

Isabel took a step forward, feeling a glut of sympathy for this poor wretch who had died in such a hideous way, when the woman's eyes suddenly shot open through the mask of mud and stared at her.

Isabel loosed a shriek as their gazes connected, and staggered back hard against the cold brick wall. The woman's eyes followed her all the way as she continued to swing in slow pendulous arcs, never blinking, but clearly focussed upon her.

Oh God, what was happening, where the hell was she? She stumbled blindly away from this apparition, her hands clamped against the wall to guide her, until she was well out of reach of the woman's hands should she try and reach for her, and then she ran headlong along the passageway away from her.

She could almost feel the tears of relief as out of

the murk ahead of her appeared a flight of stone steps that led up. She climbed them at a ragged run, the light above growing ever stronger, until she found herself fleeing a crypt and emerging into a graveyard braced on three sides by high brick walls, the stained-glass rear of a church on the fourth.

Isabel did not slow her pace until her feet had found the grass of the lawn and her skin had been touched by direct sunlight. But she turned now in tight circles, taking in the view all around her, as the bright light stung her eyes; wall, wall, wall, church. And not a single visible ghost amongst them, not even hanging from the stones themselves.

Her eyes went to the gravestones and tombs that littered the grounds, leaning and weathered like the grey teeth of some long dead giant. Isabel swallowed hard. Did these graves go down as far as the cellars that riddled the earth beneath the church? Were they burying the dead in inches of soil just above a brick ceiling? She thought all this in horror for a moment but that suddenly made no sense. With what she had seen, the crawling corpse and the hanged woman, there had been no casket, just a body thrown into a muddy hole. There had been no ceremony, no holy blessing.

Her eyes rose up to the stained-glass windows of the church, to the blackness inside the church that her sight could not penetrate. Was there something in there looking back at her, she wondered uneasily? Had it been watching her all along?

She willed her feet to move, but something was holding her to the spot. She realised that her back still stood to an open crypt that led down into that pit and her stomach turned over. Her body suddenly shook with fear, and it was enough to jerk her into motion, forcing her feet to move and carry herself out of the graveyard, away from the tunnels beneath them and the dead that tumbled from their ungodly graves.

# ELEVEN

## DISOWNED

The woods were almost entirely dark, darker than they had been before. Not even through the trees could Kyle make out any light, and he dreaded the truth that the day had slipped totally away into night, at least here beneath its canopy, a stronger domain for those that lived inside it.

The demon had killed Isabel and Emily, and Kyle wanted vengeance to be his final deed. If it killed him in turn then all well and good, but he would see it dead first - he still had powers and he would use them. Whatever had forced him to despatch his sister - the voices in his head, the deeds behind his hands - had gone from him now, and presumably had simply left her to rot. He would have his revenge, if it meant taking apart every abhorrent cohort that hung from the branches of its lair.

He set off through the undergrowth, his hands out in front of him, feeling his route between trees and low-hanging limbs in the almost impenetrable murk. With no living creatures in the wood, it was impossible to see through their eyes, and yet something nagged inside his head, goading him that something was there to be seen. He tried to force his vision between the trees, but there was only that same uncertain shifting blackness. His heart pounded inside his chest as twigs snapped around him, leaves and floating matter tumbling past his face, his imagination conjuring far worse things surely than anything that could be around him, watching his approach.

He wanted to see just one of their number, to take it apart like a brutal savage, to claw it back to its basest parts for the others to see. But they would not show themselves, if indeed they were really there, yet still his skin continued to itch with the thought of their proximity.

He halted suddenly as a stench of decay soured the air, as though he'd passed through a wall of death, of unnatural venom. The sound of breaking twigs ceased, the motions falling past his face died, and he was left in an eerie silent blackness. Not even the air moved, no breeze found its way in this far anyway, and his skin crawled with the thought that he was getting closer, that the demon at the heart of the wood was somewhere near.

He tried once again to see where his own eyes could not, and once again that insistent nagging found its way into his head. There was only blackness here, unfathomable blackness, and yet he relented and allowed the scene that demanded his attention to play out inside his head.

It startled him to see not the wood, but the inside of the office building where Isabel had hidden from him, and for only a moment he questioned her ability to not only be alive, but to return there so quickly. The spiders in the ceiling found their target, however, before he could question it, and relayed what they had wanted him to see - the coming of the shadows, despatched by the spirit that had so nurtured him for its own device, come to punish him further.

He had so very little control, other than seeing the events inside the office building, and yet he had the insects hidden away to warn her. They had crawled through the electrical systems for him, chewed and scratched and conducted vast currents through their blotchy bodies in order to save one of the last remaining members of his family. It hadn't been much, but it had managed at least some partial distraction, allowing her brief escape.

His powers had given her time to slip their grasp, time to take flight through the billowing fire, but the wood had been quicker than he, smarter than he, and had dragged his magic out of him with both agony and speed.

Kyle stumbled to the ground, his hands clutching his skull as though it would crack in two. Shapes pounded inside his head the colour of bruised flesh, as his body was stripped of everything that had once been granted him. His fingers began to bleed, his eyes too, and his lungs burned with a furious fire as though the wood sought to demand back even the air that it had allowed him to breathe.

He cried out his mother's name with what little breath he had left, but his words, rather than echoing between the trees, were simply swallowed, sucked whole into the darkness.

His skin crawled with fear now that he had been stripped of his ability to battle the things that lived here, and a freezing shiver ran down the back of his neck. What could make this wood so dark, he wanted to know, so empty, so consuming? What did he have left now that could possibly harm it?

He prayed for death to come quickly and extinguish his life before any tortures could be exacted upon him. But he knew that no prayers he made to any god would be answered kindly.

Then the air suddenly turned to ice, his breath fogging visibly in front of him. He stared straight ahead, certain that something was looking at him, certain that the demon had found him at last.

There was blackness all around him, nothing had form except for the few trees within yards of him, and yet he knew there was something there. The air almost had a drone buzzing inside it, a resonance that found its way deep inside his chest, penetrating him, searching his insides, his head. He loathed the feeling, despised its touch inside him, but he was powerless now against it.

His thoughts were skipping insanely, his eyes trying to make sense out of the blackness ahead of him, trying to paint some kind of image for him to see, a face to hate, but there was nothing, nothing but a consuming void.

"Get gone," Kyle hissed, his voice seething with panicking rage but choked as though his throat was packed with dirt.

The air shimmered in front of him with a momentary disturbance, the buzz guttering. The darkness suddenly came close like a physical presence, pressing against the skin of his hands, his cheek. He shivered. His breath halted in front of him.

"Go back to wherever the fuck you came from. I don't want you here any more."

The air shook again, the growl thumping his face, as ice slivers slashed downward from the canopy overhead, piercing his flesh like razor scars. Kyle flinched with pain, gasping at the cold that was already seeking to take over him. His hands went numb, and he clenched them into fists and blew breaths of fogging air over them to bring the blood back.

"Where's my sister?" he demanded now, turning in circles, firing his hatred at the entire wood. "What have you done to my family?"

The growl that hung in the air rumbled like a guttural snarl, shaking the wood around him with its thunder, and he staggered back a step away from it. His arms shook with the unutterable cold and he hugged them to his chest to try and keep it out of his bones.

"Just leave us alone," he screamed. "In God's name, just fuck off, get lost, goodbye."

Suddenly the trees around him shuddered horribly and then splintered, vast slabs of cracking timber tumbling down towards him out of the darkness from the tops of the trees. Kyle lurched awkwardly to avoid them, but the swathes of branches coming at him were too dense to dodge, so full were their thick plumes of needles, and they knocked him hard to the ground.

The branches scratched and tore at his face as though they were living writhing things, drawing blood swiftly to the surface of his skin. Twisting and contorting even as he tried to claw his way out, they snatched at his arms and legs as unnatural life pumped through them with the intention of throttling him, wrapping around him and crushing him like a thousand constricting snakes.

Needles found their way into his mouth as he gasped for breath, silencing the screams of terror before they'd even found their way out of his throat. Twigs and roots squirmed like graveyard worms, wrapping themselves around his wrists and ankles, holding him down, restricting his movements, burrowing beneath his flesh. He cried out again with frustration and fury, telling whatever was trying to destroy him to leave the wood, leave this world, but his voice was hopelessly drowned.

He glanced down at his right forearm as a sudden pain seared through it, and saw with horror that something was roving beneath the surface of his skin. He went to clamp his other hand to it, to stop its progress, but found his left wrist bound by pulsing tree roots. The intruder beneath his skin contorted at the elbow, bringing agony as it struggled past the joint, and Kyle bent forward to take hold of it with his mouth before it found its way any further.

His tongue tasted salt and grit on his skin as he clamped his teeth around it, but he also felt the wriggling form of whatever had entered his body writhing insanely. Forcing pressure around it, he winced with pain as his bite threatened to break his own skin. Pain was already mounting as his muscle was slowly being torn apart from the inside, the intruder literally chewing its way through him, and clenching his eyes shut, he bit down hard upon it.

Blood pumped in pulsing torrents into his mouth as the agony of the wound overtook him. Pain seared like a livid flame through a body not used to surviving naturally, but somehow he managed to find strength to keep biting down, to keep forcing his teeth down hard through his own flesh, drawing the intruder out even as he began to gag on his own blood.

His arm knotted with shock, shuddering from the wound he was inflicting, but he did not release his bite until he felt something enter his mouth and begin to struggle.

Kyle turned sharply away as he vomited both the contents of his stomach as well as the mouthful of blood he'd taken in. Out went the two inch long worm too, but he had only an uncertain moment to see the texture of bark across its soiled slick back before it was gone, down into the muck and leaf litter of the black earth.

He lay choking for a moment, blood running freely from his mouth like sick gruel, as the splintered trees continued to crawl all around him. The wound in his arm was raw and running with blood, and even in the darkness he could see the deep pink of his muscle, the flash of white bone beneath, and the map of veins that bound it all together. His stomach turned again, but he fought it back. He had to be gone, and quickly, before the thing that would have made him prince of all this shit despatched something new to take him over.

It was trying to make him part of the wood, that was all he could think as he struggled to find his feet, trying to fuse him with the roots and stone like it had his father. He shot a hateful glance back into the void of darkness behind him, but there was still nothing to focus his hate on, no face or human figure, nothing but the wood itself coming to get him.

With one arm useless, Kyle had only one hand to claw the tendrils of roots away from him. They'd slackened their attempts by a few degrees, perhaps because their internal mutilation had failed, and he managed to find his feet quickly, stumbling swiftly away from where the trees had fallen, but almost casting himself back down into the dirt so keen was he to get out of the wood.

He ran awkwardly on, supporting his wounded arm in his left hand, numbness coursing down the right hand side of his body, blackening his head, his thoughts. Nausea returned too as he tasted blood still thick around his lips, but he had no time to vomit, no time to rest. Even as he dared a glance behind him, to see what might be at his heels, strange and disorientating visions flooded into his head, like images from different films spliced together by some maniac projectionist: scarlet eyes that ran with tears of molten lead as rabid needle teeth snapped at him from above; children that danced upon stages of lurid flame while dogs made of filthy straw ran headlong into the fury to fuel their songs; horses that burned and trees that bore living fruit, houses that collapsed and men that ate from the muck in which they lay. Every image came rapidly after the last and sought to cast him into a pool of swirling madness and white noise. But he stumbled blindly on through the trees, his sight straining to see what was real and what was in front of him.

The images faded as he neared the edge of the wood, and he dared hope that he might even see the open heavens above him once again. But even before he managed to find the treeline the ground beneath his feet began to shudder afresh, tearing great trenches across the earth in front of him, inviting him into its fissures of hell.

The earth shook violently, thumping from beneath as though an earthquake was coming upward one huge footstep at a time. Kyle stumbled across the uneven ground as tremors ran across the wood, shaking the trees, shaking fissures and canyons across the black earth.

His foot gave way beneath one crack as it gaped wildly, and he slid partway into it, his boots finding little purchase on the damp slick soil, agony searing through his open wound as his arms flailed to take hold of anything to keep him upright.

Needles fell in blankets like suffocating snow, drifting across his head and body as he tried to drag himself to his feet, burying him, hiding him. The blinding shroud disorientated him, so heavy was its downfall, and he struggled to make out anything through its veil. But he managed to start away, back the way he'd come, until he noticed a sliver of open sky that appeared fleetingly between the trees. The edge of the wood was in view now, even if it was only a half-seen glimpse, and all he had to do was reach it. But even as he threw himself towards it, the maelstrom continued to build, branches cracking to block his path, to snatch at his hair and face, to prevent his escape.

With his arms up to protect himself, Kyle dashed the last few yards like a blind man. Something struck his shin hard, he heard the crack of bone as he fell headlong to the ground, tasting his blood on his tongue yet again as his head hit something solid. Tree roots sought out his body immediately as he lay dizzied, but he would not be denied the sight of the open sky this close to its beauty.

Heaving himself onto his hands, he pushed with whatever strength he had left, and pulled away from the knotting roots. Some snapped, others held their prey, but inch by inch he forced himself forward, the light from the moon appearing brighter and brighter as it penetrated more of the wood's dense canopy.

The ground ceased its shaking, halted its great thumping footsteps too, as he at last heaved himself the last few yards past the treeline and out onto the old rutted track that circled the wood. The roots that had taken hold of him slunk back into the undergrowth like slithering serpents, and a fresh breeze rose up to chill his sweat-soaked hair that had plastered itself across his forehead.

Kyle lay for a few moments just breathing it in, just feeling it on his skin, a welcome coldness, a natural coldness, as his muscles throbbed around his body, his broken bones screaming. Only then did he force himself unsteadily back up onto his feet and start away from the wood, keeping it always at his back, always behind him.

# TWELVE

## SANCTITY

The shadows had delivered her into the wood, its depths deathly silent and still. The blackness between the trees had been hypnotic and shapes had swirled and ebbed before her eyes, the agitated creatures that had carried her here.

Irene turned her head, averting her eyes from the swirling blackness, but the shapes still moved, behind her eyes, inside her skull. They'd gotten in, she thought with a sickening terror. They were inside her, searching her thoughts, her memories.

They defiled the air in front of her like God's first sketches of a monkey, awkward and misshapen; flashes of white bone and needle teeth visible in some, absent in others; five fingered claws for tree-climbers, raw stumps for the leaf-litter crawlers. She pitied some of them, seeing a mirror in their wretched state, while others she retreated from, their fangs slick with menace and spit.

Nothing moved except the writhing forms that now urged her forward, down into a deep dark hollow that sank down and down into the black ground. There was no breeze, no warmth either, and it felt as though nature had decided it best to leave this place alone.

It was dark beneath the earth, unutterably dark, darker than the night, darker than the shadows that had brought her to this place. Somewhere down below waited whatever had summoned her, the deathly spectre that had crawled inside the attic of their cottage, had thumped behind its walls, and destroyed the family that she had so longed for.

She felt a dread as she moved slowly along the dank passageway, a creeping dread that gnawed at her insides. She was not afraid to die, again, and would indeed welcome the end to the thing that she'd become; but she was terrified of what this creature might do to her, what horrible curse it might affect that could be worse than death, a living painful hell that would just go on and on without any hope or reason. That was what chilled her crooked bones.

She'd wanted only to be with her husband, to be at the side of the one she'd promised vows to, to love and cherish her children and have a life spent together - albeit when life had made some sense, and faith in God had rarely been tested.

Were things so different now, she wondered? Was she still not praying for a victory of good over evil? If, indeed, there was an evil. Perhaps things just existed. Perhaps the creatures above too held lucid thoughts, and sought hope from the condition that had been forced upon them?

Irene glanced over her shoulder and saw that the dark forms had now closed in to seal off the path behind her. She remembered Custer, circled by indians, remembered too how that had ended, his fate beneath the vengeful hands of those that had wanted for him something more than mere death - humiliation, bloodsport, revenge.

Returning her gaze to the passage ahead, Irene

forced herself forward once more. If this was where they wanted her, if this was where the demon awaited her, then she had only one choice, to venture into the darkness and learn the final truth. No more running, no more hiding - the end had come at last.

But as the single corridor, a single route carved out of the thick black soil, began to widen, a faint glimmer began to grow, a pale luminescence that lit the way ahead. But at its end she found not the devil or a monster in his guise, but some other sight, her husband, hanging like a prisoner inside a cage of living detritus.

She recognised him immediately despite the roots and branches that contorted and grew through his frame, but after so long away from him no tears of sadness came, as she'd thought they might, but instead came a blossoming joy at being with him again, in spite of the circumstances of their reunion.

Crossing the final divide of black earth between them, beneath the studied gaze of a thousand unnatural eyes that hung from the vaulted ceiling, Irene felt the touch of her husband's flesh for the first time in over two decades.

Pressing her face against the curve of his neck, she felt the coarse bark that now grew there, the harsh prickle of its rough texture against her own skin, now as dry as parchment. She laid one hand against his chest, part flesh, part tree, and felt his breath against her as he exhaled with laboured pleasure. He tried to hold her, she could feel the jagged contraction of his limbs, but the roots that crossed and re-crossed his body held his movements, bound him to his single pose.

He whispered her name as though he had been tempted a thousand times by similar visions, only to have his dreams dashed and dissolved; yet so real did this last visitation seem that he dared hope it could be true. They had both changed, both become something far monstrous than any nightmare could have made them, and yet to find each other again, to feel each other's touch, brought bliss that outweighed any physical mutation.

"It's me," Irene whispered into the space where his ear had once been. A broken tree stump grew from his skull now, twisted and blackened with either blood or soil, but he heard her nevertheless.

"You came here. I dared not hope -"

She hushed him. Pressed a kiss against his cheek.

"It doesn't matter," she told him. "Not any more."

"What happened to us?" he wept, his words skipping over themselves, demanding answers. "We started out so happily. We had the perfect start."

"It doesn't matter," Irene said again, attempting to rock his bulky frame in her arms. "We're together once more, as we should be, no matter what happens now."

"These creatures watch me, they haunt my every sight. I want an end to this, Irene, take me away from all this, I beg you."

"I would if I could, my love, but I don't know how. What is this thing that holds us here? What does it want?"

He tried to shake his head, his eyes clenched with frustration.

"I don't know," he said desperately to her.

"You've never seen it? In all these years it's never come before you?"

"I've seen things, heard bellows and screams, but nothing with a face, nothing with words to reason with. Just these creatures that come to haunt me,

344

come to watch me with their soulless eyes."

Irene hushed him again, and kissed his lips lightly, but even they had been possessed by whatever grew here, the soft flesh fused with coarse bark and lichen. Tears came now for him, for what he had endured for so long, alone and without her. Then she heard the whispers above her.

She lifted her head and saw the creatures knitted from the night crawling over themselves like a grisly tide towards them. From the cavernous vaulted ceiling they came, sliding and slithering as a single soup, roiling like bruised bile, seething like boiling shit. Irene clenched Michael's frame, felt his own trembling embrace as his arms cracked from his efforts, defying the structure that now made up so much of his body.

Shadowed hands now found them both, fingers seeking out their feet, their legs, swallowing them inch by inch. Husband and wife kissed, keeping their lips pressed tight as the creatures sought to find their way inside, reaching for their eyes, their nostrils, their mouths. Irene could feel them tugging at her hair, their claws raking the flesh of her back as they ripped at her clothes. Their touch was clammy and cold, and smothered her skin like a plague of rats swarming towards freedom. This was it, was all she could think, this was how they would die; drowned by creatures barely made, barely dreamed of, except in nightmares and lunatic delirium.

But what happened next happened in the space of two heartbeats. A guttural roar shook the belly of the cavern, shaking mud down from the ceiling as though it might collapse in upon them and crush their bones even before the air had been stolen from their lungs.

The shadow creatures halted their movements, simply froze in a nervous state of limbo. And then as the bellow shrank rapidly back, so too did their crawling forms, sweeping away from the cavern altogether, disappearing from the earth all around them, as though they had never been there at all.

Irene wanted to weep with relief but her eyes were dry, grating inside barren sockets. And Michael, partially broken away from the roots that had bound him so totally, tumbled awkwardly towards her arms. She held him up with what diminishing strength she now possessed, and kissed his coarse cheek. But the air now possessed a discordant drone that found its way inside her head like a dull ache.

"What's happening?" Irene murmured, staring round at the dark cavern.

But dirt was already beginning to patter down, stealing Michael's response. Whatever possessed the wood was in there with them, of that there was no doubt, and as the drone became gradually louder, so the ground began to vibrate with an ominous fury.

"I love you," Michael whispered beside her. "I always have."

Irene looked at him, her eyes wide with fear for what was coming for them. She tried to smile, tried to show him love upon her face, but it just wouldn't come. They were about to face the beast that had decimated their family, and even though they would do so together, she was still terrified for the worst.

"I love you too, Michael," she managed to say, clasping his hand in hers and squeezing it as tightly as she could.

But even as she said these words, his head cricked to one side and his eyes rolled up into his skull, his jaw slackening like a puppet's. She felt the strength slip from his touch, as though something had given inside him, and she gasped with fear as she urged him to come back to her, urged him not to leave her alone.

The drone that filled the air now buzzed inside him, she could feel it vibrating in his hands, could see the motions in his slack lips. She tried to pull away from him, but his hands not only held her firmly now, but tendrils had sprouted to entwine around the crooks of her elbows, holding her solid. She gazed into his eyes but they were still rolled up into his skull, his mouth still hanging open, as that same infernal discordant drone emanated from his body.

She pulled at the bonds that shackled her to him, but the roots grew thicker the more she struggled, wrapping and knotting themselves across her flesh, binding the two of them together. Then she felt something shift inside her head, a motion as fluid as quicksilver, and she realised that something else was inside her head apart from herself.

Her muscles stiffened as the motions increased, roving slickly beneath her scalp, until a bright white fluid began to seep across her eyes, distorting her vision. Terror overtook her as her hands began to shake violently. Something began punching at the inside of her skull, thudding against the bone, while the heavy discordant drone berated the air in front of her.

Her mind raced back to the night of the ouija, recalling every event, every incident, every word that was said. The pointer had moved, it had spelt the name Ben, she remembered that distinctly; but there had been another, one without a name, something else entirely that had been summoned to their home.

Her mind now sought to trace the disappearance of the first spirit, but even as she struggled to order her thoughts through the maelstrom still escalating inside her head, the spirit that had called itself Ben suddenly emerged from its refuge of over twenty years.

Blood ran from her eyes and throat as it left, and she could make out little through the blazing haze of scarlet, just a ball of burning light trailing limbs like a comet. Something left Michael too, she could make out a burgeoning black carcass barrelling out of him like a thunderhead, bruising the very air as it swallowed the brighter form immediately like a vacuum.

Her sight failed as the strength went out of her, and she collapsed onto her knees as unconsciousness threatened. Only the tendrils wrapped around her arms kept her from falling headlong into the dirt, but even their desire was slipping as they began to uncoil and retract.

Irene managed to lift her head to look up at Michael's face. Part of the mask of bark and tree roots had fallen away, leaving a bloodied track of raw new flesh. Even as she watched, the tendrils that bound him were slackening, shrinking back into the black earth, recoiling, dying. With a glance behind her, she saw the entrance to the chamber that had delivered her into this pit, its ceiling cracking as the rain of earth intensified, and she dared hope for the first time that they might still escape this place intact and see the open heavens once more together.

Forcing strength into her legs that she didn't think she had, Irene hauled herself up onto two unsteady feet and began tugging at the vines that still held Michael prisoner. It startled her how readily they relinquished him, some of them cracking like old timber, others simply crumbling to dust in her hands. The slabs of rock she levered away from Michael's legs, but even though his eyes were still vacant and his jaw hung loose, she could feel at least some limited cooperation in his lifeless limbs as though he was still partially with her.

The roiling thunderhead turned and crackled overhead like a vast raging storm, shafts of lightning breaking its perimeter, piercing the shit of its matter, fighting for escape. But beneath it, Irene fought to keep Michael upright as they staggered awkwardly for the entrance to the passageway. Black earth continued to rain down on them as the cavern continued to collapse, threatening to break at any moment and bury them all. The thunderhead had its victim; they were nothing to it now.

The walls of the passage were shaking as they made their way along its length at a slow ragged pace, Michael's arm slung limply across her shoulder, supporting his full weight. It was difficult to make swifter progress, so dark was the air now thick with debris, but then she felt the touch of a fresh breeze against her face, lifting her hair matted with muck and sweat, urging her on to feel it fully.

Brightness suddenly penetrated the route ahead, a shaft of frail light spilling down like a rope to illuminate a passage almost destroyed by its own weight. She glanced to her side and saw Michael lift his head up towards it, his eyes half-open, squinting at daylight that had been denied him for over two decades.

Slowly the ground began to rise, forcing Irene to lift her steps higher to ascend the uneven ground strewn with fallen debris. Michael's feet snagged against the mud, twisting his weight in her arms and catching her off balance, and they stumbled down together onto their knees.

Irene cried out with effort as she tried to keep them both upright, but the impact of their fall had been enough to destabilise the already fractured walls. Clods of earth fell in upon them, slabs from the ceiling too, as the whole passageway cracked and then toppled, crumbling down with the speed and weight of an avalanche.

Beneath the torrent of heavy earth, Irene had managed to keep herself up on her hands and knees, forcing strength into arms as weakened as rotten wood, keeping a pitiful space of inches just in front of her, a space of soured air. Michael was lying half-buried at her side, his breaths laboured, but at least regular.

With a huge breath of effort, she began to dig, slowly at first, but gathering momentum, scrabbling like a dog after a rabbit. But daylight was her prey, and she wanted Michael to see it with his own eyes once again, not dying just yards from its touch, not buried here in this filthy tomb.

Dirt clogged her hands as she pulled at its suffocating weight, hauling it into the tiny space beneath her, as she in turn hauled both of them towards that place where the daylight had touched. But the space filled quickly, and no light penetrated the holes that she tore open, yet still she forced her fingers outward, hoping to break through the surface of fallen dirt.

But the pitch blackness would not yield. The air grew stale, denying them oxygen, and the earth pressed down on them even harder as if to bury them where they lay forever.

## THIRTEEN

## SIBLINGS

Isabel stood at the bottom of the hill and watched as a hunched figure made his ragged path along the rutted track towards her. It was early dawn, and the gentle light struggled to illuminate him, but as he staggered steadily nearer, she saw that it was her brother.

She could see that his injuries were severe, the way that he carried one arm, his torn leg dragging dust up in his wake, but she made no move towards him, but rather regarded him with suspicion, daring not to trust him for a moment.

She knew his eyes had found her before he had even halved the distance between them, and yet neither of them acknowledged one another. Only once Kyle was within yards of her did he stop and offer her any words.

"I should have known death wouldn't kill you."

Isabel said nothing. His humour was sick.

She watched his every move, his bloodied fingers that held the flesh of his wounded arm together.

"It wasn't me," Kyle added, his face ashen.

"I know," Isabel replied quietly.

The two siblings gazed at each other uneasily. All

malice seemed to have drained out of him, all of his strength too. His eyes were still bright, however, his brain still firing, but of his body, that had taken a toll.

"I have something for you," Kyle said suddenly, reaching into his pocket, the movement creasing his face with agony. Isabel wanted to move to help him, but she kept her distance, her eyes still fixed on his fingers, his pocket.

But what he retrieved from his jeans pocket shocked her like a slap across her face. The gold of the necklace glittered in the crescent of the new sun arcing across the hillside, and she stared in utter disbelief as he offered it out to her at arms length.

Isabel took the locket delicately in both hands, opened palms out, as if it was some ancient artefact that might crumble to dust beneath clumsy attention. Gently she pried open the gold clasp and stared down at the two old photographs inside. Tears threatened as a smile creased her lips, and looking back up at her brother, saw the shame across his face.

"I'm sorry," was all he said.

She went to him now, her suspicion fading, as she saw the brother she had once known before the rot had set in. His wounds needed tending, and she reached out her hands towards them. But he stopped her, taking an awkward step back.

"Leave them," he said to her. "I don't want them healed."

"But your pain..."

"Leave them," he said again. "The only thing I want to ask -"

"Yes?"

He took a breath, his eyes closed now, his head turned slightly away.

"Your forgiveness," Kyle murmured.

"It's not me you should be asking."

Kyle looked up at her, his expression vexed.

"Mum," was all she said, and Kyle dropped his eyes to the dirt at his feet.

"If we go back to the building -"

"She's not there."

Isabel was already asking one of a dozen questions, but Kyle cut her short.

"They came for her. Took her away."

"But why?"

"It wasn't her they wanted, it never was. It was the spirit that had taken refuge inside her. They used me to search for it, used me to hunt you down, butcher you for the truth."

"Where did they take her?" she wanted to know, but she already knew, even before Kyle turned back towards the wood on top of the hill and nodded towards it.

There was nothing more to be said. Kyle had battled his sire, and lost. Mum was its enemy. What fate could she have possibly faced, what hope of survival? And yet, perhaps in the end she might have gotten her wish, finding peace with her stowaway found and taken.

Isabel looked back at Kyle, his body crippled and bloody, and wondered just what kind of future they could possibly have now? Yes, they were still brother and sister, and after years of antagonism they had come full circle and found one another again. The evil that had turned their family against each other seemed gone, leaving terrible memories and the bones of the dead in its wake. And what of the suicides? Would they continue to madden in the limbo between Heaven and Hell, or dissipate into a state of calm? She had no idea, but all she knew was that her brother was here, standing in front of her, asking to be allowed back into her life, asking for them both to start afresh.

She had no better place to be, and after twenty years spent outside the rest of the human race, a partner in the madness that was to come would be welcome. Family, that was all she had left.

# FOURTEEN

## EVERMORE

In September of that year, a new story began. The Oates farm was sold to a buyer from Somerset, a young man with a new wife and family.

While exploring the wood on top of the hill, he came upon a hollow beneath a tall tree. Inside that hollow was an opening, a shaft that looked as if it had been dug out of the earth by human hands. He thought no more of it, but as he was leaving the wood his eye was caught by what he thought were two figures standing huddled together. It was only the briefest of glimpses, but it was gone a moment later.

He was not a man to be easily scared, and indeed he felt nothing sinister in their presence, but it was to be the first of many sightings of a strange couple seen holding hands in the wood on top of the hill.

The End

# Eden

## Paul Stuart Kemp

There is a gateway to paradise, and it exists in the most unlikely of places, the very heart of London. If someone owns it, it can be bought. If no one owns it, it can be claimed. The race is on to hold possession of the eighth wonder of the known world, and the name of that eighth wonder shall be called Eden.

Jenner Hoard is now a prophet for what few vampires remain in London, guiding those that would not open his throat towards the gateway that would lead them home. Catherine Calleh, the most vicious of all vampires, is forced to endure the mortal world she loathes as she searches for her dead husband now risen from the grave. Her journey between worlds will not be without suffering and loss, but only at its end will she learn the truth about love, hate and devotion, as well as the responsibility of existence itself.

Paul Stuart Kemp is one of England's darkest writers. Eden is the long awaited sequel to his best-selling novel Bloodgod, and continues the reader's descent into the dark underworld of the vampire gods of Kar'mi'shah.

ISBN 0 9538215 6 0

# The Business Of Fear

## Paul Stuart Kemp

A young thief steals a mystical deck of cards, only to incur the wrath of their unnatural owner.

A mother is tormented by forms that seem to move within the shadows of her house.

A man stops at midnight to fix a flat tyre and sees eyes watching him from the blackness of the woods.

From malevolent ghosts to carnivorous cats, from street-walking angels to life-loving zombies, The Business Of Fear is a collection of twenty four dark tales that unravels the mind and makes us face our most primal nightmares.

Paul Stuart Kemp is one of England's darkest writers, and with this book, his first collection of short stories, he takes us on an exploration of the human capacity for fear, playing on our emotions, and exploring what it means to be afraid.

ISBN 0 9538215 5 2

# Bloodgod

## Paul Stuart Kemp

An archaeological expedition to a desert region uncovers both an ancient temple with strange hieroglyphics as well as an old man with a story to tell. Merricah speaks of a creature that decimated most of two tribes, and relays the whereabouts of a magical box that contains the Master of Kar'mi'shah. He has remained in isolation inside the buried temple for hundreds of years, waiting for the tribes to return, and for someone to release his Master.

Jenner Hoard is a thief recently released from prison. Montague, his benefactor, does not want him to quit working for him, and already has two lucrative jobs lined up for an anonymous customer, a deal involving the Blood Of The Ancients, and the theft of a mysterious box from an apartment building in London.

Times have never been more desperate for the vampire community living in the darkest depths of London. Alexia is one such vampire who has a brutal encounter with The Howler of Westminster after a butchered corpse is found floating in the Thames.

Human vampire hunters, known as Skulkers, have become more skillful and connected over the years, and find easy prey in those demons who are too careless about their actions. Join Alexia as she struggles to survive in a dark and foreboding world, where even demons suffer anguish, and in death there is still a fight.

ISBN 0 9538215 2 8

# Ascension

## Paul Stuart Kemp

Hampton, England 1172: After witnessing the death of her family in a frenzied witch-drowning ritual, Gaia, an eight year old girl, flees for her life. Alone and afraid, she stumbles upon a magical young boy who takes her on a journey to meet Calista, a spirit capable of harnessing both dreams and time, with promises of so much more.

Makara, Kenya 2589: There are desperate times at the end of the human race. Kiala is a man living at one of the last stations on Earth, a planet where all life has been eradicated by snow and ice. With his future hinted at, could he hold the key to preserving what little life remains, and if so, why is Calista intent on stopping him?

London, England 1994: When Carly Maddison's fiance is suddenly abducted under very strange circumstances and her fleeing brother is accused of his demise, she finds herself trapped in the depths of a dark and secret world. Her love for them both draws her deeper into that world, and if she is to discover both its rules and, ultimately, its solution, then she must face the past as well as the future, in order to learn truths that she would previously have thought unimaginable.

Witchcraft, alien abduction, ritual murders; all unfathomable mysteries, all with a human heart. Paul Stuart Kemp's science fiction horror fantasy takes the reader on an extraordinary journey, where such mysteries are found to be sown into the human soul, unable to be removed, and unable to be revoked.

ISBN 0 9538215 0 1